TO WED A QUEEN
QUEENMAKERS SAGA XII

BY
BERNADETTE ROWLEY

ACKNOWLEDGEMENTS

Deep thanks must go to my beta readers Nic Page and Kyra Halland. Their generosity in being my first readers for *To Wed a Queen* is so appreciated. Thanks also to Nic Page, Rachel Cass, and many of my newsletter subscribers for their critical feedback during cover creation.

To Duncan Carling-Rodgers for his assistance during the *To Wed a Queen* edits and for the formatting.

To Dar Albert for her stunning cover.

To my husband, Michael, my sons and their ladies for their unending love and support, and for sharing the disappointments and triumphs of a writing life.

TITLES BY
BERNADETTE ROWLEY

(in suggested reading order)

TABLE OF CONTENTS

CHAPTER ONE

BRIGHTCASTLE Keep's ballroom had never looked more glorious. On Kain Arenil's arm, Queen Alecia Zialni waited to be announced. She felt like a patchwork quilt that a child had stitched together. This was her coronation ball, but nothing felt right. Vard had left, his father was missing, and she was unsure whom she could trust.

If only her life would assume a semblance of order, she might feel she had achieved something. This was not how she had envisioned her rule beginning. And she certainly hadn't imagined she'd do this without Vard. She sighed, a tremor passing through her at the thought of how alone she felt.

"Why the sigh, Alecia?" Kain asked, placing his hand over hers. "The entire court awaits you. This will be a grand celebration."

Her eyes met his. "The reality of my new station is sinking in," she said, her attention returning to the brightly-lit room where her guests laughed and danced. "They all sound so happy, and yet I feel such hostile undercurrents. I'm already tired of their scheming."

He smiled. "I know what you mean."

And he really did. Kain had recently stepped into the position of high prince of the *Lenweri*, the elven people whose home was Selinore in the northern mountains. He was only half-elven, and hadn't known of his heritage until a year ago. Since then, Kain had given up command of the Thorian army, embraced his new people, moved to Selinore, and was destined to become supreme elven king.

Alecia sighed again. Yes, Kain knew *exactly* how she felt. "How did *you* do it?"

"Acceptance," he said, running his fingers through his dark hair as if the recent change in his status was not all pleasant. "I railed against my sister and her wishes, however, in the end, I stepped up." He focused on her. "But you *wanted* this, Alecia. It should make your transition to queen easier."

Her temper flared at his words, but she reminded herself he was trying to help. Her difficulties weren't his fault, and this wasn't his duty, but Vard's after all.

"You're right," she said. "I wanted this role and still do." She nodded to the assistant steward, who was the announcer tonight.

"Her Majesty Queen Alecia Zialni, and His Highness the High Prince Kain Arenil."

Alecia descended the last few steps to the anteroom and paused with Kain at the doorway into the ballroom. Thunderous applause greeted her. She smiled at those gathered while pondering which of them were trustworthy. If the recent vote was any indication, many didn't support her.

But tonight wasn't the time to allow negative thoughts to flourish. She must shore up her support and convince her detractors that she would be a great queen.

Pasting on a smile, Alecia approached her aunt, Dowager Queen Adriana, widow of the late King Beniel who died in the Battle of Wildecoast. The handsome woman wore a splendid gown of emerald satin which left much of her shoulders and a good deal of bosom bare.

She stopped before Adriana, waiting for the older woman to curtsey. Seconds ticked by as Alecia endured her aunt's censure. Finally, Adriana dropped into a moderate curtsey, and Alecia slowly released the breath she held. A wave of dizziness hit her, and she was grateful for Kain's support on her arm. Thank the Goddess he hadn't let go!

As Adriana rose, she smiled. "You look very nice this evening, My Queen." Her smirk insinuated her words were the kindest thing she could say about Alecia's ensemble.

The hide of the woman! Alecia knew she looked her best. She wore another of Isadore Bellemont's creations, a striking crimson, black, and silver sheath with a short train of heavy silver lace.

"Thank you, Adriana." She would stop calling the woman "aunt". Perhaps then the dowager would see her as queen, instead of the little girl she imagined. "You look magnificent, as always. I hope you enjoy the night." Alecia moved on, Kain nodding to Adriana as she dropped into a curtsey for the *Lenweri* high prince—a curtsey deeper than the one Alecia received!

She took measured breaths as she approached her advisors Linnet Perfore and Lady Henrietta Guiote. At least here she was among friends. They embraced her warmly, just as they would have before her recent ascension.

Lin clasped her hands together, delight in her eyes. "That dress is perfect, Your Majesty. It complements your coloring wonderfully."

"It seems a small thing when balanced against the kingdom's problems," Alecia said, "but I must convey the right image, new as I am to the role."

"And defying the recent custom of kings," offered Lady Henrietta.

She wore a grey gown adorned with silver lace at the neck, sleeves, and hem. Alecia had trouble coming to terms with the fact that Hetty the witch and this polished noblewoman were the same person. Her identity was a closely guarded secret until Alecia could be sure Hetty was safe. Many frowned upon witchcraft, though Vard and Alecia weren't in that camp.

"I thought being queen would be a little easier than this." She drew Hetty away toward the buffet tables.

"And you imagined Vard would be here to help." Hetty's tone held a decent measure of censure.

Alecia fixed her friend and advisor with a stern eye. "Vard is where he needs to be. He must find his father. Besides, I wish Lyam to give me away. He's now the closest thing I have to a father."

She reflected on the possibility that Hetty's magic may have contributed to the death of her father, Prince Jiseve Zialni. Ramón Zorba, then Guardian of Brightcastle, had asked for Hetty's help in protecting Benae Zialni from her abusive husband, Jiseve. The goal was to make the man impotent, but Alecia's father had died in the sexual act while wearing the ring Hetty enchanted.

At least Hetty had the grace to blush at Alecia's words. "Prince Zialni's death wasn't my fault, as I have told you too many times to count. Let it go, girl, or this will continue to cause problems between us. If you can't forget, at least forgive me for interfering."

Alecia spied Ramón Zorba walking her way and sighed. "I suppose you're right. I love you. I don't want bad feeling between us." If Lyam was the closest thing Alecia had to a father, Hetty had stepped into the role of mother. "I'll try to forgive your meddling, Lady Henrietta. You're too important to me, and I know you didn't intend any permanent hurt to befall my father."

Hetty appeared only slightly mollified by Alecia's words. She would have to try very hard indeed to forgive her old friend, as she couldn't bear to lose her. Besides, Hetty was a powerful force for good in her life and had always offered support. That counted for much.

"My Queen." Ramón swept a low bow, his thick blond forelock, falling across his eyes. "Lady Henrietta." He offered Hetty a much smaller bow and fixed his gaze on Alecia. "You look splendid this evening, Your Majesty." He lowered his voice. "Any news of Anton?"

Ramón would always refer to Vard by his last name, she suspected. There was no love lost between them, especially from Ramón's side. He had never believed Vard was good enough for Alecia, and wasn't likely to change his mind.

Alecia squared her shoulders. "No, I've not heard from him. As much as I hate to admit it, I've had no word from any of my sources regarding his movements, or those of Samael Delacost." Samael, a tall, green-eyed ex-pirate, had accompanied Vard on his mission to find Lyam. He had been a wonderful supporter of Vard, and Alecia felt confident he was equal to the task of protecting her man.

Ramón scowled. "Typical. Now that you're queen, I hoped Anton would quit his wandering ways, and stay home with his family. Though he's not much of a father, Iona certainly needs him in her life."

Alecia huffed out a breath. "Mind your tongue! I'll thank you to keep your feelings about Vard to yourself in the future, especially since I recently learned just how much you hate him." Ramón had finally admitted to ordering an assassin to kill Vard on the night of her betrothal ball, before she fled into a twelve-month exile.

"Do you think this is the time or place to discuss this, Alecia?" Ramón snapped. "I'd rather not have the court know about my actions on that night. And I hope I've somewhat redeemed myself by finding him for you when he was... lost."

Ramón didn't know half of what that meant. He didn't know Vard was a Defender, a shapeshifter dedicated to protecting the weak, or that Vard could shift into wolf, hawk or bear. Ramón referred to the time when Vard became trapped in his wolf form. It was Ramón's brave acts to find and return Vard to Alecia that freed him from the wolf and allowed him to save his newborn daughter's life. Yes, Ramón *had* rather redeemed himself.

She swallowed hard, the emotion of that day sweeping over her. "I'll always be grateful for your actions. You never gave up looking for me, and you risked your life finding and bringing Vard back... I wouldn't be here if not for his return."

He reached for her hand and swept it to his lips. "I'd do it all again in a moment. Your friendship means a great deal to me. I regret hiring that assassin and everything that happened after. I'm glad you know the truth, but can you please forgive me? So we can move forward?"

He was sincere. Alecia could see that much. His clear blue eyes pleaded with her to understand and forgive. If only he hadn't been involved in the enchantment of her father's signet ring. If only he and Benae hadn't betrayed her father. Had Alecia been present during those troubled days, she would know the truth, and might understand how her father could have abused Benae.

"You and I have many things to discuss before I can forgive you all your transgressions against my family. You're asking too much right now, Ramón." She took a step back. "Enjoy my ball."

She swept away, tears in her eyes that she simply couldn't spill. When would the loss of her father stop hurting? When would she stop being angry at Ramón and Benae? They were so in love, while Jiseve Zialni was cold in his grave. And even if she forgave, how could she forget?

A bevy of loveliness awaited her near the musicians' stage. Alecia stopped to admire her temporary ladies-in-waiting. Temporary because they all had other jobs besides attending the new queen.

Blonde-haired Lady Alique Jazara's blue eyes were fixed on Kain as he and Alecia approached. The lady was Kain's wife and a skilled healer. All the ladies-in-waiting were dressed in white to avoid clashing with Alecia's gown. Alique wore an elven-style gown with wide sleeves and stunning silver embroidery at neck, waist and cuffs. She bowed deeply to Alecia then reached for Kain's hand.

Stunning crimson-haired Merielle Cosara's white sheath dress showed off her voluptuous figure to advantage, while the gray ruffled hem imitated the foamy wash of a post-storm ocean. Intricate braids restrained her hair, and pride glowed in her eyes as she embraced her new queen.

"You look enchanting, Your Majesty," she whispered, though Alecia felt herself pale in comparison to the admiral's wife.

"Thank you, Meri. Where is your husband?" Admiral Nikolas Cosara was one of Alecia's new advisors, whose estate lay close to Wildecoast.

"He is attending to a last-minute problem, but said he would not be long."

"Enjoy this night, Merielle," Alecia said, smiling.

Lady Esta Delacost, of house Aranati near Wildecoast, curtsied stiffly. She hadn't voted for Alecia and appeared to be in two minds about her duties as an attendant. She had chosen a white ballgown with a full skirt covered with black embroidery and pearls. It was striking. Her aunt was the royal seamstress in Wildecoast, so perhaps that explained the splendid dress.

"Your Majesty, that gown is stunning," Esta said. "Another of Isadore Bellemont's creations?"

Alecia nodded and smiled. "The woman is a marvel. I hope you aren't missing your husband too much?" Esta's husband was Samael Delacost.

Esta's eyes clouded. "Alas, he occupies my thoughts night and day. It's a good thing I have Mika to distract me." Her seven-month-old son was one of the most active babies Alecia had ever encountered. Iona had spent time with the infant, and loved him already.

"I know how you feel," Alecia said. "Surely they will return before too long. There's a wedding to attend, after all." Even as she said the words, a shiver prickled her skull and ran down her spine. No, she would not fear the worst. Vard and Sam would return, and Lyam would be with them. The wedding would go ahead as planned, and she and Vard could finally be together as husband and wife.

Esta's jaw clenched, but she nodded. "As you say, all will be well."

Alecia's gaze found Katrine Aranati, née Tomel, who seemed to carry a shadow with her wherever she went. The beautiful dark-haired noblewoman was Esta's younger sister and a powerful sorceress, though few knew it. She wasn't one to draw attention to herself, even dressed as she was in white with a tulle skirt and a fitted silver-worked bodice that left the shoulders bare. A silver lace train fell from her shoulders and was attached to her wrists with delicate silver links.

Seeing Alecia's eyes upon her, she straightened herself and dropped into a curtsey.

"I trust you are well, My Queen," she said, rising gracefully.

Alecia frowned, but then smoothed her brow. These ladies and anyone watching would note her facial expression. She didn't wish her guests to think she found fault with her ladies-in-waiting, though to be honest, Esta and Katrine could have been more welcoming to her.

Sighing, she smiled. "You all look splendid tonight, my friends. I hope you find time to enjoy the festivities. It has been a busy and trying month, but we have much to celebrate."

She signaled to the musicians, and they struck up a lively dance tune. Alecia accepted a goblet of wine from her taster and handed Kain to his wife for a dance. She smiled as they sailed away amidst the merry crowd.

The Coronation Ball would be a success, and she would try to forget her troubles and enjoy herself, too.

Alecia danced with Nikolas Cosara, whose honey-colored hair lay in its tangled locks, restrained by a black ribbon. His black naval uniform showed off broad shoulders and his aqua eyes were more relaxed than they had been lately. Despite his dislike of Vard and his suspicion of her ascension to queen, the man had been an excellent counselor thus far. She deemed him an honest man, so perhaps he truly wished to help her assume the responsibilities of the throne of Thorius. On the negative side, he *was* Dowager Queen Adriana's cousin.

Nikolas was light on his feet and easy on the eye, and she enjoyed dancing with him. Merielle was a lucky woman. They were almost at the end of their dance when a harried-looking Captain Estevot tapped Nikolas on the shoulder. Nikolas relinquished her to the captain, whose customary graceful movements were absent.

"My Queen," he said, his pale-blue eyes panicked. "The Princess Iona is not in her room." The captain referred to her seventeen-month-old daughter.

Alecia almost tripped over her own feet, and Estevot steadied her. "How can she not be in her room?" Her heart raced and thumped. "I only just checked in on her and she was asleep."

"Keep dancing, Your Majesty," he said, guiding her around a group of laughing lords.

Alecia tried to do as he advised, but dizziness betrayed her. "What do you know?" she asked.

"The nanny heard a noise from the nursery, and when she attended the child, the crib was empty. The window was open. I've conducted a brief search of the immediate area and the castle grounds, but there's no sign of the princess."

Iona *missing*? How? Where? "There must be some mistake."

"I hope you're right, My Queen," Estevot said as he guided her to her ladies-in-waiting. "I'll continue to search and gain clues, Your Majesty." He addressed the ladies. "The queen has had concerning news. Her daughter is missing. I bid you care for her."

He whirled and strode away. Katrine stiffened, then excused herself, hurrying after the captain.

CHAPTER TWO

ALECIA barely heard her ladies as she struggled to accept Estevot's news. Iona couldn't really be missing. She was walking now and a devil to keep track of. She must have crawled from her crib and wandered off. Why would anyone steal her? Alecia's breath caught in her throat. There were more than enough reasons someone might kidnap her daughter.

"What will you do?" Alique hissed, her fingers clutching Alecia's.

She shook her head and focused on her blonde lady-in-waiting. "I must go to her room and see for myself. If you would come with me, ladies?" She took off toward the ballroom exit, trying for composure but failing miserably.

The three noblewomen nodded and followed her. On the way, Alecia motioned for Lady Henrietta and Lin to join them. Alecia felt lightheaded, but she couldn't allow this shock to weaken her. She would find her daughter, and Iona would be well. It was all a big mistake.

Hetty gripped her hand. "What's amiss, Your Majesty?"

Alecia spoke between gritted teeth. "Estevot says Iona is missing."

Hetty's face lost all its color while Lin, overhearing, immediately signaled to Alecia's female guards, who loitered just inside the ballroom entrance.

"Get to the nursery, quickly," Lin snapped.

The three guards, Arelle, Cretia, and Kenna, rushed to the stairs and ascended into the gloom. Doors banged from the direction of the royal nursery.

Alecia gulped and followed them, her heart pounding and palms moist. When she arrived at the door into Iona's nursery, every light in the room blazed. Her ladies made a hasty search, but there was nothing to be found. Alecia wandered to the crib and rested her fingers where her daughter's head had so recently laid.

"Don't fret," Merielle said, placing her arm around Alecia. "We will find her safe and well."

Alecia pulled from her embrace and stalked to the window overlooking the courtyard. It too was ablaze with torches, both in their sconces and being held by hurrying soldiers and servants. Was it true? Iona was the victim of a kidnapping?

Alecia swallowed hard and left the room, determined to find Estevot and discover all he knew. Out in the hall, servants hurried about their duties. She heard a booming voice from the ballroom and went to investigate. Soldiers blocked the door into the ballroom, but allowed her and her companions through. Alecia noted that soldiers guarded all the exits.

Nikolas Cosara stood on the musicians' platform. "I must have complete silence."

As the crowd hushed, the admiral spoke. "Princess Iona is missing." Alecia's fists bunched as she steeled herself to accept his words. "No one may leave this room until I have personally spoken with them." A low murmur of shock, and no little anger, followed.

The need to be out looking for her child made Alecia's skin itch and her stomach queasy. But, as queen, should she do that? Search for Iona? She looked for Hetty and found her right beside her.

"I need to join this search, Lady Henrietta. I can't just sit here and wait for news."

Hetty motioned to follow her to a quiet corner. "I wouldn't advise you join the search, My Queen. This may be what they want—to lure you out of the castle and attack you."

Alecia shook her head. "I don't care. The only important thing is Iona. She'll be scared. I must find her before she's... hurt."

Hetty's dark eyes softened with what looked like pity.

Alecia flung up her arm. "Don't say it! Don't even *think* it. Iona will be well. The Goddess has protected her in the past and she will do so now."

Hetty closed her eyes, and when she opened them, the pity was gone. "Send whomever you wish to find the child, but *you* need to strategize."

Lin joined them. "She's right, My Queen. *If* Iona has been taken, we must uncover the reason *why*. She could have gone wandering by herself."

Alecia heaved a deep breath. "I might tell myself that, but I don't believe it. We can't afford to think that." She examined the room. Nikolas had made the partygoers line up, and was speaking to them. Once interviewed, he allowed each guest to leave the room.

Estevot entered and approached her. "My Queen, we have completed our initial search of the castle and grounds. Princess Iona is nowhere to be found, but deep scratches on her windowsill indicate she may have been taken from the nursery through the window. Perhaps a grappling hook was used."

"Estevot, we must get her back. Tonight!"

His eyes held pity and grief. "I'll do everything I can, Your Majesty."

"What can *I* do, Captain?" Alecia asked.

"Please stay in the castle, My Queen. I fear for your life if you venture outside these grounds. I'll get her back. You have my word on that."

Alecia nodded stiffly, and Estevot left. Her eyes met those of Merielle, who stuck close to her queen.

"Will you keep me company, Lady Merielle?" Alecia asked. "I'm retiring to my room and don't wish to be alone."

Meri nodded, and Alecia turned to Lady Henrietta and Lin. "I'd appreciate it if you could supervise the search, ladies. Make sure no stone is left unturned."

When Alecia would have walked away, Lady Henrietta caught her arm. "Don't do anything stupid, girl," she muttered under her breath.

Alecia's brows rose. "Of course not." She left the ballroom before anyone else could delay her.

* * *

Katrine crouched with her hounds in a small grove of trees outside the castle wall. She had shed her skirt, under which she always wore breeches, and donned a light travel cloak with a hood which was thin enough to fold and place in a hidden pocket of her bodice. Her shoes were soft leather, like the elves wore. Not much good for dancing, but perfect for questing through the dark forest with her hounds.

The beasts were ecstatic to spend time with her. They had been apart too often lately and had caused problems for the townsfolk. So far, she had kept them under control, and they had only frightened a handful of people. But how long would it be before there was a more serious incident?

She knew how they felt. Her magic bubbled within, seeking a release. Trapped by court life, the king's funeral, recovery from the recent war, and preparations for the queen's wedding, there had been little time lately for escape. Tonight, she would remedy that.

Night Dancer, her smallest hound, a black female, stalked the castle grounds as she waited. Kat had let her in via a small access gate and given strict instructions to remain unseen, but to seek a scent trail. The most likely place to find this was under the nursery window. Kat believed Princess Iona had been taken from there.

She sent her mind waves out into the castle grounds, seeking her hound, trying to see through her eyes. Lately, if she concentrated, Kat could use the eyes of her hounds to see what they saw—if they were close. Night Dancer was one of the three hounds she had the most success with.

Nothing! She tried again, but instead of forcing her mind out, she tried to relax and let her hound's connection come to her. At first the images that came were blurry and dark, but as she concentrated, they cleared. She recognized the paving at the foot of the castle. It appeared close to where she imagined a scent might be found. Night Dancer froze as she smelled the ground, then growled. Kat sensed fear from the hound, and the impression of a dark cloud descending. The hound sniffed for a while longer, and then spun, making Kat dizzy as the stone wall of the castle flashed by. Then Night Dancer was running.

Kat bolted for the gate she had left open and stood watch for her hound, relieved when she appeared moments later, running as if a demon was on her tail. Something about the search had spooked her, but what? The dog charged through the gate and slid to a halt outside the castle wall. Kat laid her hand on the beast's head, willing her to quiet, but Night Dancer trembled, red eyes glowing in the dark. Closing the gate, Kat turned and trotted back to her pack, Night Dancer on her heels.

She squatted with the hounds as they welcomed their friend, breathing deeply to get her ragged emotions under control. She felt too much of what the hounds did, and they lived on the edge, ready to leap into fight mode and tear the throat out of any who threatened them. Kat knew they wouldn't hurt her, but how far did her control of them extend?

"Night Dancer," she said, once the doggy greeting ceremony had been completed. The hound fixed its daunting gaze on her. "Follow the scent."

Night Dancer raced back to the gate and sniffed along the wall then took off toward the town center. Kat set her two senior female hounds to track Night Dancer, then followed with the rest of her beasts.

* * *

Merielle spun to face Alecia as she bustled the red-headed lady into the Queen's Chambers.

"What do you plan, Alecia? I have not known you long, but I know that muley expression means you do not intend to sit quietly in this chamber and talk."

Alecia smiled at her friend as she quickly sized up the other woman. At a stretch, her own clothes would fit Meri. A good thing she hadn't thrown her street outfits away. She strode to her wardrobe and fished around in it, pulling out two pairs of breeches and tunics, shoes, and a light cloak.

"Dress in these," she said, tossing Meri a set of drab brown clothes, "and be sure to bind your hair and keep it covered, unless you wish Nikolas to know you have helped me."

Merielle looked at her over her shoulder as she tied her hair up and started undressing. "As if I care what Nikolas knows."

Alecia raised her brow.

"Well, perhaps I didn't express myself properly," Meri said. "I only meant I do what I like, and I can manage Nikolas if he is angry. He loves me too deeply to stay mad for long."

Alecia squeezed her arm. "We'll try not to bring his wrath down upon you, if for no other reason than it will make it more difficult for you to help next time."

A chill swept over her, and she wondered where Iona was at that very minute. Was she terrified? Missing her mother? Was she even alive?

Alecia didn't realize she had frozen, staring into space, until Meri stood before her.

"We will get her back, my friend," she said. "For now, you must have faith in your Goddess that Iona will be well."

Alecia swallowed the lump in her throat. "I keep thinking about the reason for taking her. Is it for money, power, to lure me out of the castle? Is it revenge? Surely Piotr must be behind it."

Meri, who had quickly dressed in the street clothes, helped Alecia out of her ballgown and laid it over a chair. Then she assisted the queen in donning her disguise.

"Let us investigate and see what we find," Meri said. "There! I would hardly recognize you myself, assuming you also have a cloak with a hood."

Alecia pulled herself from her anxious thoughts and fetched her oldest cloak from a peg near her wardrobe. She drew it on and pulled the hood over her blonde hair.

Meri nodded with approval. "Now, what is next?"

"You'll never believe this." Alecia strode to the tapestry of Queen Izebel and pulled it aside. She felt around on the stonework until she found the hidden latch and triggered it. A low grinding sounded as the stone swung outward, creating a narrow opening into darkness.

Meri's eyes widened. "A hidden passage. Oh, my friend! Thank you for trusting me with this."

Alecia fetched and lit a lantern, holding it up as she peered into the passage. The heavy strands of spider webs suggested that it had been some time since it was last used.

"Just tell no one about this. Now come with me. Grab that candle."

After an unpleasant journey through the passage that eventually became a tunnel under the castle perimeter wall, Alecia and Meri emerged through a trapdoor in a small grove of trees. They replaced the tunnel cover and dusted dirt over it to conceal it.

Alecia looked around to get her bearings.

"What is your plan?" Meri asked.

"I must get out of the castle or go crazy. This way I can move and think without all those eyes on me."

"Forgive me, my friend, but, as queen, surely you expect to be the object of scrutiny?"

"Of course, but you know how it can be." She began walking toward the town. "Let's take a stroll."

They journeyed in the forest as far as they could, then entered the streets of Brightcastle. Alecia was keen to check her old haunts and the houses of the nobility. Perhaps their servants had heard something. Brightcastle was a hive of activity with many residents enjoying the street party being held in the Central Square to celebrate her coronation. They joined the crowd, steering clear of the soldiers on duty. The people seemed oblivious to the drama that was unfolding in the castle, but, by their heightened vigilance, it appeared word had reached the soldiers.

Again, Alecia knew a flood of fear. How would she go on if she never got Iona back?

Their first stop was The Dancing Lion, a tavern Alecia had visited before her exile. She had never been inside, but now she pulled Meri in with her and took a seat in a shadowy corner.

Meri leaned across the table. "Are you certain this is wise? I have terrible memories of an establishment like this one."

Alecia smiled, her gaze flicking around the room rather than resting on her companion. "If we don't associate with the masses, we won't discover anything."

The Dancing Lion was full of merrymakers, mainly comprising off-duty soldiers and mercenaries, many of whom had ladies on their knee. Others were dancing, and there was a juggler in the far corner on a low stage. To say the place reeked was an understatement. Alecia wanted to place her hand over her nose, but that would draw too much attention. This was not an establishment the nobility frequented, and only a noble would notice the stench.

Meri drew a deep breath and coughed. "It is long since I smelt anything so distasteful. Even on the estate we have fresh air!"

"Voice down, Meri," Alecia whispered. "We mustn't draw unwanted attention." She sipped the ale the barmaid brought them and pondered her next move. Perhaps this was a stupid place to start the search. Shuddering, she remembered a previous visit to this tavern and how it led to her killing of the Devil. She had slain men since, but the mercenary was her first.

Suddenly, she spotted a familiar face. "Damn!" She grabbed Meri's hand and pulled her to her feet. "Make your way outside, and we'll meet in the alley behind."

Alecia immediately exited the tavern, eyes down and praying to the Goddess for concealment. She made it to the alley and rested her back against the wall. Meri soon joined her.

"That was close. I don't want anyone knowing we have been out this night."

Meri cast a worried look back to the alley entrance. "Who was it?"

"Vortek Cruzen," Alecia said. "I don't know him well, but he's a colleague of Vard's."

"That's a strange word to describe him," Merielle said. "A colleague? You mean they work together, but aren't friends?"

Alecia sighed. Vortek was a Defender like Vard, but for her, he was an unknown quantity. She didn't know if Vard trusted him, or if Vortek had been sent to watch her. He could be working for anyone. However, Defenders were oath bound to protect the innocent, so perhaps he was looking for Iona. Vortek was also a shifter.

"I don't know him well. He's a man of considerable fighting ability; one I don't want to come against."

Meri smiled. "Do not worry. Some say that I am as strong as a man. I will see that no harm comes to you."

Alecia scowled at her friend. "Strength won't matter if he sneaks up and slits your throat. Take this seriously, or I'll find another companion next time."

Meri's jaw clenched as if she was angry. She appeared to relax with effort and nodded. "I am sorry. This is serious, Alecia. Your daughter is missing, and we must find her."

Alecia nodded. "Come on. Let's go back to the street party. Keep your eyes open."

CHAPTER THREE

KATRINE kept to the shadows, following her hounds through the streets of the city. Night Dancer had disappeared into the darkness, but she could feel the hound and the two females who tracked her. The others spread out, keeping in touch with the small black female through their bond. Her mind wandered to James, her husband and head of the Queen's Intelligence Network. Where was he?

As she worried over James, a group of men staggered out of an alley, laughing and slapping each other on the back. She froze against the nearby wall, wrapping herself in a glamour that would encourage them not to notice her. Their state of inebriation helped, and the group meandered up the street. They were no real threat, especially with the hounds to guard her, but she could do without attention being drawn to her charges. Even one suspicious death in Brightcastle would not be helpful. And should her hounds kill a man, it would be obvious an animal was involved.

Her hounds were the size of large dogs, with fearsome teeth and hind feet sporting sheathed claws like a cat's. Those claws could disembowel a man, and the teeth could tear out a throat with one bite. No, there would be no mistaking a serious predator was responsible. And if she was attacked on the street, she wouldn't be able to stop them from defending her.

Kat slipped into a narrow alley, intending to take a few seconds to compose herself, before rejoining the hounds. She leaned her head against the stone wall of a small manor house, welcoming the cold against her cheek. What was she doing here? It was a question she'd asked herself many times in the last few weeks as her life spiraled out of control. In fact, things had been chaotic for months.

It wasn't long ago that she was only the second daughter of an impoverished estate, albeit a second daughter with magical powers. She had honed her craft aboard her smuggler sister's ship, protecting it against pirates, riding the waves in stormy seas and calm. Esta had used the smuggling to help keep the Aranati family estate viable, and she and Kat had traveled incognito. Those had been simpler days, even though she had suffered persistent melancholy.

Her mood had lifted more recently, but she was not where she wished to be. She had certainly never asked to be mistress of twenty night hounds, creatures of legend who had, until recently, been absent from the kingdom for more than five decades. She had also not asked to be a lady-in-waiting to the first ruling kingdom queen in centuries. At least that was temporary. How could she refuse when Alecia had raised James to the esteemed position of head of kingdom intelligence? Not so long ago, her husband had fallen out of favor with King Beniel and been lucky to escape with his life.

She sighed. They had Vard Anton to thank for his escape. He convinced the then-king to release James under his supervision. Although it had chafed her husband, he and Vard seemed to have fallen into an uneasy friendship. Kat was grateful—she really was—but it irked her they owed so much to Alecia Zialni and her fiancé.

Kat drew on her magic and sent a tendril coursing up the nearby streets, both feeling the mood and searching for her hounds. She felt a spike of excitement from Night Dancer and hoped the beast hadn't gotten herself into trouble. Kat ordered the hound back, and was surprised when the black female bounded up to her with an object in her mouth. So excited was she that she wouldn't let the object go.

It was fabric. Kat knew better than to try forcing the hound's jaws apart. That was the surest way to be bitten, despite how much sway she held over the beasts. She sent a picture into Night Dancer's mind, as near as she could form it, of her dropping the cloth. After several failed attempts to communicate her wishes, finally the hound dropped the object on Kat's boot.

As she bent to retrieve it, several warning growls sounded from other hounds nearby. Kat lashed her magic out to cow the animals, and they whined softly. That would teach them to growl at their mistress!

Their insubordination angered and scared her. If she lost control of the beasts… well, that was a situation she could not allow to happen. She picked up the fabric, but the alley was too dark to identify it. It was soft cloth, perhaps a sock? She sniffed the material. Night Dancer's foul-smelling saliva was all over it, but beneath that the faint scent of… lavender?

Kat closed her eyes and reached into Night Dancer's mind, trying to discover where the sock had been found. It was a tedious exercise—the hound wanted to hunt prey—but finally she formed a vague picture of the back of the building she leaned against. At least Kat thought that was what the hound meant. Some days she needed an instruction manual for these beasts! Most days, actually!

Mentally, she ordered the hounds to stay where they were and slid through the shadows to the back of the mansion. All was quiet. No lights burned in the windows that she could see. Night Dancer had followed her, and now sniffed back and forth near a pile of wooden boxes left out for collection. That must be where the sock had been found. But was it relevant to Iona's disappearance? Though Alecia favored the lavender fragrance, so did many others.

Kat peered up at the darkened windows, trying to memorize the look of the house, then studied the others on either side. There was no point in investigating further this night. She must find out if this sock belonged to Iona. Besides, the hounds grew restless and there was a limit to her control of them. She must allow them to hunt before they defied her.

Turning for the castle, she gave the night hounds permission to disperse to the northern forests for their hunt. Their gleeful agreement made her smile.

* * *

Alecia's heart lay heavy in her chest. It seemed her idea of prowling the city streets for clues regarding Iona's disappearance had not been sound. The roads and alleys were a mess of heaving humanity, with more than half of the merry makers severely inebriated. If there were any clues to be found, the partygoers would hide them. Tears pricked her eyes at the total waste of time. Iona could be hurt, and she was surely scared—and her mother was doing nothing useful.

She sighed heavily and looked for Merielle whom she had last seen climbing the fountain to get a bird's-eye view of the main market square. Her friend was not to be found.

"I am here, Alecia," Meri said, popping up at her elbow. "I saw nothing unusual. Perhaps you should have been the one to climb. These are your people. You may recognize someone."

"Iona could be anywhere by now," Alecia muttered. "Did you see anything at all?"

"I glimpsed a cloaked and hooded couple heading toward the houses of the nobility. It could have been a man and a woman, but they were similar in height. They were looking about them as though searching for or trying to avoid someone."

"Can we follow them?"

She shook her head. "A glimpse was all I got. They vanished as soon as they appeared. Perhaps they ducked down one of the narrow alleys." Meri wrinkled her face. "This city is like a warren for rabbits. I prefer Wildecoast."

Alecia sighed. "What rotten luck." Her shoulders slumped, and she drew her cloak around her ears. "I think we should return to the keep. I may have been missed, and I must discover if anyone has news of Iona."

They began moving toward the dingy streets that led to the keep.

"How will we enter without drawing attention?" Merielle asked.

"I've been giving that some thought," Alecia said. "You should enter via the servants' access and go to my chamber. If anyone is there, lure them outside so I can enter via the tunnel. If no one is there, lock the door and wait for me."

"Won't I get asked questions regarding where I've been?" Meri asked.

"Better you than me. I'll say I've been prowling the castle, searching for clues."

"And what of me? Why am I dressed like this? It's clear I've been outside and not at the ball."

"Try not to draw any attention and perhaps you can rejoin the party in the ballroom. Though I doubt there is much happening there. If you can reappear in your ballgown, that would be ideal."

Meri nodded. "I'll pose as a servant until I get back to your chambers."

The hairs on Alecia's neck rose, and she spun to find three men close behind them. Meri followed her lead as they confronted their drunken assailants.

"Well, lads, what do we have here?" the shortest man said. Though none too steady on his feet, his eyes held menace. "Seems a couple of ladies of the night have fallen into our laps."

The other two laughed.

"Could be our lucky night, chaps." This from a taller blond man with a scruffy beard.

Merielle gasped. "You will keep your distance or be sorry," she snapped, brandishing her knife.

Alecia had drawn two of her knives, but kept them hidden in the folds of her cloak. Intoxicated or not, they couldn't afford to underestimate these three. "Try not to kill anyone," she said under her breath.

Out of the corner of her eye, she saw Meri's sharp glance at her words. "Why ever not?"

"Too messy!"

"Now ladies," the short man said, "we won't hurt ye if ye cooperate."

The three inched closer, but hadn't drawn weapons that Alecia could see. She forced her body to relax, trying to lull the men into a false sense that she would go along with them. It worked, for they stepped within range.

Alecia lunged at the closest who was the blond man. By the surprise on his face, it was the last thing he expected. She swung her elbow at his jaw and heard a satisfying snap before the man went down in a heap. He stirred and groaned, and she kicked him in the side of the head before a hand closed around her neck.

"Now that's no way to welcome us, darlin'," the short man breathed near her ear. His muscled arm clamped her neck and squeezed, causing spots to dance before her eyes. Alecia stabbed him in the thigh with the knife in her left hand, and he let go, cursing and grasping his wound. She brought her knee up under his chin in another jaw-breaking blow, and he went down like a sack of flour. Neither of the men she had engaged made a sound, but their chests rose and fell.

Alecia took her first deep breath since the fight began and turned to find Meri behind the third man, his arm wrenched up his back, her knife at his throat. He was of a height with Meri, albeit heavier, but she held him easily.

Alecia approached, but stayed out of kicking range. "I suggest you leave this area now if you value your life. Perhaps leave the city." She paused as if to consider. "Yes, that would be best. I have memorized your face and will have the watch keep an eye out for you."

Meri dug her knife a little harder into his throat and a trickle of blood oozed down his neck. The sharp metallic scent of his life force brought memories of the night she had killed the Devil.

"Let him go, friend," she said to Meri.

Meri stepped back and shoved him hard away from her, growling as she did so. She sounded ferocious. The man landed on his face, but surged to his feet and ran off, tripping over his boots in his haste to be away from them.

Alecia grabbed Meri's hand and led her into the nearest alley, heading for the keep.

They reached the west side of the keep without further incident, and Meri helped Alecia raise the trapdoor and light the lamp, watching as she descended the ladder into the tunnel. The cover settled into place, and Alecia was alone. She hoped Meri would make her way safely to the east wall of the keep, which lay close to the kitchens. Meri assured her that was the best way, and that she could climb the wall with no help.

Alecia hadn't used that side of the keep wall much, but she didn't recall any overhanging trees or vines that would assist passage over the wall. She hoped Meri didn't break her neck! Shrugging off fears for her friend, Alecia made her way along the dank passage up through the wall of the castle and eventually stopped outside her chamber. She froze, ear pressed to the stone, careful not to trigger the mechanism that would swing the wall inward.

"Someone must know where the queen is!"

Estevot's voice carried to her while the answer did not. So, there were at least two people in her chambers. She swallowed hard, praying that her friend could draw Estevot out of the room.

Alecia slid to the wooden floor of the passage, prepared for a long wait.

CHAPTER FOUR

MERI had discovered some time ago that she was proficient at climbing. It had been a shock. Climbing shouldn't be an innate skill for a woman who once had a finned tail instead of two legs. But she was naturally skilled at many physical activities, so why not climbing?

The keep wall posed little difficulty with its finger and toe holes— just right for her delicate digits. With her extreme strength, a small crevice was all she required to scale the keep outer wall, which was three times her height. She made it to the top, listening for the patrol. Slowing her breath, she cast her hearing out, sorting through the sounds that came to her… the faint whoosh of wings as an owl took off in flight, the far-off howl of a wolf, and the sigh of the light breeze through the bushes below her. What she wouldn't give for a large tree to climb down.

The sound of boots on dirt floated to her ears seconds before two guards marched toward her perch. They weren't looking up, but she flattened herself against the top of the wall, hoping the crescent moon wouldn't give her away. Fingers crossed. The footsteps stopped just past her hiding place, and she held her breath. *Keep moving!* Meri let out her held breath as she smelled, then heard one man urinating below.

After what seemed ages, the tinkle of urine stopped, and the two guards continued their watch. Meri listened for further guards, but the night was quiet of bootsteps. Lowering her feet over the wall, she carefully descended, her fingertips and toes finding the gaps. Once down, she pulled her shoes from the front of her shirt and slipped them on, then searched for the cloak she had tossed over earlier.

Meri closed her eyes and cursed as she discovered her urine-soaked cloak. *Damn him!* She held it up, wrinkling her nose as urine dripped onto the dirt, then wrapped the garment wet side in and tucked it under her arm. Alecia might need the cloak in future, even urine soaked as it now was. The stench of the bodily waste traveled with her as she slipped into the gardens along the eastern side of the keep proper and found the servant's entrance. Saying a prayer to Llyr, God of the Sea, Meri turned the door handle and slipped inside.

Fleetingly, she thought perhaps she should have converted to Nikolas's Goddess by now, but certain things, especially the worship of a deity, were difficult to change. Again, Meri cast her senses out to the surrounding corridor. Footsteps sounded in the distance, and there was the usual kitchen noise. Alecia's chamber was in the west wing, the opposite to her current location, and on the fourth floor. She could use the servants' corridor for now and then find the access point to the upper floors.

Get moving before someone finds you! She considered leaving the cloak at the laundry entrance, but kept it with her. No sense creating suspicion by leaving it somewhere and having the house mistress ask questions about who owned it. A small thing perhaps, but Nikolas had taught her to pay attention to detail.

As she stalked the halls, the only sound she made was a soft swish as her pants brushed together. There was more than enough local noise to cover her secretive sounds. A pity she had nothing to mask the horrid cloak she carried. At last, she found the narrow stairs to the upper levels, stepping on them as close as she could to the wall to avoid creaks. Mostly this worked, and she counted past two exits until she reached the fourth-floor exit.

Meri peered around the doorway and immediately darted back. Someone was in the corridor, walking her way. She flattened herself against the side of the exit and held her breath. He strode past, heading to the west wing. When his footfalls faded, she slipped into the corridor and followed. The trouble was, there was nowhere to hide should he turn or someone else come along.

And then he disappeared! One moment he had been there, and now the corridor was empty. Meri froze, swallowing sudden nerves, and then an arm like a band of steel encircled her shoulders and a hand clamped over her mouth.

"Don't scream," a voice growled in her ear, male and not familiar. "Why are you skulking the corridors in that costume, Lady Merielle?"

So, he knew her. She closed her eyes, desperately trying to think of an excuse. The truth was not an option, especially when she didn't know him. He was confident, so perhaps a guard or soldier? The way his arm and hand gripped her spoke of competence in the martial arts.

His hand loosened. "Well? Are you involved in the princess's disappearance?"

Meri took advantage of a slight loosening of his hold and elbowed him as hard as she could in the gut, then spun out of his grip. Facing him, she dropped the putrid cloak and fended him off, hands outstretched. He was familiar. Had they met before?

"Who are you?" she snapped, reaching for the knife in her sleeve and menacing him with it.

He smirked. "Do you think you could lay steel on me, My Lady?"

She scowled and assumed a fighting stance.

He raised one brow. "Perhaps you could at that." He took a step backward. "Put the knife away and answer my question. Do you know where the Princess Iona is?"

Meri slowly lowered her blade, but kept it pointed at him. "Of course, I don't. Alecia and I are friends."

"Tonight, no one is above suspicion. You are from Wildecoast, your husband kin of King Beniel's widow."

Meri narrowed her eyes at the man. "And who are you to judge? You still haven't told me your name. You were lurking in this hall. I could have you arrested for laying hands on my person." She kept her hands and body ready to move. He would not catch her unawares.

The man raised his chin. "I am Vortek Cruzen, one of Lord Anton's Rangers. He has asked me to see that the queen is safe. I imagine he will not be impressed when he learns his daughter is missing." He fixed his direct gaze on her.

A door up the hall opened. "Who's there? Ah, Ranger Cruzen. About time you reported to me."

It was Captain Estevot's voice.

Meri watched as Vortek spoke, never taking his eyes off her. "I have the Lady Merielle here, Captain. She is dressed for the streets. I thought you may wish to question her."

"What?" Estevot strode into her field of vision, and she met his startled gaze. "My Lady? Why are you garbed so? And what is that smell?"

Estevot picked up the cloak. "She carried this and was on her way toward the Queen's Chamber."

Meri still struggled to think of a viable story to explain her garb and the cloak. Though…

Estevot stepped closer, his eyes hard. "My Lady Cosara. Explain yourself."

"The cloak I found in the bushes inside the keep's east wall. I wanted to help with the search for Princess Iona and thought I would be less conspicuous in this outfit." She showed her dark and rather tattered clothes. "I wanted to help. And it seems I did. Unless you can explain who belongs to this cloak, and why it was lying in the garden."

Neither man appeared convinced of her story. Time ticked by. If she didn't get rid of these men, Alecia would come through the tunnel and expose her secret. Meri didn't wish for Nikolas to learn of her activities this night, but he would understand. After all, she had fought in the battle to thwart the *Sis Lenweri*. Prowling the night in a man's costume was just the sort of activity he might expect from her.

"I was bringing the cloak to Alecia, thinking it might be important in the princess's disappearance. Now that she isn't here, could we perhaps inform my husband? He is, after all, one of the queen's advisors."

Estevot's right brow shot up. "I'm an advisor to the queen as well, so we hardly need to seek Admiral Cosara's help, but perhaps he needs to be informed of his wife's nocturnal wanderings." He turned to Vortek. "You stand guard outside the Queen's Chamber. No one is to go in or come out."

As she followed Estevot back down the hall, Meri struggled to not groan out loud.

* * *

Alecia sat up from her place against the stone wall. Her chambers were quiet. She strained her ears to hear, but not a sound came. Of course, that didn't mean the rooms were empty, but it might! Best to make sure. She relaxed back against the stone, listening as she counted slowly to five hundred.

Counting finished without hearing sounds of occupation, Alecia stood, stretching stiff muscles, and listened again. Still nothing. She reached along the stone and found the trigger, rewarded by the low rumble of the wall swinging inward. When the gap was wide enough, she stepped through into a blessedly empty sitting room. A flick of her fingers against the stone closed the access to the passage.

Heart pounding, Alecia took two deep breaths to bring her tormented nerves into order. It didn't work, but perhaps action would calm her. Why wasn't Merielle here? It must have been she who drew Estevot away. She slipped across to the outer door and placed her ear to the wood. A slight scuff of a boot against the floor outside told her the door was guarded. She slipped back deeper into the room, then entered her bedchamber. Best to get out of these clothes and hide them.

Placing a small log on the banked fireplace in her room, a cheery blaze soon warmed her. She lit a taper, and then her candles. Merielle's ball gown lay on the bed alongside hers. What if Estevot had searched her bedchamber? He wouldn't dare, surely. There would be no reason to. After all, she was the queen—unless he thought she too had been abducted like her daughter. Her heart seized at the pain of knowing she may never see Iona again.

She stiffened her spine and hung their ball gowns in her wardrobe, then dressed in a modest blue gown suitable for the discussions she knew would continue until dawn. Her street clothes she rolled up and stuffed in the bottom of the wardrobe, and her knives she hid in the wood box in the sitting room. Her stomach grumbled, reminding her she had missed dinner.

When her chambers were in order, Alecia sighed, not wanting to face whoever stood without. She strode to the door and pulled it open, only to be confronted by Vortek Cruzen, in a fight-ready crouch.

He snapped upright. "My Queen!"

Alecia lifted her chin and raised a brow at the man. "Who did you expect? These are my chambers, after all."

He narrowed his gaze. "I wasn't aware you were present. Captain Estevot couldn't find you, and he asked me to stand watch when he left."

"Oh, well, that explains it. He obviously didn't search my bedchamber. I felt unwell and went to lie down."

Vortek frowned. "You… yes, that must be it."

Smart man—very smart to trust his queen and not argue with her.

Alecia tilted her head to the side. "Can you tell me if you have seen Lady Merielle? She advised she needed to speak with me."

"I *have* seen the lady, but she left with the captain to find her husband."

"Can you have her brought here? And I would speak with the captain and the admiral as well. I need to know what is happening in the search for the princess."

"My Queen, I can't leave my post. Unless someone comes to relieve me, here I must stay."

"Then accompany me to the Cosara apartment."

"I can't do that either, Your Majesty. The captain asked me not to let anyone out of this chamber."

Alecia's volatile feelings bubbled up. After everything she had been through tonight, this man wanted to imprison her?

"Excuse me, Ranger, I thought you just refused to escort me to find Merielle Cosara. I must be mishearing, as you certainly would never do that."

Even in the dim hall, Alecia watched crimson creep up Vortek's neck. "Please, Your Majesty, don't take this the wrong way. I must do my duty."

"And you think Captain Estevot meant for you to keep me in my room?"

"I can't interpret it any other way, My Queen."

Alecia allowed the full force of her stare to rest upon Vortek while she puzzled over this impasse. She had no wish to be known as a queen who threw tantrums when she didn't get her way. But this was going too far. She refused to be confined to her room in her own castle. She also wouldn't force Vortek to physically restrain her from leaving. *How to save her dignity?*

She turned and reentered her room, tugging on the bell rope. While she waited, Alecia poured herself a goblet of red wine and took a bite of the cheese that lay on the table before the fire. She cast a sidelong glance toward the open door and smirked as Vortek stood stiffly at attention, giving the impression this was all in a day's work for him.

Millie appeared, hesitant to enter when she spied Vortek and the open door.

"You rang, Your Majesty?"

"Ah, Millie, please come in, but the door must remain open." She addressed Vortek. "I assume you have no objections, Ranger?"

Vortek stiffened but he gave a small shake of the head.

Millie entered, wringing her hands. "Marm, I blame myself for the princess's disappearance. I took time off to visit my sick mother tonight, and my replacement… If I had been on duty, this wouldn't have happened."

Alecia drew the maid to a chair and pressed a glass of wine into her hands.

"Drink, Millie," she said, waiting as the maid obeyed. "I don't blame you. However, that's information I didn't know. I shall tell the captain. Can you ask the chamberlain to send a senior Ranger, or someone of comparable rank, to relieve Vortek, please? I need to run an errand, and Vortek will escort me. I don't wish to leave my room unguarded."

Millie sprang to her feet, placing the goblet on the table. "I'll do that right away, Your Majesty. Thank you for not blaming me. I love that little girl like she was my own. I wouldn't ever let anything happen to her."

Alecia took a deep breath before she could speak. "I know, Millie. We'll find her, I promise."

Millie nodded and curtseyed, then hurried out. Vortek ignored her as if he hadn't heard the arrangement. She would move freely about her own home, and neither the captain nor Vortek would stop her.

Alecia sipped on her wine as she waited for Vortek's replacement, even though she wanted to down the entire goblet and pour another. It would do no one any good, least of all Iona, if she got drunk.

Before long, and to her surprise, Ramón Zorba arrived. He was still in his ball attire, his hair tussled. He slipped inside and closed the door, leaving Vortek outside.

"Alecia! Where have you been?" His eyes darted to the tapestry which hid the entry to the secret passage.

Oh yes, of course. *He* suspected she had been out and about. He knew her old habits might persist even once she was queen. But there was no need to confirm his suspicions. He had caused too much harm recently to have earned her honesty.

She gathered her nerve. "I've been right here in my rooms." There, let him call her a liar.

"Oh, you have?"

"I felt poorly and lay down on the bed. I must've fallen asleep."

His brows climbed his forehead. "With Iona missing, you fell asleep?"

"I know it sounds strange, but that's what happened." She fixed him with a look which she hoped would still his tongue. They had a long history. He should know a fruitless line of questioning when he saw it.

"I'm here because Millie informed me you needed an errand run. Can I help?"

"I need to speak with the admiral and the captain. You can escort me there, if you please."

"Of course." He stepped back and gestured to the door. "After you, Your Majesty." Ramón bowed, allowing Alecia to sweep past, rolling her eyes as she went. Their relationship was complex, and they had yet to settle into the new reality of her ascension and his demotion.

She nodded to Vortek and stalked down the corridor, leaving Ramón to catch up as best he could.

CHAPTER FIVE

ALECIA headed for the small audience chamber, recently the hub for strategy meetings during the battle against the Sis Lenweri. That branch of the dark elves had tried to wrest control of the kingdom of Thorius from the human "occupiers". They were a troublesome and aggressive segment of the dark elven race, and their peaceful cousins, the Lenweri, had helped thwart them.

As she entered, Alecia was relieved to see Estevot, Admiral Cosara and Merielle in deep conversation. She had been worried for Merielle's safety when they parted at the trapdoor, though it appeared she need not have concerned herself. Her friend still wore her street clothes but was missing her cloak. Nikolas Cosara stared at his wife with poorly concealed frustration, which was mirrored on Estevot's face. After all her success in the battle for Brightcastle, the men should have known she could look after herself.

And then Alecia listened to her own thoughts, and realized she had been as worried for Merielle as the men were.

"My Queen!" Estevot said, striding to her and bowing low. "I'm delighted to see you safe and well."

"Of course I'm safe," Alecia said, catching herself short of snapping his head off. "Best you concern yourself with finding my daughter rather than worrying about me."

"Am I not supposed to worry when I can't find you, so soon after the princess's abduction?" he asked, anger flaring in his eyes.

Alecia took a deep breath. Those words! They made the situation with Iona more real. Her mother's heart still rejected the possibility.

"You're sure Iona has been taken?" Her usually firm voice sounded panicked to her ears. She cleared her throat. "I mean, you have more evidence?"

Nikolas answered, his eyes full of pity. "The scratches on the windowsill and footprints below her room are all we have at this time, Your Majesty."

"What is being done, Nikolas?" Merielle's voice held a deal of censure. "You take me to task for checking the grounds, and yet what actions have you taken to find the princess? We need all the help we can get!"

One of the admiral's eyebrows rose. "You were checking the grounds and found this urine-soaked cloak, yes?" He held up a brown cloak that reeked of urine.

Meri lifted her chin and met his gaze. "Yes! Surely it is connected to the disappearance of the princess?"

Alecia frowned. That was the cloak she had loaned Meri to accompany her to the marketplace. Why was she declaring it had something to do with Iona's disappearance?

Merielle turned to Alecia. "My husband thinks I have been in the city. I am sorry he is letting this issue distract him when we need to find your daughter."

Nikolas looked like he would erupt, but clenched his jaw and took a deep breath. "You're right, Merielle. We can discuss this later." He turned to Alecia and bowed.

"Your Majesty, let me take this opportunity to let you know I'll move heaven and earth to find your daughter."

Alecia nodded. "So, you believe someone has taken her?"

He sighed. "After an extensive search of the keep and grounds, we couldn't find any sign of the princess. We believe she was taken through the window of her room." He looked at his wife. "This cloak my wife found may or may not be relevant. It may have lain there for some time."

Alecia fought fear that she might never see Iona again, at least not in this lifetime. She must hold herself together and try to stay positive. Vard would want that.

"What is your next move, Captain?" Alecia asked.

Estevot stepped closer. "Your Majesty, I have every available soldier combing the town, but the dark hampers us. The moment the first rays of light break the horizon, they will retrace their steps. I want to ensure we have missed no clues."

Though Estevot's words gave her some hope, Alecia couldn't help thinking that Iona could already be many miles away.

A knock at the door heralded the head steward. He gave a low bow then rose. "Your Majesty, Lady Katrine Aranati asks for an audience."

Out of the corner of her eye, she saw Nikolas stiffen and wondered why.

"Show her in, Master Etis." The man was new to his position, the former steward having retired because of his advanced age.

Katrine entered the room, seeming cloaked in shadows. She wore a midnight blue dress and navy-blue cloak with the hood pulled back. Her dark tresses cascaded over her shoulders. The candles seemed to dim in her presence, and the silver sparkles in her irises drew Alecia's attention. Someone behind her, either Ramón or Estevot, gasped. The sorceress had an imposing presence, especially for those not used to her.

She held something in her hand, and Alecia suddenly felt cold.

"You are welcome to this meeting, Lady Katrine," Alecia said, "though I thought you might have sought your bed."

Katrine's eyes flared. "How should I seek my rest when the princess is missing? You made me your lady-in-waiting and I take the position seriously. I will rest when you do."

Merielle joined Katrine. "That goes for me as well."

Alecia lay her hand on Meri's arm. "Thank you, my friend." She looked back at Katrine. "And I appreciate your support, Lady Katrine. Could you explain why you need to see us?"

Katrine held up the item in her hand, and Alecia's breath thickened, trying to choke her.

"Where did you find that?" Her voice came out a strangled rasp.

Katrine handed her the sock. "I found it in the town, Your Majesty. Close to the marketplace, but in the nobility quarter in an alley behind a mansion. I can take you there."

Alecia clutched Katrine's hands and nodded. "Yes, please, lead me there."

Nikolas Cosara cleared his throat, and Alecia realized what she had said. She turned and looked at him, then at Estevot and Ramón.

"You are all going to say I may not be involved in the rescue of my daughter." Tears threatened, but she fought them.

Ramón appeared bursting to have his say, but trying to allow the other men to speak first. After all, he wasn't her advisor, and had never been so.

"Your Majesty," the admiral said, "although I understand your need to control the search for your daughter and be involved, you must stay here. Let us act on your behalf, and if we should apprehend a suspect, you will be safe. Furthermore, there can be no claim of bias."

Alecia drew in a long breath. This was what she had feared when she became queen. She had no wish to be a figurehead, but a real monarch who acted rather than merely advising. If she were a man, there would not be this concern—or not so much. It seemed merely agreeing to a queen was not enough to change society. She wondered what her idol, the battle queen Iona, would have done in this situation. Alecia clenched her teeth so hard it hurt.

"Were I a man, you would welcome me to the scene of the crime." Alecia's words were measured, but her tone was hot.

Nikolas Cosara narrowed his eyes. "Would you have this tragedy worsened by harm coming to our queen?"

Alecia raised her eyes to his, nose in the air. "I fought in the battle against the *Sis Lenweri*. I faced down a dragon and lived to tell the tale."

Nikolas nodded. "So you did, and you and Thorius were lucky—on that occasion." His shoulders dropped, and he looked away, then turned back to her. "I understand you have a drive to be involved, but please stay here in safety. I'm sure, if he were here, Vard Anton would agree with my words. We don't need the added worry of your security. Let us do our jobs, and you do yours."

She looked at the ceiling, praying for patience. "I will stay here for now, but hear this—things will change before much longer. I will not sit idly by while men fight for me, die for me. I will lead my people in a very visible sense, and you must all accept that."

Nikolas raised one brow, but only nodded. He gestured to Katrine, and she preceded him out of the room, followed by Estevot. Meri moved to stand beside her, the woman's body fairly vibrating with tension. It seemed she, too, wanted to head back into the night. Or perhaps she was angry at her husband. Or both.

"I vow I will make the changes needed to free women in this kingdom, Meri. If I can't do it as monarch, it cannot be done. But I don't believe that."

A snort came from the other side of her, and she remembered Ramón.

"Do you have something to say?" she asked, turning to him.

"Women are better off as they are," Ramón said. "You'll be sorry if you interfere with the natural way of things."

"Is that a threat?"

"Of course not. In case you've forgotten, Alecia, I'm fond of you, and I want nothing but your happiness. That Iona is missing is killing me, and Benae is the same. You wanted to be queen, and now you have your wish. I believe you would be foolish to push for dramatic change in Thorius. It will only lead to heartache."

"You believe a person or persons hostile to my reign has taken Iona?"

"Don't you?" Ramón paused, as if he needed time to gather his thoughts. "You've been crowned a week, and Iona goes missing. What other explanation could there be?"

"Ransom?" Her heart cracked at the possibilities. There was no guarantee she would ever see Iona again. Anyone could be responsible for her daughter's disappearance. Top of her list were Piotr Zialni and Dowager Queen Adriana, either in partnership or acting on their own. And she couldn't discount *Sis Lenweri* involvement either. Then there was the possibility that whoever had taken Iona had done so for coin. Or it could be deeply personal. After all, she had killed men, both before the war and during. Their allies or families might wish revenge.

"We need to make a list of motivation and suspects," she said.

"I can help you with that." Ramón strode to a table and removed quill, ink and paper.

Alecia eyed him. Truth be told, she didn't wish to spend more time with Ramón than necessary. His lies and duplicity sickened her. But, because she was undecided, Ramón stayed. They wrote their list while eating a late supper. Meri had several excellent suggestions, and made the time spent more bearable. She had certainly been glad of her presence when Benae came to find her husband. If Alecia and Ramón had been alone, she might have jumped to the wrong conclusion.

Instead, Benae approached and curtsied to Alecia. Her eyes, when she rose, were sad.

"I regret I've not come to you before now, Alecia. The news of Iona's disappearance was shocking in the extreme, and I found I couldn't leave Solomon's side. Even now, six of our household guard him. I'm so sorry Iona is missing. We will do everything we can to help return her to you."

Alecia rose and nodded. "Thank you, Benae. If there is any justice, Iona will be found safe and well. I'd be out looking for her myself if I could."

Benae's eyes widened. "Oh no! I can understand your need to be busy, but don't place yourself at risk."

Benae's words angered Alecia, but she wrestled down her temper. "What is the sense of being safe when my child is not? Really Benae, you'd be out looking if it were Solomon."

The beautiful, dark-haired woman bowed her head. "You're right, I'd be combing the streets, even if there were no clues. Are there any? Clues, I mean?"

Ramón gave her a summary of their findings. It was a short list indeed.

Benae turned to Meri. "Lady Merielle, I'm glad to see you here, supporting our queen. She shouldn't be alone." She cast a look at her husband. "If you're finished here, Ramón, I wonder if you could help me? The night grows late."

He stood and handed Alecia the list. "I bid you good night, My Queen. Please give the items on that list more thought." He looked at Meri. "You too, My Lady. A good night to you and try to get some rest."

He bowed and escorted Benae from the room.

Alecia shook her head. "As if I'll be able to get any rest, knowing Iona is out there." Then she remembered something. "That smelly cloak was the one I loaned you, Meri."

She scowled and told Alecia the story. "I had to explain my presence in your hallway. I thought the idea of finding a cloak was excellent. Except it may be a distraction in the search for Iona."

"The admiral didn't seem to think it particularly relevant, and at least *I* know how it came to be there. We shall steer them away from it as evidence. Besides, we have Iona's sock now, and hopefully that will lead us to her."

CHAPTER SIX

VARD rested against a log and stared into the flames of his campfire. He had been gone from Alecia and Iona for a full week and daily fought the urge to turn back. Over the last year, he had missed too much of their lives. He should be helping Alecia settle into her new role, not stalking the country in search of a man who likely didn't want to be found.

Sam's voice came from the other side of the fire. "What has you so morose? Or do I need to ask?" He lounged against his saddle, long legs extended to the flames, and hands behind his head.

Vard looked up into his friend's face. Sam's green eyes were tired but no less penetrating and with his tawny hair and scruffy beard, he looked every bit the ex-pirate. But Vard thanked the Goddess constantly that Samael Delacost had come into his life. Friends were scarce, especially when you were a Defender.

"I want to return to Alecia and Iona. That's where I belong, not looking for my father. What if he doesn't wish to be found?"

Sam frowned. "Why would you say that?"

"It's been rough for him over the last fifteen years. I thought the hard days were behind us when I found him, but there's a good chance he couldn't integrate back into the society Alecia and I now inhabit."

"He loves Alecia and Iona, and he must be proud as hell of you."

Vard smiled. "Sometimes loving your family isn't enough to make you happy. My Father had many demons."

"So, you think Lyam just up and left in the middle of that last battle? Slipped away when no one was looking, rather than face you like a man?"

Vard allowed his words to sink in. When Sam said it like that, it seemed unlikely. Lyam Anton *was* an honorable man, and Vard had placed him in charge of Alecia's safety. But perhaps, seeing Alecia reunited with Vard on the battlefield, he had taken his chance to escape.

No! His gut told him Lyam wouldn't leave before the task was complete. Even with the battle in its last minutes, the danger to Alecia had been great. Lyam would not have slipped away if he could help it.

Vard met Sam's gaze. "You're right. It's unlikely he'd do that. But perhaps my assessment of him is off. Maybe I misjudged his recovery when I left him in charge of Alecia's ultimate safety."

"Is there any occasion you can think of that made you wonder about his sanity?"

The question troubled Vard. His own sanity had been tested a time or two. But, thanks to his mentor Melandrach, he controlled his bear now, and his shapeshifting gift. He would never have to battle insanity again.

"No," he said, unable to disguise his unease, "Melandrach wouldn't have released Lyam if he wasn't sure of his ability to function in the world. I know how hard he drove me to ensure I was sound. I don't think he could be fooled."

There was a light of triumph in Sam's gaze. "There you go then! Lyam didn't leave of his own free will. He was taken, likely by the enemy. As much as you want to return to Alecia and Iona, you must continue the search. Furthermore, if the enemy has him, we know where we must go."

While Vard's heart had soared at the thought of seeing Iona and Alecia again, now his stomach crashed to imagine his father in the hands of the *Sis Lenweri*. Though defeated in battle, perhaps they hadn't crawled away to lick their wounds. And if they had Lyam, it would take more than the two of them to rescue him.

"We're close to Amitania," Vard said. "We'll call in and see Gwaethe Arenil and Jacques Vorasava. I'm sure they'll be interested to hear our suspicions."

They were up before first light, but Vard had already scouted ahead in his wolf form. Sam knew Vard was a shifter, but they barely discussed it, and Vard preferred to keep private his nighttime scouting as the wolf. Sam realized he did it, but knowing and seeing were two different things. Sam was the first friend he had made in a long time, and there was no point making him more uncomfortable than necessary.

Vard had covered a lot of territory as the wolf in the three hours after midnight, coming across several tracks leading north. During the last week, he and Sam had crisscrossed the country to the north and east of Brightcastle, searching for evidence of Lyam's presence, but with so many tracks made by elves, men, and horses, even Vard's superior tracking had been inadequate.

He had thought these areas were most likely to have been used by his father to escape the battle and also by the fleeing *Sis Lenweri*. Now he was more convinced that Lyam had not left of his own accord, it was easier to predict the direction of flight.

Since the defeated *Sis Lenweri* had traveled north after the battle, it made sense that they had taken Lyam with them. Of course, his father could be dead, but why kill the man if they could use him for leverage in the future? That didn't rule out the possibility of them torturing Lyam. He pushed the thought from his mind.

After returning from his scouting, he had snatched two hours of broken sleep before Sam had woken him. The hours of nightly scouting were taking their toll. He wasn't getting any younger. Shaking off the negative thought, Vard forced himself to be alert as he rode his horse, Trax, through the scrubby forest that led to the Usetar Mountain Range.

By midday, they narrowed the tracks down to two which could be linked to Lyam's disappearance. Men had made the other trails, possibly kingdom patrols sent to ensure the elven invaders left

Thorius. It was difficult to follow the two paths of elven prints, and they had horses and ponies with them which muddied the tracks. Lyam's mare had broken its leg at the end of the battle, so he might be on foot if he could walk.

If he could walk… which begged the question—if Lyam could walk, why hadn't he simply transformed into the bear or wolf and made his escape? Vard had given the matter much thought over the days since his father's disappearance, and was yet to come up with a reason. Unless he was dead. His heart squeezed tight in his chest, and he closed his eyes, allowing Trax to pick his way through the trees with free rein.

"What's wrong?" Sam's voice came from the right.

Vard opened his eyes and looked at his friend. "Nothing more than usual. I was trying to understand why my father hadn't transformed in order to escape. That leads me to think he might be dead."

Sam sighed. "Of course, that could be the case, or he could have been badly injured and unable to transform, been unconscious. They could have used bribery on him."

Vard cast him a doubtful look. "Bribed with what? Lyam can't be bribed."

"Last night you told me you thought he had fled of his own accord, and now you say he can't be bribed? Make up your mind, Vard. Is he a sinner or a saint?"

"I can't imagine what threat would keep him with the *Sis Lenweri*."

Samael laughed. "No one said you had a brilliant imagination." He slapped his chest. "I, on the other hand, have an excellent grasp of possibilities. And I'm not heavily emotionally involved with Lyam, so I'm not hindered by that."

Vard rolled his eyes. "Oh, really?" This was why he enjoyed Sam's company. The man could usually brighten the darkest day. "Do I want to hear your imaginings?"

Sam cocked a brow. "Perhaps not, but I think we need to consider them." He paused, frowning. "Your suggestions are valid, of course. Lyam may be dead, unconscious, or have been forced to go along with the *Sis Lenweri*. For example, a potion could keep him dazed or unable to transform. And I've heard the elves have certain magics at their disposal."

Vard frowned. "How come you to have this knowledge of that branch of the dark elves?"

"For my sins, when I roamed the high seas, I had a *Sis Lenweri* crew. It was just me and the dark elves. At first, I thought them only elven, but soon deduced they were a kind I hadn't heard of."

Vard inhaled deep and long. "The *Lenweri* have magics, but I've seen nothing that could overcome the power of a Defender." And if they did harbor talent that strong, Vard feared for the future. What would stop them from taking advantage of those Defenders who protected the kingdom? The *Sis Lenweri* surrender was yet to be finalized, despite the deaths of their leader, Faenwelar, and his son, Gorin.

"Perhaps it's a talent exclusive to the *Sis Lenweri*. We can ask Princess Gwaethe and her elders when we arrive in Amitania."

"We can ill afford the time for discussions, but we need reinforcements, and it's not far out of our way—perhaps not out of our way at all. If I could determine... What's that?"

They were following the more eastern tracks, and Vard's keen eye had fallen on something stuck in a tree. He trotted Trax closer, Sam on his heels. Wedged in a rough piece of bark were several dark strands of hair. Vard pulled the fibers loose and held them up for Sam to study.

"They're not elven," Vard said. "They're too coarse, and have a slight wave, though the color is right." Almost all the elves, *Lenweri* and *Sis Lenweri*, had dark brown to black hair. Vard's own hair was nearly black, and Lyam's was an identical color. Vard pulled a few strands of his own tresses out and compared them. "Almost the same." He looked up at Sam, who stared at him as though mystified.

"How did you see those hairs at that distance? It should be impossible, even considering your gift."

Vard shrugged. "I got lucky. I think the wind moved them. and I was looking in the right direction."

Sam frowned deeper. "Are you sure you don't carry more magic than just your shifter abilities?"

"That's a story for another day. This eastern trail is the one we need to follow. Those hairs must belong to my father. He placed them there, or his head brushed the tree."

"Or someone placed them in the tree, hoping to divert us."

Vard's gut tightened. The *Sis Lenweri* were cunning enough to do that. "The enemy could be drawing us in or trying to divert us, but for now I'm going to assume Lyam is either deliberately or accidentally leaving a sign."

With the help of Vard's animal forms, they had been monitoring both trails made by the elves. Both seemed of a similar age, and both groups had horses. They followed the eastern path with Vard covering sections of the more western path as the wolf or the hawk. The hawk had superb vision and could easily spot tiny clues of the passage of the elves through the open forest. The wolf's sense of smell might be keen enough to sniff out Lyam, but, to date, Vard hadn't detected his father's scent. There was only *Sis Lenweri*, horse, and the assorted metal, leather, and foodstuff that went along with an army.

He thumped his thigh with a fist, and then again, feeling no less frustrated.

"I'll scout ahead, Sam, and take a look at the other trail on my return." He was tired enough to fall asleep on Trax, not having had proper rest for over a week. "You follow at a quick walk or trot with the horses. I'll meet you at nightfall." By that time, they would enter the mountains.

Vard dismounted and handed Sam his reins before jogging into the trees.

"Take care!"

Vard raised his hand at Sam's words, but his mind was all on the transformation, forming the picture of the large gold and black hawk in his mind. In minutes, he perched on a branch in one of the taller trees, watching as Sam rode past.

* * *

The hawk launched itself and climbed out of the forest to fly above the canopy. The man below would examine the trail while the hawk would wing its way north. In a matter of minutes, it outdistanced the man and flew on until well ahead. It dropped amongst the trees, and trained its eyes on the slightly flattened path below. The hawk had no real notion of why it behaved this way, but knew a powerful drive to explore anything not natural to the forest—like that thing there. Something glinted under a tree, almost hidden by forest detritus.

The bird landed and grasped the bright round thing in its beak, then took to the air again. It flew northward, into the wind, but the gusts gained intensity. Before long, it must turn back or exhaust itself. It flew west and south, looking for the other path the elves had taken. It came across a diagonal trail that appeared to originate from the western trail. By this time, the bird's strength had almost failed, and it was all it could do to flap back to the eastern trail.

* * *

Vard leaned against a tree and spat a feather and something else from his mouth. He flicked the feather away and examined the silver button as he brought his breathing under control. He had vague memories of picking the button up from the side of the trail, and stronger memories of it resting on the cuffs of Lyam's coat. It belonged to his father; he was sure of it. Was he conscious enough to be leaving signs for them to follow?

He shook his head, shivering in the cooling air. The light would soon be gone. A noise came from the south, and he picked up the sound of a horse approaching—no, *more* than one. He stayed hidden, waiting for the horses to come into view. When they did, he spotted Trax, and let out a relieved breath. He was in no condition to fight.

Vard attempted to join Sam on the trail, but his legs went from under him, and he sprawled on his hands and knees. In seconds, Sam was beside him.

"Are you injured?" he asked, feeling over Vard.

Vard shook his head and waited for it to stop spinning. "Just tired. I was out too long, and the wind was too strong for flying in. I left it too late to turn back. One of the risks of the hawk."

He tried to rise, and Sam helped, guiding him back to Trax, and into the saddle.

"Let's find a spot to camp," Sam said, casting him a worried look before trotting up the trail.

Vard left Trax free to follow, and chewed on a stale biscuit he had stored in his saddlebags. By the time Sam found a suitable campsite away from the road and the wind, Vard was feeling more himself. Sam surveyed him warily and well he might, for he had never seen him so weakened.

Vard met his friend's gaze. "I'm fine."

Sam huffed. "I've seen you tired, and it barely affects you. That was downright almost dead!"

Vard shook his head. "No need for anger. I'll be right as rain with warm food and a little rest."

Sam's face appeared in front of him, too close for comfort. "No need for anger! You could have died, and where would that leave us? Damn you, man! The kingdom needs you; Alecia needs you." He stared at Vard, but evidently didn't get the response he was hoping for. "Well, if you die, don't expect me to carry your sorry ass back to Brightcastle. How would I explain to the queen what happened to her fiancé? Eh? How?"

Vard held up his hands. "Sorry, okay? I miscalculated. It won't happen again. I'll use the wolf instead, except I would never have found this as the wolf—not this soon anyhow." He held out the silver button, and his friend looked at it as if it were a deadly spider.

"Looks like a button," Sam said, voice surly and frown evident. "Is it Lyam's?"

"It is. He's leaving a trail for us." Sam started to object, but Vard held up his hand. "I know it could be a false trail, but I don't believe it is. Perhaps we missed an earlier clue, or maybe he was unconscious for several days then began leaving them later into the journey. And there's something else."

Sam cocked a brow at him. "Well?"

"It appears those who made the western trail have merged with this one. You'll soon see it coming in from the left if I'm correct. The hawk was weary, but I'm pretty sure that's what it saw."

Sam peered skyward, as though praying for divine help, and then began settling his horse and collecting firewood. Vard attended to Trax and started a fire with the wood Sam found. Neither of them spoke as they made dinner then ate. They finished their meal with strong tea, and lay back against their blanket rolls, feet outstretched to the fire.

"What's bothering you, Sam?" Vard asked.

He was quiet for so long that Vard thought he hadn't heard.

"You don't realize how valued you are, or understand that you aren't on your own anymore. You can depend on me and many others, but still you act as a one-man band. It's infuriating when you risk your life, never thinking how it will affect those around you."

Vard inhaled a long breath. "I *do* think about it. But I'm a loner and can't see that changing. Perhaps, at my age, it's not possible."

Sam narrowed his eyes. "I was a loner too, until Esta came along. Believe me, I understand feeling alone, even when you have an entire crew around you. Though with a *Sis Lenweri* crew, all speaking their foreign language, it's isolating." He paused and seemed many miles away. "Anyhow, now I have family and friends. I have no desire to lose any of them before they live a long and happy life." His green eyes tore through Vard. "That includes you. So next time you push yourself too hard, think of all those you would leave behind—including your father. You're not much help to him dead."

Sam threw the rest of his tea on the fire, pulled his blanket over himself, and rolled with his back to Vard. It looked like he had the first watch. His instincts screamed at him to take the wolf form and prowl the forest, but he suppressed the beast. His body needed rest. He dropped into a half sleep that would allow him to hear if enemies approached.

CHAPTER SEVEN

KATRINE led Estevot and the admiral back to the street where she had found the sock. All the while, her hounds were a presence in her mind, urging her to leave the men, and run in the hunt with her. Their wild joy called to something deep within, but she walled the emotions off and concentrated on the task at hand.

"This is the place," she said, stopping in an alley across the street.

"Do you know who owns that house, Estevot?" Nikolas asked.

Estevot conferred with the half-dozen men with him. "Lady Stenmore, Admiral."

A prickle ran down Kat's neck. The woman had been engaged to James for a time, and was a key player in the intelligence service. Was there more to her than it appeared? Why would she be involved in Iona's kidnapping? Or was the sock dropped near her manor house without any connection to her?

"She may not be involved," Nikolas said, "but we must search her residence." He motioned for half his men to cover the back of the house, and set off for the main entrance with the rest of the soldiers. Estevot and Katrine followed.

They paused before the impressive dwelling, and the admiral turned to her. "My Lady, please wait here. It may be dangerous."

She crossed her arms, wanting to be involved, but not wishing her magic to be exposed. If there was danger, she would find it difficult not to unleash her gift. She nodded and stepped aside to lean against the wall beside the door.

Nikolas motioned for Estevot to knock. The sound rang up the street which had quieted as the party wound down. The door opened, and Estevot requested Lady Stenmore. They gained entry, leaving two men outside with Kat. She strained her ears for any indication of what was happening in the house, but all she heard were two bumps like doors being flung back.

Lights bloomed in the manor, and Kat stepped cautiously over the threshold, despite the protests of the men with her. Raised voices carried to her from upstairs.

A manservant was arguing with the captain.

"Her ladyship won't be pleased at this intrusion."

"Search the house, and leave nothing unturned."

Estevot's order was followed by the clatter of cupboard doors being opened and belongings being moved around.

Unable to dampen her curiosity, Kat carried on into the lower rooms, using a tendril of magic to light enough candles to see by. After a short debate, neither of her minders followed her, wanting to ensure the front door was guarded.

No, Melanis Stenmore would not be pleased. She was a member of the previous king's intelligence network, that much James had told Kat. According to him, she was above reproach. Kat wasn't so sure. She had recently met Lady Stenmore, and the woman made her uncomfortable. Of course, that might have been jealousy that she had loved James first. But Kat didn't think it was only that. There was something "off" about the woman.

By the time the admiral found Katrine looking about, she had unearthed nothing.

"There was a reason I asked you to remain outside, My Lady." His voice was crisp, disapproving. She knew he didn't like her, perhaps didn't trust her.

"Without me, you'd have no evidence, Admiral." She fixed her eyes on him, knowing that in the candlelight, the swirling silver in her irises would be evident.

His gaze darted away, and he whirled to begin going through papers on a desk.

"There's nothing there. I already looked. I assume Lady Stenmore isn't at home?"

"You assume correctly."

"Any clue where she is?" Kat asked, peering into several silver containers on the mantel. They contained small strips of paper, possibly used for notes which could then be attached to pigeons or ravens.

"The servants aren't forthcoming. I doubt they know her location, but I'll take the steward in for questioning."

"So far no sign of Iona." Kat muttered, chewing a strand of her hair.

Estevot appeared in the doorway. "The serving girl says Lady Stenmore has an estate outside the city. I think we should search there."

The admiral sighed. "Yes, you see to that, and I'll question the steward. He's most likely to know the lady's business."

* * *

The morning after her Coronation Ball, Alecia awoke from a fitful sleep just after dawn. She squinted at the weak light coming through the chink in her heavy curtains, and moaned. Iona was missing, along with her heart. As she sorted through the events of last evening, she realized they were no closer to finding her daughter than when she first vanished. What she wouldn't give for Vard to be here to handle the search. But he was somewhere to the north, and didn't know of her desperate need for him.

She pushed herself up, swung her legs over the edge of the bed, and spotted Lady Merielle asleep against the wall beside the fireplace. Her friend wore a dressing gown over her sleeping attire, her legs drawn up, arms resting upon her knees, and her head on her forearms.

Alecia shook her head. She didn't wish to disturb the woman, but she couldn't allow her to take her rest in such an uncomfortable situation.

"Lady Merielle," Alecia said, bending over and gently patting her shoulder. "Wake up."

Merielle groaned. "I feel like I have slept in a hole."

Alecia smiled. "No wonder. You fell asleep against my wall."

Meri's head rose, and she blinked sleepily at Alecia. Then her green eyes sharpened.

"I'm sorry, My Queen! Even after all that wine we imbibed, I could not rest. When I came to keep you company, you were asleep. So, I sat beside the fire, pondering who had Iona. Sometimes staring into the flames helps me think. Not so this time. I must have fallen asleep."

Alecia offered her hand, and helped Meri to her feet. "I'll ring the bell for breakfast. Then we can tackle the day ahead."

Meri helped Alecia dress as they waited for the food to arrive. And thank goodness for Meri's help, as it was more than Alecia could cope with to decide the proper gown—considering the circumstances. What she wanted to wear was her breeches, tunic, and armor. She longed to saddle Silver and take to the road in search of her daughter. But they had no clue of which path to take.

Her heart cracked as she recalled the last update from Nikolas. Lady Stenmore was absent, and her household servants couldn't say where she was, or when she would return. Or when she left. She wondered if Captain Estevot had discovered anything at the noblewoman's country house.

"There!" Meri said, stepping back to admire her handiwork. "The silver and red gown suits you very well. It is fitting for your station without being somber. You must stay positive. The people will look to you for their mood today."

Alecia shook her head. "Then they will need cheering up. How can I put on a brave face at this time? Iona is missing, perhaps dead, certainly terrified. We have no idea who is responsible. What if we never find her?"

She heard her voice rise and couldn't do a thing to stop it. Meri grasped her hands, and her touch pulled Alecia back from the edge. She took a deep breath and met Meri's eyes. There was so much strength there, and Alecia knew she could rely on her. But her heart betrayed her. What use was Meri's strength when she might have lost Iona?

"Stop it!" Meri's voice struck Alecia like a whip. "You cannot despair, but must remain strong for your daughter and your people. You will believe in yourself and your staff. We will see Iona returned to you. Rely on it."

"But—"

Meri's hand flew up, index finger pointing upward. "You will believe in us, and you will stay strong and determined. There is no other option." The red-haired woman's piercing gaze held Alecia spellbound. When Meri said it like that, she could believe.

"My Queen?"

A young maid paused in the doorway of her bedchamber. She dropped a curtsey first to Alecia, and then Meri. "I've laid the breakfast in the sitting room before the fire." She paused, her gaze flicking between her two betters. "And Captain Estevot is outside. He asks for an audience with Your Majesty."

Alecia drew a deep breath. "Thank you, Claudette. I would say send the captain in, but Lady Cosara is in her sleeping robes."

Merielle made a dismissive sound. "I do not care if the good captain sees me like this. It is more respectable than some of my ball gowns, after all."

"Then send the captain in, Claudette."

The maid bobbed a curtsey and left the room. Alecia and Meri followed, finding the small table in the sitting room laid for two with tea, sweet rolls, and an assortment of preserves. Meri fell on the feast like a woman starving while Alecia poured the tea, wondering if she could stomach any food.

A clearing of the throat nearby brought her out of her pondering. Estevot bowed low to both ladies.

"Your Majesty; Lady Cosara," he said. "I'm sorry to disturb your breakfast, but wanted to speak with you before I attended to the day's duties."

Alecia nodded as she sipped her tea. Meri merely waved a hand at the man.

"What do you have to report, Captain?" Alecia asked.

Estevot sighed, not quite meeting her gaze. "I traveled to the country estate of the Lady Stenmore overnight. I didn't find her there. The servants—a housekeeper, maid and manager—said they hadn't seen her in several weeks."

"But you don't believe them?"

Estevot tilted his head. "I'm not sure. It was quiet as the grave out there, but the servants seemed nervous where there should have been no reason for it... unless they have been up to no good, or they know something they're not telling."

Alecia clenched her teeth and placed her cup and saucer back on the table. "Another dead end! When will we discover something which might lead to my daughter?"

"My Queen," Estevot said. "I'm sure if we can find Lady Stenmore, we will rescue Princess Iona."

Alecia stood. "I'd like to take comfort from your words, Captain, but there is simply no reason to. Melanis Stenmore may have something to do with Iona's kidnapping, but so could several others we haven't yet discussed."

"You're referring to Prince Piotr?"

"Not only him." Alecia walked across the room to the window which overlooked the courtyard. "As you know, Dowager Queen Adriana is not happy with her decline in status. She was seen talking to Piotr. Perhaps they have hatched a plot together." She turned back to face Estevot. "And there's also the *Sis Lenweri*. They appear to have retreated to their mountain home, but what if they are behind Iona's disappearance?"

"How would they benefit from such an action?"

"It could be simply an attempt to get money from Thorius in return for Iona's release. Or perhaps they are trying to undermine my rule by removing one of my heirs."

Estevot looked doubtful. "Perhaps."

Alecia continued. "And then there is Lyam Anton's disappearance. I strongly suspect the *Sis Lenweri* took him, though Vard wasn't convinced of that. I know Lyam would not have abandoned me in the heat of battle."

And Vard would realize that, too, once he thought it through properly. She hoped Vard was close to finding his father, so he could return for his daughter's sake... and hers.

"Your Majesty," Estevot said, sounding far from convinced. "Why would the enemy take your fiancé's father?"

"Ransom? Or perhaps he has something they need. What if they want to draw Vard away from me at this critical time, and that was the way they chose?"

"Well, if so, it worked," Estevot muttered.

Alecia folded her arms and glared at her army commander. "I've given this much thought in the time since Lyam and now Iona disappeared. We can't afford to rule out any motive. I expect you and Admiral Cosara to follow all leads, no matter how unlikely. Keep your minds open, and your eyes. You're dismissed."

Estevot frowned at her words, but stood to attention, bowed deeply, and left the room.

Alecia flopped into her chair. "Men! If they spent more time thinking and less effort trying to keep women in their proper place, the kingdom would be better for it."

Meri used her moistened finger to pick the crumbs from her empty plate. "My Nikolas thinks a great deal. I believe you are being unfair to both he and Captain Estevot."

"Do you? Nikolas maybe, but Estevot was a thorn in my side during the recent battle against the *Sis Lenweri*. I had to fight tooth and nail to get anything I needed. He only respects me now because he must." She drained her teacup. "They all think they know better than I, even though I've proven myself time and again."

Merielle handed her a plate with two sweet buns. "Eat these and feel better, my friend. Then we shall tackle the day."

* * *

Katrine hung up her cloak on the stand in the entrance hall of her townhouse, and turned to find James frowning at her, hands on hips.

"I've barely seen you these last twenty-four hours, Katrine," he said. "Where have you been?"

Kat sighed, noting the formal use of her name. "I have business to attend to, as you do. And I'm Alecia's lady-in-waiting. It has been a trying night."

"Of course it has." James approached and kissed her on each cheek, holding her close for precious moments. "I was worried about you, that's all. I'm always worried about you these days."

"You don't need to be. I have the hounds for protection."

"It's them I worry about most. You can't deny they pose a risk to your safety."

"I don't believe they do," she said, shaking her head. "Unless you mean the consequences for me if one of them is killed." She shuddered, remembering the horrific pain Dawngazer's injury had recently caused her. Her mind shied away from the fact that James had killed the hound to save Kat's life. It was a mercy killing, but she hadn't accepted that at the time. Eventually, she had come to terms with James's actions.

She tightened her arms around him and rested her head on his chest. "If only things could be the way they were when we first were married. We were in control of our lives then."

James laughed wryly. "You think? I haven't felt in control of my destiny since I met you."

"Since you were almost run over by me, you mean?" She basked in the warmth of his adoring gaze as she remembered careening into James, who had stopped on the road with his cart and pony. "I'm glad you've now taken to riding horseback instead of relying on a pony and trap to get about."

She looked up at him and melted as his lips descended to hers. His demanding mouth and tongue soon swept her away to a place only James could transport her. How had she once believed she could live without this man? Kat slid her arms around his neck as his hands roved her body, pressing her curves against the bulge in his breeches.

Next thing she knew, Kat lay before the dancing flames of the fire, skirts around her waist and James inside her. In mere moments, she was on the edge of orgasm, his clever fingers fondling her nub as his lips slid over her neck. With a last thrust, James stiffened and groaned. Kat shuddered hard, screaming her ecstasy. As she came back to reality, she wondered if this would be the lovemaking that led to a baby. She so wanted one, but the responsibility of caring for a child terrified her.

"I'm sorry, my love," James said, taking his weight on his arms as he looked down at her. "I was desperate to have you. It was too quick, I know. We can go again when I'm ready, and I promise to take it slower."

She fondled his cheek. "I wanted it fast and furious. You're not the only one who has been desperate for connection. It seems like we are never in the same place at the same time anymore. Either that, or I am exhausted from running after the hounds and the queen."

James rolled off her and lowered her skirts to make her decent. "Tell Alecia you can no longer be her attendant, then. She has many who could take your place."

"That might be true, but do they have her best interests at heart? Or the kingdom's? It's no accident that she chose us four to attend her. We might not be her best friends, but we are loyal, and can be relied upon to tell her the truth."

James nodded. "Those are rare qualities, and not to be undervalued." He frowned. "How is Alecia holding up? I heard they found the child's sock in town."

Kat hesitated. "Yes, outside Melanis Stenmore's townhouse."

"You know Melanis can't be responsible for the abduction, don't you? She was a member of King Beniel's intelligence network, so we can't question her integrity."

Kat's gut churned at the thought of James's former betrothed. She couldn't be impartial where Melanis was concerned. She'd tried not to interact with her on the few social occasions they'd run into each other. Luckily, Melanis seemed equally reluctant to engage.

But just as Kat couldn't be impartial, neither could James.

"I beg to differ," she said. "If we don't keep an open mind, we might overlook important clues. Indeed, Estevot has already traveled to the lady's country estate to speak with her. She is nowhere to be found, and none of her servants are talking."

James frowned deeply. "That *is* strange. Melanis rarely leaves the city, and her country estate is the only place she resides on the rare occasions she travels outside Brightcastle. No sign of a struggle at her mansion?"

"None. I hate to say it, James, but Lady Stenmore had better show herself soon, or she'll be our chief suspect."

"I'll look into the matter." His gaze flicked back to her and darkened with desire. "But before I do, let me attend to your urgent needs, My Lady." He bent his head, and Kat giggled with delight.

CHAPTER EIGHT

VARD and Sam rode hard all day and made it through the mountain passes, arriving in Amitania after dark. They crouched behind a bramble bush at the base of one of the gigantic forest trees that grew close to the eastern wall of the city.

Vard cast his senses out—smell, hearing, and that sixth sense that never failed him. He perceived only the occasional stealthy footfall or kicked stone—guards going about their business. The patrols could be elven or human, for both lived in this multicultural city. True to her word, Princess Gwaethe wished her people and her husband's to exist in harmony.

Gesturing to Sam, Vard left the brambles and ghosted to the stone of the city wall, noting the repairs made since his last visit. The stonemasons had been busy. He felt rather than heard Sam behind him and nodded to himself. His friend moved as quietly as an elf. There was little light in most of the streets, and the moon was new. Perfect for creeping through the elven city without notice. They would be welcome enough if announced, but Vard wanted to arrive and leave with the minimum of fuss.

It was relatively easy to navigate the dark streets if they kept their wits about them. He spared a thought for their horses, secreted in a nearby clearing. Hopefully, they would be safe until they returned. His stallion, Trax, certainly could handle any wolves that threatened him, though Vard had sensed none this close to Amitania. All would be well.

Nonetheless, unease squirmed in his gut. The first time he visited this city was with Alecia in her year of exile. They had been on the run from her father, and seeking a mentor to help Vard master the bear. Alen Leck, a sorcerer, had lived in Amitania then, and it had been the home of a band of *Sis Lenweri* who were training there.

Vard had hoped the sorcerer, another shifter, might be his mentor. However, the longer they dwelled there, the worse things became for him, and for Alecia. To his shame, the sorcerer had coerced him into training the elves with the sword and in hand-to-hand combat—skills they had used in the eventual war with the kingdom. He clenched his jaw in shame at the thought.

In the end, he and Alecia fled, and, when Leck tracked him down, Vard killed him. That time was foggy in his memory. Suffering injuries sustained in the fight with the sorcerer, Vard morphed into the wolf to save his life. He became trapped in that form. Alecia had left him, staying on a farmstead, pregnant with his child. It was a dark period in his life and still gave him nightmares.

He shook off the chill that the memories brought and focused on the large stone edifice ahead. Likely that was Gwaethe and Jacques's home now, though it had housed the treacherous sorcerer in the past. They skirted the square that lay before the building and were about to mount the stairs when a dozen elves materialized before them. Vard froze as the guards snapped at them in elvish.

He drew back his shoulders. "If you wish us to do as you say, speak the kingdom tongue," he snapped.

The leader stepped forward, taller than Vard and almost as heavy. He brandished no weapon, but had no need of it when all his men trained arrows on the pair of intruders.

"Remove your swords and knives, and place them on the ground, kingdom man," the leader said.

Vard was surprised by his tone, particularly the contemptuous way he spoke the words "kingdom man", but he complied with the request.

"What is your name?"

"I am Vard Anton, and this is Samael Delacost. We come in peace to speak with Princess Gwaethe and Lord Vorasava."

Vard could see the elf had heard of him from the slight stiffening of his body.

"If you come in peace, why do you I find you sneaking about the streets, *Lord* Anton?"

Vard ground his teeth. "We must carry out our mission in the utmost secrecy for the sake of Thorius."

The guard leader sneered. "Indeed! Well, we shall see how Princess Gwaethe feels about her rest being disturbed, and her city invaded. Follow me." The man turned and strode toward the palace, flicking his fingers at his men, who closed in around Vard and Sam.

As the guards herded Vard toward his goal, he wondered again at the attitude of the elves who had intercepted them, coming close to violence before giving them a chance to explain themselves. But would he have been as aggressive in their shoes?

His gaze took in the building he had once called his home, however briefly. It was difficult to tell in the dark how much it might have changed from the ruins the *Sis Lenweri* had inhabited. Inside, the shadows revealed a little more furniture than in the past, and there were wall hangings in abundance which he couldn't remember being there. They were hustled through the reception area and climbed the massive staircase, then were deposited into Leck's old office. Six guards were positioned around the room, and the rest left. They didn't extend any hospitality.

Sam huffed out a breath. "Well, this is a fine mess you got us into. I thought you said we'd be welcome here?" He lounged on an overstuffed chair, one leg over the side. One thing about Sam, he never seemed to be upset or anxious. He usually gave the appearance of being composed, and Vard appreciated that trait more than usual.

"I thought we would be, but it seems I misjudged the manner in which we entered... or perhaps the stealth required."

"We should've announced ourselves or waited for dawn. Now I guess we'll cool our heels until daylight." Sam pulled out a pipe, filled it, and lit it with a taper from the fire. All the while, the guards kept an eagle eye on them.

Vard paced in the small area of the room available.

"Sit down, and I'll let you share my pipe," Sam growled.

Vard grunted. "I'm not one for smoking, normally." He kept pacing.

"That was *not* a suggestion," Sam said, puffing a fat smoke ring into the air.

Vard glared at his friend, who returned the look with a cold one of his own. So much for the previous way of things between them, where he led and Sam followed.

He hmphed out a breath and sat, arms crossed. Sam handed the pipe over, but Vard ignored him. He had to maintain his position in this relationship somehow. If he caved in now, he would never live it down.

"Look," Sam said, "we may as well relax and enjoy ourselves before the axe falls—if it does. That's why you asked me along, to advise and guard your back… isn't it?"

Vard allowed Sam's words to sink in as his eyes lingered on the coals of the fire. In the end, he reached for the pipe and sucked on it. The tobacco was a superior blend from the Goddess knew where. Perhaps Sam still had pirating contacts or smugglers who could get the stuff. Then again, Vard was no expert in tobacco.

"There," Sam said, and, without looking, Vard heard the smile in his friend's voice. "Isn't that better? You look more relaxed already. I always say when you don't have a drink, a smoke is the next best thing."

Vard looked over at Sam to find him grinning like a loon. Despite himself, Vard couldn't help smiling. And yes, he *was* more relaxed!

Sam clapped him on the back, took the pipe, and puffed contentedly, closing his eyes. It wasn't the first time Vard had been grateful to have the company of a friend instead of his habitual solitude. He felt a pang of guilt at thinking that, knowing that Alecia would consider herself Vard's best friend. Indeed, she was, but having a male friend was a revelation. He knew he wasn't the most likeable or approachable person—far from it—but Sam appeared to accept him, faults and all.

He was deep in thought about the changes Sam had brought to his life when the door opened, and the guard commander strode into the room, standing stiffly to attention.

"Princess Gwaethe Arenil and Lord Vorasava," he announced in a loud voice.

As Vard rose from his seat, Vorasava and the princess entered the room and paused, taking in their guests. Gwaethe wore a high-necked formal gown with silver details and full sleeves with points in the elven tradition. There was a haughtiness to her visage that made her even more beautiful. Vorasava was in full uniform, but not that of Thorius. It was green and silver, and reminiscent of elven garb, but with silver rope, shoulder decorations, and buttons. The livery was quite something. His face looked like thunder.

Vard bowed low and noticed Sam do the same. "Princess, My Lord. I must apologize for the lateness of our arrival."

"Yes," Vorasava snapped, "you must, Lord Anton. This is rude even for you."

Vard's brows climbed his forehead before he could guard his expression. Was this the same man whom he had risked much to save?

"I'm aware the time and style of our arrival might seem the height of rudeness, but I beg you to listen to our reasons, Lord Vorasava."

The man opened his mouth, thunder on his face, but Gwaethe placed her hand on his shoulder, and he remained silent.

"Tell us your story, Lord Anton," she said. "There is much friendship between our cities." She pushed her hands out, palms down, as if smoothing choppy waters. "After the troubles this city has endured, you will understand we are on high alert. And we believe the recent *Sis Lenweri* surrender was merely a ploy."

Vard's stomach leaped into his throat. "That is fell news indeed."

Gwaethe spoke quietly to one of her guards and continued into the room, leading her husband by the hand.

"Please be seated." She drew Jacques down onto a loveseat positioned opposite the couch Sam and Vard occupied. A low table stood between the chairs, and servants laid a late supper, including red wine.

The guard leader approached. "What are your wishes in relation to these intruders, Princess?"

"You are to leave us in private. Two guards may wait outside, otherwise please return to your duties."

"Your Highness?" The elf seemed speechless at her dismissal.

"That will be all."

The elf looked at Vorasava, who flicked his fingers in dismissal. With a stony face, the leader left the room, taking his men with him.

Vard cleared his throat. "Again, I sincerely apologize. I would not have invaded your city unannounced had our need not been crucial."

"Invaded is a good word," Vorasava snapped. "It is fortunate there were only two of you. The guards may have shot first and asked questions later. What brings you here?"

Vard considered. Perhaps it would be best to explain their situation first, and then ask for help.

"You would know my father disappeared in the last minutes of the battle?"

"Of course," Vorasava said. "I'm sorry."

"Thank you. Master Delacost and I are looking for him. Our search has led us into these mountains. It appears the *Sis Lenweri* have taken him."

"Why do you believe that?' Gwaethe asked, folding her hands in her lap.

"We saw signs, likely left by my father. But two men aren't enough to rescue him if the *Sis Lenweri* have him."

Gwaethe snorted indelicately. "Are we never to have a moment's peace from their plotting?"

"Why would they take your father?" Vorasava asked.

"Who knows why the *Sis Lenweri* do anything?" Vard snapped, not missing the hard look Vorasava gave him. He sighed. "I've tried to answer that question. Perhaps they wish to draw us into their territory in a rescue attempt. But there is no guarantee anyone would come for my father. As it is, we initially thought he had run away of his own accord."

"And why would he do that?" Gwaethe asked, leaning forward.

"I can't know my father's mind. He has led a troubled life this past decade, and we have just found each other again. However, Sam led me to see that Father wouldn't have left his post, which was to protect Alecia."

Vorasava smirked. "From what I observed, Queen Alecia isn't easy to protect."

"Damn near impossible," Vard muttered. He took a swig of the wine. It felt good as it burned its way down his gullet. "Regardless, my father went north with the retreating *Sis Lenweri*. We ask for your help in retrieving him."

Gwaethe and her husband looked at each other for long moments. Finally, Vorasava nodded.

Then Gwaethe turned to Vard. "We will be glad to help, but I think we should bring my brother Kain into this hunt. He is the king apparent of my people, and, if you are correct and the *Sis Lenweri* are responsible for Lyam's disappearance, Kain will want to know. I have a means of contacting him."

"We should inform Prince Arenil," Vard said. "We could certainly use his help."

"Tell him to summon the black dragon," Sam said.

Gwaethe and Vorasava cast the ex-pirate identical sharp looks.

"Nugoriem doesn't come when Kain snaps his fingers," Gwaethe said. "He is an ancient and regal beast with his own agenda."

Sam's reply was a smirk.

"I'm sorry if my companion's comment offended you, Princess," Vard said. "Please contact Prince Arenil and inform him of our suspicions. It will be up to him how he acts upon the information."

Gwaethe nodded and stood, the fingers of one hand fiddling with a ring on her other hand. She left the room, accompanied by her husband.

Sam slumped in his chair and huffed out a breath. "That was tense. Worse than an interview with my brother Nik." Sam referred to his half-brother, Nikolas Cosara, the kingdom Admiral.

Vard frowned. Cosara was a hard and prickly individual at the best of times and often seemed to resent Sam's presence. Additionally, the admiral had no love for Vard, who had run afoul of him more than once.

"Watch your words with those two. We don't want to offend them."

Sam shrugged. "I *was* watching my words."

Vard barked a laugh.

Sam took a mouthful of wine before continuing. "I wonder what this 'means of contacting' Princess Gwaethe is talking about? Do you think it's magical?"

Vard shrugged. "If it is, then I have no objection. I've heard of witches communicating over distances." He wondered if Sam knew his own sister-in-law was a sorceress. Lady Katrine Tomel née Aranati was not only in control of the night hounds, but in command of powerful magic. Her sister Esta must surely know of her talents, but it wasn't a topic one wanted spread around.

The two men finished their meal and drinks while they waited for their hosts to return. When the door finally opened, Gwaethe was on her own, and her eyes were wide. She looked at Vard and swallowed hard.

Vard leaped to his feet. "What is it, Princess?"

Gwaethe's jaw was tight as she approached them. "I have fell news from my brother." She stopped before Vard and placed her hand on his shoulder.

Vard's heart almost stopped. What news would make her act thus? Had someone discovered his father dead? Did Kain have some other ill news? *Alecia!*

"Just tell me, Princess," he ground out.

"Kain is in Brightcastle. The keep is like a kicked ant's nest. Your daughter, Iona, she is missing!"

Vard's heart not only stopped, but cracked in half. *Iona!* "When did this happen? What is known? Is Alecia well?"

Vard felt Sam's big hand land on his other shoulder and was glad of the support.

"Your daughter went missing the night of the Coronation Ball. It appears she was taken from her room through the window. As it has only been a matter of two days, investigations have uncovered few clues regarding the exact method of and reason for her disappearance." Gwaethe explained what was known. "My brother has summoned Nugoriem, who has agreed to help in the search. I told him what you feared regarding your father's disappearance, and Kain thinks it is too much of a coincidence that two of your family are missing. He will travel here when the black dragon arrives."

Vard clenched his jaw with such force that he was surprised his teeth didn't crack. His composure evaporated like smoke on a breeze. Alecia would be beside herself with fear over Iona's disappearance. He needed to be there for her, and he needed her presence more than ever.

"Is Alecia coming here?" he croaked. "She will want to help in the search."

Gwaethe's chin rose. "Alecia is now the Queen of Thorius. She cannot act as she once would have. Her advisors will keep her in Brightcastle."

The princess was correct, of course, but… Just when they had all they ever wanted—to think that everything might be snatched away. In that moment, he realized that if Iona could be found alive and well, he would never ask the Goddess for another thing.

"Who would take her?" he asked. Sam's fingers tightened on his shoulder.

"There was no time to discuss theories with Kain," Gwaethe said, "but if my elven cousins have taken your father, could they not also be responsible for Iona's kidnapping?"

Vard raked his fingers through his hair, pulling his leather head band out. His dark waves fell over his face, and he was grateful for the shield they provided against the sharp eyes of the princess. So cool and in charge she sounded—but then her daughter wasn't at risk.

"It could be the case," Vard said, the words reluctant on his tongue. But all *Lenweri* valued children of any race. They wouldn't hurt his daughter, surely? Perhaps not, but there was always the chance of accidental death when the stakes were high. And Iona would be terrified. This could change her forever.

As if he knew what Vard was thinking, Sam spoke. "Iona is *your* daughter, Vard. She'll come out of this happy and well. If there is any trauma, you and Alecia will deal with it."

Vard sighed. "I can't even think about that until we have her back safe with us."

Iona's disappearance must be linked with Alecia becoming queen, he considered, no matter if it was *Sis Lenweri*, a ransom attempt, or something else. Alecia had drawn attention to herself and her family with her desire to become the ultimate ruler of Thorius.

"Your thoughts, Lord Anton?" Gwaethe said, her dark eyes probing.

If his heart wasn't frozen, Vard would have laughed. His only thought was to charge back to Brightcastle and track down his daughter; to take Alecia in his arms and make her believe all would be well. "I leave for Brightcastle as soon as I can gather more provisions."

"No!" Gwaethe snapped. "Now is the time for calm reason, not knee-jerk reactions, My Lord. You will lose valuable time should you return to Brightcastle. I urge you to wait until Kain arrives with Nugoriem. He has said he can be here by midday tomorrow. Nugoriem can travel magically to Brightcastle, but will need to fly here, hence the delay."

"Delay?" Sam said. "I count that very swift indeed." He eyed Vard. "We should resume our search at dawn. The dragon can catch up with us." He turned his attention to Gwaethe. "Are you able to supply soldiers and scouts to aid our quest, Princess?"

Gwaethe held up her hand, and Sam fell silent.

"Lord Anton, your thoughts?" she asked.

Vard felt foolish. He had never been this "at sea" before. What sort of leader was he to go all to pieces when his family was threatened? What use could he be to them? He was the best tracker he knew, for obvious reasons, and could be useful in Brightcastle, tracing his daughter's kidnappers.

He thought back to Prince Gorin's rescue from his tower prison in Wildecoast. A dragon had aided the *Sis Lenweri* prince's escape, and one could be involved now—if the enemy was again behind Iona's disappearance. Tracking a dragon would be impossible, but he had other skills that could help.

Though he wondered how Alecia fared and longed to support and comfort her, he sighed and faced Gwaethe.

"As much as my heart urges me to race to Alecia's side, that might well be the wrong action to take." He paused, closing his eyes and looking deep to discover the best course to follow. Once sure, he opened his eyes. "I'll resume the search for my father, and Kain can catch us up. Hopefully, he'll bring more news with him."

Vorasava entered the room. "I have thirty men and elves ready to help you, Lord Anton."

Gwaethe cleared her throat. "I too will accompany you," she said.

Gwaethe's husband snapped, "Out of the question!"

"Princess," Vard interjected, "if Alecia can't lead the search for Iona, then how can *you* be spared here?"

"My thoughts exactly," Vorasava ground out. "You must stay here, Gwaethe. It's too risky."

"Besides, Princess," Vard said, "once your brother joins us, you can help with communications back to Amitania at least. It will do no good if you are both present in the same location."

Gwaethe scowled. Vard held her gaze.

It seemed the *Lenweri* princess wasn't above making mistakes when there was an adventure to be had. At last, she nodded.

"You are right, Lord Anton. Even though it grates to be bound to this city, I will stay so I can relay information. It is a pity there are not three of us, so we could have someone in Brightcastle."

Vard nodded. "Yes, that would be ideal." He mused a moment on Hetty's use of fire for scrying—a handy tool for communication across distances—then shook the thought away. "Kain should be able to find us easily enough once he and the dragon reach Amitania."

CHAPTER NINE

ALECIA paced back and forth across her small audience chamber. Her maid had roused her from bed with a request from Kain Arenil for an audience. It must be urgent for him to wake her. Not that she was asleep. She had slept only fitfully since the night Iona vanished. Perhaps mulled wine would settle her stomach. That too had been more queasy than usual the last day or so.

Telling herself that wine wouldn't help, she poured some anyway, and sipped the fragrant liquid. A pleasing warmth burned its way down to her stomach and she took a deep breath. If only she could "do" something. She had always been more inclined to action than waiting. Now, as queen, everything had changed.

There was a sharp knock at the door, which kicked her heart up in pace. The deputy steward, who took care of night duty, stuck his head around the door.

"Prince Arenil to see you, Your Majesty."

"Send him in."

Kain swept into the chamber, eyes tight and hand gripping his sword. "My apologies for disturbing your slumber, Majesty."

Alecia gave a ladylike snort. "It is of no concern, Kain. Tell me your news."

His eyebrows rose. "I do indeed have news—from Amitania."

"Oh?"

"Vard Anton has arrived there."

Alecia's heart lurched. "He is well?"

"Yes. He and Master Delacost are both in good health. But their path has revealed signs that the *Sis Lenweri* may have taken Lyam Anton. Items belonging to Lord Anton's father have turned up on one trail the *Sis Lenweri* took after they left the field of battle."

Alecia's chin rose. "I *knew* they must be involved, but even Vard thought Lyam might have run away of his own accord." She paused, taking deep breaths before asking the next question. "Does he know about Iona?"

"Lord Anton has been informed of the princess's disappearance."

Alecia felt her mind slow, thoughts frozen by an image of Vard, getting that news when he was far from home. Would he charge back and take control of the search? A very large part of Alecia wished he would.

"What was his reaction?" she asked, sounding calm to her ears but battling to keep the wine in her stomach.

"He was distraught, as expected. He wanted to be by your side and help in the search, but he has been persuaded to continue the hunt for his father."

Alecia nodded, deeply conflicted.

"He sends his love and prayers for your fortification during this difficult time."

Her eyes snapped to Kain's.

"They were not his words."

"No, but I couldn't repeat what he said, Majesty, not in polite company." Kain's neck was a blooming shade of red.

Alecia straightened her shoulders, and looked him in the eye. "We shall manage well enough without him." Her words made him shift his feet.

"What else, High Prince Arenil? Your discomfiture speaks of more tidings and ones I won't like."

He cleared his throat. "I've summoned Nugoriem, and will fly on him to meet Lord Anton and Master Delacost north of Amitania."

"No! I can't spare you, no matter how important finding Lyam is." Her heart squeezed at the thought of managing without his support.

Kain advanced and grasped her hand. "Alecia, I believe there's a good chance the two disappearances are linked, and that Iona could also be on the way to the holds of the *Sis Lenweri*. Gwaethe has made men and elves available to accompany us." His eyes hardened. "As the leader of the peaceful elves, and the heir apparent of the entire elven people, I must act against this threat. I cannot stay here and do nothing!"

Alecia almost snapped back, "*I* have to stay here!" but ground her teeth on the words. She was a queen now, and she would try to control her emotions, no matter how difficult it was.

"I understand. We will manage. Who will you take with you?"

A voice carried from the door.

"You must take me, Your Highness."

Katrine Aranati stepped into the chamber and dropped curtsies for the two leaders. She wore a blood red gown over sleeping attire of a similar shade, but dark shadows lay beneath her eyes as if she had not yet taken her rest.

Kain eyed her. "Why should I take *you*, My Lady?" One of his eyebrows rose, but it was the only sign that he didn't take her seriously.

Alecia crossed her arms, curious to hear Katrine's reasoning. She thought she knew, but was still surprised the woman had offered.

"Your Highness, I have heard you can communicate with Princess Gwaethe via a magic talisman?"

Kain stiffened. "How did you hear that?"

Katrine tossed her head, reminding Alecia of a highly bred and flighty mare. "That doesn't matter. Is it true?"

Kain stared hard at Katrine before nodding. "It is. I'd appreciate it if you could keep that information to yourself."

"By the lack of surprise on the queen's face," Katrine said, "it appears *she* was already aware."

"As the kingdom ruler, I was privy to this information," Alecia said stiffly.

"Whatever," Katrine said. "I understand you wish to keep this information to yourselves." She fixed Kain with irises that swirled silver. "I understand because I also have a magical means of communication. If I accompany you, I could keep the queen updated on the search. Also, I have 'friends' who can be formidable fighters."

"Lady Aranati," Kain said, "are you aware that I intend to fly to Amitania and beyond on the back of a dragon?"

Katrine's chin rose. "I do. It will not be a problem."

Alecia stepped forward. "Will your 'friends' be able to follow you?"

Katrine smiled. "They will need to catch up, but yes, they will have no difficulties, one way or another." The silver sparkles in her eyes flared in the candlelight, and a jolt of unease chilled Alecia's neck. As unconcerned as she was about witchcraft—having spent so much time around Hetty—it seemed Katrine had talents Alecia could only guess at.

Kain looked from one to the other. "I don't appreciate your secrecy, ladies. This feels like a club, and I'm denied admission."

Katrine switched her attention to him. "Don't be concerned, Your Highness. All will be revealed should it be necessary. I'm glad to be of help, but the nature of my gifts must remain hidden, at least for now. Perhaps it will not always be so."

"If you speak of magic, I accepted that long ago," Kain snapped.

Again, Alecia interrupted. "This is wasting time, Kain. I'm sure you have preparations to be made, and now so does Katrine. My Lady, I give you leave to travel with High Prince Arenil. Do not be concerned about your duties here. I can manage."

Katrine curtsied. "Then I'll be about my packing."

"Travel light, Lady Katrine," Kain said, his voice cold as the stones on a winter's morning.

Katrine nodded, then swept from the room.

Kain glared at her retreating form, then turned to Alecia. "If I must travel with her, at least I should know a little of her magic. She is a sorceress?"

Alecia sighed. "I know little of her gifts, Kain, but I can vouch for her. Lady Henrietta knows her well."

"And these friends of hers? Who are they?"

"I cannot say, but Vard is aware of them. They are formidable, but you have no cause for concern."

Kain growled. "I'd like to be the one to make that judgement!"

"You'll be flying a massive fire-breathing dragon! I think you can deal with whatever Katrine brings with her!"

Kain's gaze turned chilly, but he managed a respectful bow before wishing her a good evening and departing. She would not like to be on that man's bad side. What an unusual night this had turned out to be!

* * *

Two hours later, Katrine stood beneath a tree at the edge of the archery range north of Brightcastle. Her hounds surrounded the range, hidden in the forest. She counted them in her mind, and spoke words of love and encouragement. The thought of a dragon spooked them, having dealt with the beasts in ancient times.

Kat wasn't too keen on dragons either, for that matter. She had once scared one off with her fireballs when it attacked James. She still didn't know where that beast had come from. It had been black or a very dark green. Nugoriem was black, and a green dragon was involved in the battle of Brightcastle. She had witnessed none of their attacks in the battle, but had heard plenty.

A shiver ran through her. Kain should be here by now. Unless he had given her the wrong location and was already on his way north. But soon hoofbeats sounded from the trail, and Kain appeared on his black horse, accompanied by his elven guard of twelve. They would take the horses back to the keep. Kat patted her mare's soft nose, and the creature snorted.

"Good of you to join me, Your Highness," Kat said. "I was wondering if you were still coming."

It wasn't dark enough to hide the man's raised left brow. "Not that I must explain myself to you, My Lady, but there was more to organize than I expected. And I had to see Alique." Kain's wife wasn't happy he was haring off across the kingdom on a dragon's back. She had told Kat herself when she had come to her room, and begged her to keep her husband safe. She had, of course, promised she would—but what did Alique imagine she could do? Kat wasn't a warrior, and Alique didn't know of her witchcraft. At least she should *not* know of it... She must have scowled because Kain held up his hands.

"Let us not begin this journey on a sour note," he said. "I'm glad of the company, and if you can do what you say you can, it will be an immense help."

"I can," Kat assured him. "Where is the dragon?"

Kain smiled. "Dragons have only a vague sense of time. Nugoriem will come when he comes, and it would pay for you to be polite."

"Of course, I shall! I don't appreciate you implying I might offend the creature."

"Just watch what you say, anyway."

Kat folded her arms while Kain dismounted, collected her horse, and led the two beasts to his guard commander. The two had a low-voiced exchange, and then the commander spread his squad around the clearing.

Kat steeled herself for the dragon's arrival, hoping he wouldn't prove to be the same beast she had encountered before. If he was, that would *not* be a great way to start their mission.

It seemed she wasn't the only one on edge. Kain strode back and forth across the open area, his gaze occasionally flicking to the sky. The silhouette of the distant mountains appeared, heralding the sunrise. They were supposed to be away before now, the first leg of their flight undertaken in darkness.

Birds resting in the surrounding trees twittered as they prepared to greet the sun. Kat always enjoyed this time of the morning, when the day was full of promise and mystery. A flowering tree close by lent the perfume of its flowers to the dawn, and she breathed deeply of the intoxicating scent. Her heart slowed, and she smiled to herself.

But then the bird calls fell silent as if a heavy blanket had fallen over the trees. A low "whopping" sound sent a shiver down her spine. It came from the north. A glance in that direction revealed a dark spot that rapidly enlarged, revealing itself as a huge flying beast. The first rays of the sun struck its scales, causing them to glow faintly. She glanced over at Kain, who observed the approach of the beast with quiet intensity.

"Nugoriem, I assume?" Kat asked, taking a deep breath to settle her pounding heart. Clenching her teeth, she wrestled her fear back under control and waited, arms folded across her chest.

"He won't hurt you," Kain said quietly. "Just don't offend him."

She snorted. "How does one *not* offend a dragon? Apart from being 'polite', of course." Her very presence here could offend!

Kain cast her a last frown and raised a finger to his lips, leading Kat to clench her teeth. She longed to teach him a lesson he wouldn't soon forget.

When Nugoriem finally hovered over them and sank to the grass, Kat steeled herself not to take a step back. The creature was enormous—certainly much larger than the one that had attacked James. Some of the tension left her shoulders at that realization. At least she could start this trip without that weighing her down.

Kain approached and bowed low. The dragon inclined his head, and Kain appeared to be listening to something. Kat heard no sound. Then Nugoriem's gaze swung to her, his one remaining reptilian eye plunging ice into her core. She bowed low as Kain had, but the dragon stayed frozen, unblinking.

Kat dropped her gaze before the beast, trying not to upset him.

"Raise your eyes, sorceress!" Nugoriem rumbled. His voice sounded in her head rather than in the air, and she wondered if that was the only way he could communicate. In her peripheral vision, she saw Kain stiffen.

She peered up at Nugoriem, noting the brilliant yellow of his iris and the elongated slit of his pupil. This close, she felt the heat of his breath. He opened his mouth, and Kat swore she saw fire in the back of his throat. If he attacked, she would have to try a quenching spell and hope that would be enough to save her.

"It is long since I have seen a human witch. Why do you come now? I sense you are not alone."

He must mean the hounds. She didn't want her dominion over them revealed to Kain. Not yet anyway. It must be her secret—though James, Samael and Vard knew… and now, Alecia. *Not much of a secret after all.*

Kat sent Nugoriem a meaningful glance, hoping he would understand. "There aren't many of us left, though I hope that changes. And, as you can see, I stand here with Prince Arenil, heir apparent of the kingdom of the *Lenweri.*"

Nugoriem's gaze narrowed, and Kat felt sliced through. "I know the high prince. We shall not speak of the others yet. But we *will* speak of them." Kat took a shaky breath as his attention switched to Kain. She sent her magic into the shadows, seeking her hounds, and found them a safe distance away. They would follow her wherever she went, but Nugoriem unnerved them. They had no desire to meet him.

While her attention was elsewhere, Kain had loaded Nugoriem with their supplies. The dragon showed where Kain could tether saddlebags and water bottles. He wore no harness, but there were several prominences which looked to Kat as though they might come in handy when she needed a place to hold on to. She was definitely thinking twice about this voyage.

All too soon, Kain was gesturing her to mount. She buried her fears and strode over to the enormous beast, then used his foreleg, boney ridges, and bumps to climb onto his back. Kain followed and settled in front of her. Nugoriem's voice rumbled in her head.

Do not fall. I cannot catch you.

Kain chuckled, but Kat scowled. Nugoriem swung an eye to them, catching Kat's expression.

You are forewarned, little sorceress. Hold on tight, and you may yet survive this flight.

"Little sorceress indeed," Kat muttered, then yelped as Nugoriem flexed his legs and leapt into the air, his wings outstretched, carrying them quickly aloft with powerful downward sweeps.

She clutched Kain's sword belt with one hand and a thin protuberance on Nugoriem's back with her other hand. Squeezing her thighs and digging her heels in, she fought for stability, every muscle in her body tense.

In front of her, Kain appeared to have little trouble keeping his balance.

"How do you do it?" she asked, through clenched teeth. She took her right hand from the dragon and wrapped it around his waist. A semblance of calm returned at his solid security. It was difficult to get used to the motion of the dragon as he moved in the air, and wind currents buffeted them from time to time.

"Try to relax. Think of him as a giant horse. The motion is a little different, but the principles are the same. Staying calm helps, too."

Kat glared at the back of Kain's head. It wasn't often her composure suffered, especially not since she had fully embraced her powers. But this was not an ordinary situation. She admired Kain's ability to accept the challenge—indeed all the trials that had come his way over the last year or so. His life had radically changed from being general of the Wildecoast army, to discovering and embracing his elven heritage, a new family and people. Nugoriem's support had come along with that.

"I'll try. Sorry I'm using you so much for support." She had wrapped both of her arms around Kain's middle.

He chuckled. "That's fine, Lady Katrine. You're not interfering with my balance. If you don't panic, and you do as I ask, we'll be safe."

Kat again ground her teeth. Unfortunately, she had come all too close to panicking as the dragon launched into the air. However, she was becoming accustomed to the motion of the beast, and her body had loosened its death grip. If she stayed alert but relaxed, she might survive this, and not pull Kain to his death.

CHAPTER TEN

A FTER snatching a few hours of sleep, Vard and Sam accepted the bundles pressed upon them by Gwaethe and said their goodbyes. Jacques had supplied thirty men and elves to help with the expedition to the *Sis Lenweri* stronghold.

They arrived in the stables to find their companions already saddled and formed up. Four scouts approached Vard.

The leader was a short, stocky man with blonde hair and long mustaches. He bowed. "My Lord Anton, I am Tholdrek Opalgrip, and I lead the scouts. We heard of your need and wanted to help." He gestured behind him to another man who could have been his brother, and two elves. "They are Lungret Frostforge, Tanulia Venna, and Ara Olocan."

All bowed. Vard inclined his head, then studied the scouts. The two elven scouts were female. Both returned his gaze, their scents distinctly prickly, which wasn't unusual for elven females. He hoped they were nothing like Isiloe. Gwaethe's cousin was the most difficult female Vard had ever encountered.

"I am grateful for your help, Opalgrip. What is your story?"

Opalgrip frowned. "Have ye not heard of us, Lord Anton? Though we are not of this kingdom, the dwarven race is ancient, perhaps even more ancient than the elves."

"Dwarves?" Sam said, glancing at Vard, no doubt to measure his surprise against his own. "I thought your people were only a rumor at the most, a race that no longer existed."

Vard cleared his throat. "My pardon, Opalgrip. Indeed, I have heard your legends, but never met one of your race. Though, now I see you, perhaps I have come across your kin many years ago and didn't realize it."

The dwarf didn't appear mollified by Vard's words and apology. "We have been too long from the kingdom," he grumbled. "Have ye at least traveled the paths under the mountains called Usetar? Our people once mined that region."

"I have not, but I thank you for your presence today. How come you to be in Amitania?" Vard hoped the question would distract Opalgrip from his disappointment.

"Though we be rarely in Thorius, we hear news from time to time, and our people sometimes visit your kingdom. We once counted the *Sis Lenweri* as our allies, if not our friends. We have heard fell things such as civil war amongst the dark elven race, and a direct threat against Thorius."

"You heard correctly, Opalgrip. We believed we had settled the threat against the kingdom, and ended the elven civil war. It appears we may have celebrated too soon."

The dwarf nodded. "We noticed *Sis Lenweri* incursions into our lands which lie far to the north of Amitania, around and under the Northern Alps. And so, we came to investigate, keeping our eyes open on the way."

"How many of you are there?" Sam asked.

"We number thirty-four in our party. Six good men we lost on the journey, thanks to the enemy."

"All men?" Sam asked. "No women hunters, then?"

Opalgrip scowled at Sam.

"We cannot risk our females in battle. They are heavily involved in governance, and responsible for raising and educating our children."

Sam raised his palms. "Say no more, good Opalgrip. I agree wholeheartedly. However, it's not always the case that our females follow the rules of society."

"Well, ours *do*," he snapped, "and our race is stronger for their contribution. Thankful I am that they are not exposed to the peoples who foster female fighters."

Tanulia Venna and Ara Olocan, the elven scouts, raised their chins and stared coldly at the dwarf. Could this be the cause of their prickly scents?

Tanulia spoke. "You would do well to remember our presence, Tholdrek Opalgrip, or we may show you how competent female fighters can be."

Opalgrip stiffened. "Be at ease. No offence was meant, I assure ye."

"Still," Ara said, "we must work together on this mission, and statements such as the one you made do not lead to harmony between our people."

Opalgrip bowed his head. "I will heed your words." It appeared the elves weren't getting any more apology than that.

Vard concluded that a distraction was called for. "We should get underway. Please disperse your scouts, and let me know immediately of any concerns."

Opalgrip nodded and strode away, motioning for Frostforge and the two elves to follow. The glares on the elven scouts' faces, implied they would request more apologies in future.

Sam joined him. "Diplomacy not his strong suit, then?"

Vard snorted. "You might say that. However, he seems a forceful leader, and fierce."

"He'll need to be if he persists in upsetting the *Lenweri* scouts. Let's mount up and be on our way."

Vard's party rode out from the stable yard and entered a broad avenue which would take them north towards the heavily forested mountains the *Sis Lenweri* were rumored to inhabit.

* * *

It was early morning when Kain and Katrine arrived over Amitania. Somehow, Kain communicated with his sister, and Gwaethe directed him to an enormous park in the center of the city. Nugoriem landed, and they dismounted, offloading their belongings.

Gwaethe was already present, along with Jacques Vorasava, and a small group of human and elven officers. Kat had briefly met Gwaethe in Brightcastle, and the elven princess filled her with awe. Not only was she exotic and beautiful, but a princess and a battle leader. She carried herself with an assurance Kat envied, and one she would never emulate.

Nugoriem took off, his wings raising a storm of leaves and twigs, and Gwaethe stepped forward to embrace her brother. They spent a few moments conversing quietly before Gwaethe approached Kat.

"Lady Aranati," Gwaethe said, and Kat dropped into a moderate curtsey. "It is so nice to see you again, though I didn't expect it would be so soon. Please rise."

Kat straightened. "These are troubled times, Princess." She peered at the retreating form of the dragon. "And strange."

"Indeed," Gwaethe said, following her gaze. "Nugoriem is only one of the strange happenings of the last year. But he seems to be an ally for now."

Kain joined them. "You think the black dragon will betray us?"

Gwaethe tilted her head and shrugged. "Who is to say? History tells us the great dragons are fickle creatures who are ever more concerned about their own preservation."

"No different to any of us, then?" Kat asked, eyebrow raised.

Gwaethe frowned. "I like to think I have the greater good in mind in all my dealings. It is why I fought for peace in the recent battles. The *Sis Lenweri* do not want peace, but more holdings for themselves. I believe they would be happy to wipe the *Lenweri* out."

"We won't allow that to happen," Kain said, his hand on Gwaethe's shoulder. "And I'll be wary of Nugoriem."

"If he turns on you, he will be a formidable enemy," Gwaethe said.

Kat gave her attention to the park. The lush grass and shrubs were a surprise in the center of the city, especially when it had been a ruin until recently. There was even the beginning of a small forest close by. Several fountains spouted water, and stone benches were placed throughout the lawns.

She felt a presence at her shoulder, and turned to find Lord Vorasava. He smiled and nodded.

"My Lady Aranati. This must seem strange to you compared to your coastal home."

Katrine smiled up at him. "It's good to see you again, My Lord. I was indeed wondering about this place. The park is extraordinarily peaceful. I wouldn't have expected it in a ruined city."

"The park is a memorial to the elves and men lost in the battles with the *Sis Lenweri*. Since Brightcastle, we have added more souls to the park, although many were buried on the killing field."

He shook his head, a sad light in his blue eyes. "I thought the killing was over, but it seems there is more to come." His sharp gaze fixed on her. "I'm surprised to see you here with Kain."

Kat grimaced, but she should have expected questions.

"I have the means to communicate over distance, and thought I could be of help."

"Ah, some kind of sorcery? I have no objection to a little magic if it's on the side of good. How do you do it—the communicating?"

"I'd rather not say, if you don't mind."

He scowled at her. Surely the man couldn't expect her to give away all her secrets. Perhaps one day if witchcraft was no longer outlawed, she could relax her guard somewhat. Currently, even though Alecia might prove to be a champion of magic practitioners, with such instability in the kingdom, Kat wasn't trusting many. The less those in power knew of her gifts, the better.

Kat kept her nerve, and Vorasava finally nodded and turned away. He joined his wife, and they led the way out of the park, Kat and Kain following, servants behind with their baggage.

"You don't look happy, My Lady," Kain said quietly. "Is there a problem?"

Kat huffed. "Only the usual. Vorasava was being nosy about my 'skills', and I refused to enlighten him."

"You can trust him, you know."

"I can't even trust *you*, Your Highness."

Kain stiffened.

"No offence," said Kat, "but trust is earned. I came along on this jaunt to aid communication, and that's all."

"You speak with extreme forthrightness."

"I find it's best to let others know where I stand. There are fewer misunderstandings that way."

When Kain didn't respond, she continued. "Look, think of me as a thorny plant, and treat me with respect and a little distance. That way, you and I should get along fine."

Kain fixed her with a stern eye. "I don't imagine we'll be spending much time together now our journey has ended."

Kat crossed her arms over her chest. "I'll continue with the expedition. I think it's best I see the situation firsthand. And my other skills may come in handy." She almost mentioned her association with Vard, but decided not to. She and Vard each had secrets that the other knew, and an understanding that they would never reveal those secrets to others.

Kain nodded. "Then let's join the Amitanian leaders and break our fast."

They continued in silence, but Kat's mind was far from calm.

* * *

Alecia worked the sword with Arelle, one of her lady guards. Physical activity was the only way she could endure the hours of waiting to hear about Iona. Even during this mock battle with the black-haired guard, acid churned in her stomach.

"Harder," she gasped, attacking Arelle and forcing her back against the fence. "Must I thrash all of you to stop you from holding back?"

Anger burned in her opponent's blue eyes as she held Alecia's practice sword from her throat. "Enough!" She shoved Alecia, who spun to the side and knocked Arelle's legs out from under her with the wooden blade.

Kenna, another of Alecia's guards, stepped between them, giving Arelle a hand to her feet.

"Will you be next, Kenna?" Alecia asked, taking a step back and breathing hard. She rested her sword point in the dirt of the practice arena.

"This is madness!" Kenna hissed. "You'll get hurt, or hurt someone. None of us can afford to be out of action, or accused of injuring you."

Alecia quirked a brow. "I think we are all proficient enough to avoid that, don't you?"

Kenna scowled. "No. Not when you have both lost your tempers. It was obvious the next altercation would see blood spilled."

"Not to me," Alecia said through gritted teeth. "Anyhow, what's a little blood when—" She trailed off, realizing where that thought was going. She wouldn't be that woman who thought no one else mattered when her daughter was missing. Unfortunately, her guards knew her too well.

Cretia, a pretty blonde who was also a member of the lady guards, joined them. "Your Majesty, hurting each other won't bring Iona back. Neither will harsh words." The last was said quickly, and with a pleading look in her baby blue eyes.

Fury lashed through Alecia. She wanted to take that anger out on someone, but these women didn't deserve that. All three of them were loyal to her, the rock she built her reign on. Well, perhaps that was going too far when she had so many supporters in her life. Gritting her teeth, she took a long breath through her nose, then another.

Once her anger receded to a simmer, she spoke.

"You're right, Cretia. I don't wish to hurt any of you." The rest she left unsaid—that she owed them much, along with Linnet and Hetty; that these days of waiting were killing her when all she wanted to do was act. As queen, Alecia must show a strong front, must steel herself to protect the kingdom, and allow others to find Iona. The question remained though—was she tough enough to weather this storm?

She placed her practice sword back in the rack, said her goodbyes, and turned for the castle. As she neared the front door, Hetty and Ramón stepped out to meet her. Her stomach plummeted at the sight of their grim faces.

"What's wrong now?" Alecia asked, forcing her voice low.

"Your Majesty," Hetty said, "I've heard from Amitania. Prince Arenil and Lady Katrine have arrived. Lord Anton sends his deepest regards, and asks you to be strong."

"Be strong," she hissed. "That's fine for him. He has something to occupy him." She again took a long breath through her nose. "He is well?"

"He says he is," Hetty said. "It will do no good to rant, My Queen. Everything is being done to locate your daughter, and we are all praying for the best outcome. We all love Iona."

Her words took the wind from Alecia's sails. Of course, they were all worried for Iona, and were concerned for Alecia and Vard. It helped to remember she wasn't alone in her heartache.

Alecia took Hetty's hands in hers. "Thank you, my friend. It helps to be reminded of that."

Ramón scoffed. "I'd have thought that was obvious. Now, I'd like to know how this 'communication' is occurring. It's one thing to know that Kain and Gwaethe have a way of talking over distances, but how can Lady Henrietta get a message from Amitania more quickly than a raven can fly?"

Alecia flinched, and Hetty stiffened.

"Well?" Ramón insisted.

"Come to the small audience chamber, and we'll talk," Alecia said, climbing the steps. She asked her guards to wait outside the chamber, and entered with Ramón and Hetty. Once they were all seated, Alecia steeled herself.

"Ramón, you should know that Lady Henrietta is also Hetty the witch."

Ramón shot to his feet, angry eyes upon Hetty. She met his fury with outward calm.

He turned to Alecia. "All this time you've deceived me as to this woman's identity, had me treat her like a lady?"

Alecia stood. "Hetty *is* a lady. Many years ago, she was a noted socialite with a small estate and friends in the nobility. She was also my nanny before my father accused her of witchcraft, and she fled into hiding."

"You've been protecting her ever since," Ramón snapped, his finger poking at Alecia's chest. Lucky for him, he didn't touch her.

"Of course I protected her! I love her, and she has always supported me."

Ramón laughed. "That's rich, considering she may have been involved in your father's death!"

Alecia stood and took a step toward Ramón, tempted to slap him. But that would only inflame an already difficult situation. "How dare you say that when you were the one who asked her to do it?"

A cold light entered Ramón's eyes. "How many times must I say it! I had no intention of harming Prince Jiseve when I went to this... this witch."

"Keep your voice down!" Alecia snapped. "There are those who would harm her if they knew what she was."

"Perhaps those people are in the right. I expected better of you than to keep a secret like this from me, Alecia. You did, after all, roast me for keeping secrets from you."

"This is hardly the same thing! This was not my secret to reveal."

Ramón drew himself up. "If you will excuse me, I need to see my family." He turned to go, but Alecia grabbed his sleeve.

"Promise me you'll not reveal who Lady Henrietta is."

Ramón laughed. "Her secret is safe with me. For now..."

He pulled his sleeve from Alecia's grip, and stalked out without even a nod, let alone a bow.

Alecia resumed her seat across from Hetty, her heart racing.

"He could be a dangerous enemy, My Queen," Hetty said, calmly sipping a rich red wine.

Alecia reached for her goblet and took a mouthful, willing her hands to stop shaking. "He will say nothing." She wished her voice sounded stronger.

"You had better be right, or we could both be in trouble."

Alecia stared at her advisor. "Ramón will cool down, and we'll talk this out. You forget he has secrets of his own he will not want exposed. And believe me, I'll expose them in a flash if I think he will hurt you."

Hetty nodded. "Good. At least he hasn't asked questions about Katrine's involvement. She'd be furious if we revealed *her* secrets."

Alecia nodded. "We must ensure we don't." She chewed her lip. "Isn't there some way I can help in Iona's search? It's killing me sitting here doing nothing."

Hetty's face softened. "I know you ache for her return, but you are queen now, and must remember that. You can't go galloping off around the countryside as you once did."

Alecia shook her head, sighing. "What good am I to anyone, let alone Iona, if I can't take direct action? What are your informants saying?"

"I have asked James Tomel here to speak on that," Hetty said, draining her goblet. "He should be here soon."

Alecia ran through what she knew as she waited for James. Unfortunately, it was precious little.

A knock at the door heralded Linnet, her junior advisor, and spymaster James Tomel. He looked tired, and his coat was dusty.

He approached and bowed low. "My Queen."

"Master Tomel," Alecia said, rising. "Do you have any news about the disappearance of my daughter?"

"Your Majesty, Lady Stenmore must have been involved, even though I struggle to believe it. With the princess's sock being found near her residence, and now Lady Stenmore being impossible to locate—either she has met with foul play, or she has taken Princess Iona."

"Are you sure that isn't a stretch, Master Tomel?" As much as Alecia wished for news of Iona, she had no desire to take part in a wild goose chase.

"I know Melanis Stenmore well. We were once very close." James cleared his throat, red creeping up his neck. "We were engaged, in fact, and, as colleagues, we spent much time together. She doesn't just disappear with no trace. Melanis would be in her town house, or in the country at this time of year. She is in neither place, and her servants can't shed light on her whereabouts. I'm as sure as I can be that she's involved in your daughter's disappearance."

Alecia released the breath she had been holding. "At last, a sound theory on who has Iona."

James held up his hands. "It is theory only, and we don't know how your daughter was taken, or if Melanis willingly took part in the crime."

"Or what the motivation for the kidnapping is," Hetty said, her tone grim.

Alecia closed her eyes. "I have received no ransom demand, so I think we can rule that out—which leaves revenge or a political motive."

"Lady Stenmore may be involved, but who else is with her?" Hetty asked. "We should look further, especially if revenge is the motive. Has Adriana been questioned, or Piotr?"

"The admiral has briefly spoken with all who were at the coronation ball," Alecia said, "and that includes Adriana. Though invited, Piotr didn't attend. However, he was spotted speaking with Adriana in the days leading up to the ball."

Alecia gritted her teeth against saying more than that. She had wanted to question her aunt, but the admiral—the dowager queen's cousin—cautioned her against it. Well, now Alecia would hear what Adriana had to say.

James frowned. "Can we trust Nikolas Cosara to be impartial when questioning his cousin?"

Alecia shrugged. "He has much to thank Adriana for, including his lands, his title, and his position, so I guess the answer would be no."

"I've always thought he was hard but fair. However, even he might struggle to stay impartial in these circumstances." James considered her. "And you, My Queen, are not impartial either. Your relations with Adriana Zialni haven't exactly been friendly since the death of the king."

"And with good reason." Alecia clamped her lips down on the comment. She would not air her family troubles, or expose Adriana's plot to marry Vard—a plan she could never forgive Adriana for. Even the mere thought of it made her blood boil.

Oh yes, *she* could be involved in Iona's kidnapping.

James walked back and forth, pondering. "We need someone with status who *will* be impartial."

"Would Estevot suffice?" Alecia asked. "I can't think of anyone else who would be suitable, though Admiral Cosara won't be happy."

"No, he won't. But it must be your appointment as the Queen of Thorius. As such, the dowager queen must agree. I believe you could be present, but perhaps not take part. You could bring an advisor."

"Send a request for Piotr to appear as well," Alecia said. "I believe he is staying at an inn near the castle called The King's Triumph, which is well chosen should he try to oust me from the throne."

James laughed. "I think you are secure, My Queen. There's too much suspicion about Piotr's behavior during your father's death and funeral. He'll never recover from that."

"I never say never, Master Tomel. Get Piotr to attend, and ask Estevot to interview Adriana and him. We will work on the questions to be asked."

CHAPTER ELEVEN

THE venue for the interviews was Alecia's sitting room. It was a cool day, and the maid had built up the fire. Alecia's breakfast sat heavy in her stomach as she contemplated the hours ahead. A knock at the door made her pulse race until the maid ushered Hetty in.

"Good morning, Your Majesty," Hetty said, dropping a moderate curtsey, appropriate for her station. In all probability, it was as low as her old friend could manage. "I hope you're well today."

Alecia inclined her head and crossed the floor to grasp Hetty's hands. "I'm well," she said in a hushed voice, "but not looking forward to speaking with these people."

Hetty's gaze hardened. "You had better prepare yourself. Adriana is on her way."

Alecia gripped Hetty's fingers a little more tightly, and the old woman hissed. "Not so hard! I need those fingers."

Alecia let go and walked away, thoughts on the composure she needed for this morning. After all, she wouldn't be required to ask the questions. She was merely there to watch. It would be fine.

The maid arranged a desk and chairs for the interview, while Alecia and Hetty would sit on the two deep chairs before the fire. She need not even look at her aunt.

The maid attended another knock on the door to Alecia's chamber, and admitted Captain Estevot and dowager queen Adriana. Alecia stood with her arms crossed, waiting for her aunt to acknowledge her.

When she saw Alecia, Adriana crossed the room and dropped into a curtsey so deep it was a wonder she could rise again. Once upright, she grabbed Alecia and pulled her in for a hug.

Alecia stiffened. She had not expected *this*!

"Alecia, my *dear* niece," Adriana said, as she pulled back and held Alecia out for inspection. Alecia was doing some inspecting of her own. Her aunt was obviously dressed to impress. She wore a red dress with silver and black embroidery over the bodice and around the hem. There was no other word for it but magnificent.

"How *are* you?" Adriana pulled a handkerchief from her wrist and dabbed at her eyes. "You appear to be bearing up as I knew you would. The Zialnis are a tough breed."

Alecia sighed. "Thank you for your concern, Aunt. I'm as well as can be expected, and focusing my efforts on finding Iona."

"Of course you are. And that is why I am here—to shed any light I can on the events of the night of your Coronation Ball. Though I must tell you, Nikolas has already questioned me."

Estevot cleared his throat, addressing Adriana. "Lord Cosara had only the briefest of chats with those at the ball, My Lady. This talk will be more in-depth. Please be seated."

Adriana nodded and sat on the chair the maid drew out for her, the desk between her and Estevot. Alecia assessed the man chosen for this task, and was pleased at his presentation and carriage.

"Now, My Lady, can you tell me what you know of Princess Iona's disappearance?" Estevot said.

Adriana's eyes widened. "You cannot think I had anything to do with this terrible event?" She turned her attention to Alecia.

As tempted as Alecia was to answer that question, she remained silent as per her instructions. She did, however, allow her eyes to narrow ever so slightly.

"I'm not accusing you, My Lady," Estevot said. "I'm trying to discover if you know anything of importance. Please, answer the question."

Adriana's gaze returned to him, and she visibly collected herself, throwing her shoulders back. "I have no knowledge of my great niece's disappearance, or kidnapping, or whatever you wish to call it. I was at the ball the entire time, and beforehand was in the company of…"

Adriana's words tailed off. Alecia was certain she had been about to give Estevot delicate information. The former queen sat still, her hands in her lap, her face pale.

"That is my next question, My Lady." Estevot said. "Who were you with in the hours leading up to the queen's ball?"

Adriana stood and approached Alecia. "You know I love you and Iona. I've lost Beniel. Why would I wish to harm my family?"

Alecia hardened her heart. "Aunt, you must answer the question. I can't intervene or take part in this interview."

Adriana's chin rose. "I don't wish to say who I was with. It is delicate."

Now Estevot rose. "My Lady! If you don't return to your seat and answer the question, I can only draw negative conclusions."

Adriana scowled at the captain and stood her ground for a moment, but, just when Alecia thought her aunt would refuse, she strode back to the chair and sat, glaring at Estevot.

"I was with my nephew Piotr before the ball. He could not attend the event, which is why we met before. It was completely innocent."

Alecia heard Hetty's quiet scoff, and barely contained her own.

"For what purpose did you meet?"

Adriana drew in a long breath. "He wanted to know the details of Beniel's death since he had not attended the funeral. He reflected on a time when he was a child and Beniel was kind to him. He also lamented that he had not spent more time in his uncle's company."

"How many times have you and he met in the last month?"

Alecia watched Adriana's jaw muscles tighten. "Twice beside a few social occasions. I tell you our meetings are innocent." Her eyes fell upon Alecia once more. "Nothing for the queen to be concerned about."

Estevot cleared his throat. "You will forgive me for being suspicious of the reasons for your meetings. Where did this most recent one occur?"

Adriana maintained her poise. "In the private dining room of Piotr's inn. He is staying close to the palace, and is here on business. I also think he was hoping to mend bridges with the queen."

Now Alecia *did* scoff. It would be a wintry day in hell before she befriended Piotr.

"It is true, whatever you think," Adriana said to Estevot.

Estevot's eyebrows rose. "Is it not also true that you suggested to Vard Anton that you and he marry? Within hours of the former king's death, no less?"

"That is dirty gossip. Where did you hear such a thing? I was too distraught over losing Beniel to even think of the future."

"I believe the 'gossip' comes from Lord Anton himself, My Lady."

"Is he here to accuse me?" Adriana asked.

Estevot pointedly ignored her question and Alecia felt like clapping. He continued. "Is his accusation true?"

Again, Adriana's chin lifted. She was silent for a long moment. "I might have suggested such a thing to Vard, but I was crazy with grief."

"You will forgive me for asking, My Lady, but is a grieving widow normally contemplating replacing her lost husband so soon with the lover of her niece, and father of her great-niece?"

Alecia boiled inside. She could never forgive Adriana's betrayal, and it hurt to realize the woman she had admired as a child could be so callous.

Adriana's posture pleaded for understanding, but the eyes she had turned to Alecia a moment ago were cold and calculating. "I can only say again, I was insane with grief. And... Vard Anton is a man hard to resist. Combine that with the power he had inherited, and the situation was tempting."

"*Tempting*, My Lady?" Estevot said, his voice cold. "Is it also tempting to consort with Piotr Zialni, hoping that he is successful in a future challenge for the throne of this kingdom?"

Adriana's finger stabbed the air in front of Estevot's face. "I fully support my niece, and have given up all aspirations to be queen again."

Estevot raised his brow. "Then what will you do?"

Adriana drew in a slow breath, and lowered her arm. "Once Alecia decides on her seat of residence, I will settle in the other city or in the country on one of my estates."

Alecia ground her teeth. She would never be free of the woman's scheming. And if she snared Piotr as a husband, they would have a strong case for ruling Thorius, no matter what Adriana claimed.

"And you have no plans to marry Piotr Zialni?" Estevot pushed.

Adriana's eyes widened as though she had never contemplated the union. Perhaps she hadn't, but Alecia didn't believe that. Adriana was still a young woman, and had always wanted a child. With Piotr, she could have a family *and* rule Thorius.

"Let us summarize, My Lady," Estevot said. "You know nothing of the kidnapping of Iona Zialni, and though you have met with Piotr Zialni, the meetings were unrelated to the princess's disappearance. Furthermore, you are not involved in any plot to take the throne."

"That is the truth, Captain."

"Have you ever been in contact with the *Sis Lenweri,* or Melanis Stenmore?"

Adriana's eyes widened even more before she slipped her composed mask back in place. "I would never risk this kingdom by consorting with the enemy. As for Melanis Stenmore, I know of her, but have never met her."

Estevot nodded. "Then I believe that is all for now, My Lady. You may retire."

Adriana rose and nodded towards Alecia, then turned and swept from the room.

Estevot crossed to Alecia. "Are you satisfied with that interview, My Queen? I fear we learned nothing helpful."

Alecia pursed her lips. "I think we learned a little, Estevot. I don't want to believe my aunt is responsible for Iona's kidnapping, but I do think she aspires to marry Piotr. It would benefit them both. The fact that Piotr has no wife, or children he can prove are his, was a dilemma for him in his push for the throne of Thorius. He will want to correct that as soon as he can. And Adriana is young and beautiful. She also has a good head for politics. I think they would make a formidable team."

"Indeed, they would," Hetty said, lines etching her brow.

"We will leave that issue for another time," Alecia said, firmly closing a mental door on the subject of her aunt and Piotr. "Captain, have you summoned Piotr Zialni?"

"I have. Allow me to fetch him, My Queen." Estevot bowed and left Alecia's rooms.

Hetty cleared her throat. "Are you sure you're ready to confront Piotr, Alecia? He's likely to be hostile."

Alecia lifted her chin. "If I can't, I don't deserve this throne."

"Then I wish you good fortune," Hetty said.

It was late in the day before Piotr presented himself for questioning. Rather than Alecia's sitting room, this time they set up in the small audience hall. Alecia hadn't wanted Piotr anywhere near her chambers. Lin kept her company on this occasion, with Hetty trying to sleep off a headache. The trials of the last few days must be taking a toll on her friend, and Alicia determined to take better care of her.

Piotr entered, accompanied by Captain Estevot, and bowed low to Alecia. She remained seated and nodded to her cousin. He had changed of late, Alecia noted. He no longer dressed in satins and lace, and had lost weight. It looked as if there was hard muscle on that once pudgy frame. She wondered why. Had Adriana something to do with it? Or did Piotr want to present himself as a more attractive package when he tried to overthrow her rule? Alecia knew he would. It was only a matter of time.

"It's nice to see you, Your Majesty," Piotr said. "I wish it was under happier circumstances." He turned to Lin and nodded his head. "Lady Linnet."

"Welcome, cousin," Alecia said. "These are indeed dark days. I hope you can help us with information."

Estevot cleared his throat. He wouldn't want Alecia to have any input into this interview. "Your Highness, please sit, and we will begin." He waited for Piotr, then took his chair across the table. Alecia and Lin sat to the side, near the fire, and out of Piotr's line of sight.

"Your Highness," Estevot began. "Thank you for attending today. I have several questions for you." He shuffled the papers before him. "Where were you on the night of the coronation ball?"

Piotr shifted in his chair. "I was at my hotel early in the night, and then attended a meeting with some business contacts at a mansion in the nobility quarter."

"And whose mansion was that?" Estevot asked. "We would like to verify your whereabouts."

Piotr frowned. "Isn't my word as a gentleman good enough?"

Alecia snorted, and Estevot cleared his throat. "I regret to say not, Your Highness. You must reveal the business contact you visited."

Piotr stood and paced to the door. For a moment, Alecia thought he would leave the room. Her heart leaped at the thought that they may have found their culprit. But the prince stood staring at the door before turning to Estevot.

"This is not the way to treat the cousin of the queen," he snapped. "I should be above suspicion."

Estevot stood. "Your Highness, please return to your seat. If you don't answer the question, there'll be no choice but to believe you have something to hide."

"Of course I have something to hide," Piotr blustered. "My business contacts, and the matters I discuss with them are confidential. I can tell you they will not be happy if I reveal the name of the man who owns the mansion I visited the night of the coronation ball."

Privately, Alecia thought Piotr was making too much of not wanting to reveal the businessman's identity. Surely, if he was innocent, he would be happy to clear his name? She just did not know.

Piotr sat and stared at Estevot. The captain didn't wilt under her cousin's scrutiny.

Piotr sighed. "Very well then. I see I have no choice. I visited Cal Delcore, the Master Goldsmith in Brightcastle."

Alecia knew the name. Master Delcore produced exquisite jewelry, and had several shops and many apprentices. Since becoming queen, Alecia had been advised that Cal Delcore was also part of her spy network. This was an interesting development indeed.

Estevot sat back in his chair. "And you remained at Master Delcore's residence for how long?"

"I was there until after midnight. We had dinner and discussed various business opportunities. I didn't hear of the princess's disappearance until I awoke the next morning."

"Have you been in contact with Adriana Zialni since you arrived in Brightcastle?"

Piotr frowned. "I assume you've already spoken with her, since she was at the ball?"

Estevot raised his brows and folded his arms.

Piotr huffed out a breath. "Yes, I've seen Adriana since I arrived, several times in fact. She visited me the afternoon of the ball."

"Where did that meeting take place?"

"In the private dining room of The King's Triumph. We reminisced about Beniel, and the loss he was to the kingdom."

"Was it a romantic assignation?"

Piotr spluttered. "Of course not! The woman is my *aunt*."

"Only by marriage," Estevot responded. "And she is a beautiful woman still in her childbearing years. Are you telling me you and she have never discussed marriage? If you have ambition for the Thorian throne, you will need heirs. Her ladyship would seem the ideal choice."

Piotr stood, his cheeks red. "You, Captain, are out of order." He paused for several seconds. When Estevot did not react, he sat back down. "On reflection, I must say what you suggest is a good plan,

Captain. However, I had my eye on the queen here to help me onto the throne. She is not yet married, and she has been deserted by her husband-to-be in her time of need. Perhaps I might step into the breech, find Iona, and secure her mother's everlasting gratitude."

Alecia surged to her feet. "We are cousins, Piotr!" she spat. "That will never happen!"

She struggled to control her shock and horror at the course the interview had taken. She sat back down and took a deep breath. Lin handed her a goblet of mulled wine.

"Thank you, Lin," she said.

"Don't overreact, Alecia. It's what he wants," her advisor said quietly.

Estevot continued. "I apologize if I insulted your honor, Prince Zialni."

"Damn right! You're lucky I don't challenge you to a duel!"

Estevot smirked. He would have a good idea who the victor of that contest would be.

"Let's not be hasty, Your Highness. Two remaining questions. Have you had any contact with Lady Melanis Stenmore, or with the *Sis Lenweri?*"

"I know Melanis, but it is weeks since I saw her. She usually snubs me these days. As for the enemy, I would never consort with them, for business or otherwise." He directed a glare at Alecia. "Even *you* should know that, Your Majesty."

Alecia knew nothing of the sort. She raised her brow at Piotr, who scowled back.

Estevot cleared his throat again. "Then to summarize, Your Highness. You assert that you were visiting Master Cal Delcore on the night of the Coronation Ball when Princess Iona vanished. You say you met with Master Delcore on business. You have been in touch with Adriana Zialni in recent weeks, including on the afternoon of the ball, but you have nothing to do with the disappearance of the princess. Melanis Stenmore is known to you, but you haven't spoken to her recently. Nor have you consorted with the *Sis Lenweri*, recently or in the past."

Piotr stood. "That is correct, Captain. Am I free to leave?"

Estevot remained seated. "You are."

Piotr's face was wintry. "I wish I could say this has been a pleasure, Your Majesty," he said, glaring at Alecia. "Good evening." He bowed, barely low enough to avoid insult, turned, and marched from the chamber.

Estevot stood, and moved to stand before Alecia. "What do you think, My Queen?"

Alecia huffed out a breath. "That man is as guilty as sin. He was invited to the ball. Why would he decline that for a business meeting? Perhaps so he would have an alibi?"

Estevot nodded. "That could be the case. Or perhaps he saw no point in attending the ball."

Alecia shook her head. "No. There is always value in social occasions, if only so that you can speak with enemies and friends under the cover of general chitchat."

Lin stood and joined them. "Perhaps Piotr was trying to signal his lack of support for your reign by not attending?"

Alecia gave that some thought. "Perhaps, but wouldn't it be more prudent that he show visible support, lulling us into thinking he accepts me?"

"He clearly doesn't, judging by his words, Your Majesty," Linnet said.

Alecia sighed. "I don't know him well enough to judge. And his words were ludicrous. As if I'd ever consider him in place of Vard."

"Of course you wouldn't. He was baiting you," Estevot said. "Prince Piotr knows you as little as you know him. I advise you to be extremely guarded around him, My Queen."

Alecia nodded. "Good advice. Also, it wouldn't hurt me to get to know him better—assuming he challenges me for the throne, I would be better able to anticipate his next move."

"You could appear more conciliatory toward him, leading him to believe you think he is no threat." Lin's eyes were alight. She loved a good intrigue. Alecia, on the other hand, preferred matters out in the open.

"I will think on it. In the meantime, it won't hurt to build bridges with my cousin."

"Just make sure your guards and advisors are always around," Estevot said. "You are far too brave for your own good, Your Majesty." He bowed low to her and nodded to Lin. "If you'll excuse me, I have work to do."

Alecia waved him out of the room and turned to Lin. "I don't know which version of Estevot I like less. The chauvinist who won't let me take a risk, or the advisor who speaks unnecessary lessons about being 'careful'."

Lin laughed. "Neither, I would say. However, he is coming to respect you, so this version is definitely superior."

Alecia pursed her lips as she and Lin left the chamber. Time to focus on finding Iona.

CHAPTER TWELVE

VARD trotted Trax along a narrow forest path north of Amitania, his knees brushing the low branches of fir trees either side. Sam rode ahead with half the party, and the rest were behind him. He had sensed no danger, and the scouts had brought no ill news. By the look of this path, only animals had traversed it recently. Which meant the dark elves had taken his father north via a different route.

"Damned elusive vermin," Vard muttered under his breath.

"What was that?" Sam asked, throwing a glance over his shoulder. His friend sat the dun stallion easily for one accustomed to the high seas, but Vard imagined Sam could master new skills easily.

"I was talking to Trax."

"Oh, and what was his reply?"

Trax snorted loudly, and they laughed.

"I think we both know what that means," Sam said. "Do you think this path is much used?"

Vard drew in a breath. "No. I knew of it, but it's been many years since I traveled this far north. Nothing has changed much. I imagine the *Sis Lenweri* stay far away from the central mountains and Amitania."

"Until they wish to cause us grief," Sam said, his voice a low rumble.

110

"Indeed," Vard said. "I wonder how Alecia is?" He nearly said "coping", but that would reveal more of his concern for her than he wanted to, even to Sam.

"I imagine she's feeling much as you are. Worried, helpless, angry, determined..." Sam kept his voice low so those nearby couldn't hear. "You'll be back together again with Iona," he said. "There's no point thinking anything else. And we'll find your father, too."

Emotion clogged Vard's throat, so he couldn't reply. He nodded, clenching his jaw against tears that suddenly filled his eyes. That was a first! He never cried, and was rarely emotional. It was what came of opening yourself to others. It made you weak, and he couldn't afford that, not with his daughter and father missing.

"I'm fine," he snapped. "You're not my mother to be giving me advice."

Sam stiffened and faced forward, kicking his horse to place more distance between him and Trax.

Vard regretted offending Sam, but, with luck, the pirate would shrug it off sooner rather than later. They had a task to complete, and Sam wasn't one for allowing his feelings to interfere. Neither was Vard, usually. He sighed and swallowed hard as emotion again rose. He must control these unhelpful feelings!

He noticed the stillness in the trees they passed. No birds called, and the noise of their passing had hidden the fact from his companions. However, the forest creatures sensed something.

Vard raised his hand, and a low whistle sounded. The line pulled to a halt. The scouts trotted toward them from up the trail. Tholdrek Opalgrip arrived at Vard's stirrup.

"The forest waits for something, My Lord Anton. Tanulia and Ara say they feel 'prickling' up their necks." He added quietly, "Whatever that means." His eyes rose to scan the skies while Vard pushed his senses out into the forest.

"I can't detect anything, Opalgrip, but I'm loathe to ignore your warning, and our elven friends are in tune with the forest and its creatures."

"I don't like it," Opalgrip said. "We're barely a day out of Amitania. I had not thought to encounter the enemy this soon."

"Dismount and take cover," Vard said, suiting action to words. He led Trax under the trees to the left of the trail. Sam and Opalgrip followed. Once they were all hidden, Vard again sent his senses probing. This time, his questing mind touched several wolves.

We meet again, Wolf Brother

Vard started, then touched minds with the speaker. It was a she-wolf, but she seemed young for any beast he might have met.

I doubt we have met, little sister.

Our kind knows all the Wolf Brothers. Their existence is passed down through the generations as you live such long lives compared to us. We must be able to recognize your kind, or it might lead to... misunderstandings.

Vard smiled at her embarrassment. He had been in a similar situation with a young she-wolf who wouldn't back off when asked.

I see, little sister. Do you know what comes?

Vard sensed their meeting of minds, then the she-wolf, whose name seemed to be Leaps the Stream, answered.

A large bird in the air that breathes fire and carries men. We are scared the forest will burn.

Do you have a color for the beast?

It is dark as night.

Thank you, little sister. The dragon is a friend. He won't burn the trees.

We retreat. The beast isn't to be trusted.

Leaps the Stream's mind vanished, and Vard could no longer find any of the wolves.

He sighed. Kain was approaching, but he couldn't let his companions know that without explaining how he knew. He called Opalgrip over, while Sam kept watch.

"Opalgrip, there's a good chance this is our help from Brightcastle. I expect Kain Arenil to join us."

"I certainly hope that's the cause of this quiet." He scowled at Vard. "However, I prefer to expect the worst. That way I'm never disappointed."

Vard opened his mouth to reply, but at that moment, there was a rushing of leaves as from a great gale through the forest.

"What in the name of the almighty!" Opalgrip snapped. "Take cover!"

Where the dwarf expected them to take cover, Vard was unsure. Before he could move, even the fir trees around them whipped back and forth, showering them with needles and bark. Curiously, there was no wind. He looked at those around him and saw fear in their eyes as they realized the same thing.

"How can the trees shower us with leaves when there's no wind?" Sam asked.

Unlike the others, Vard had experienced this before. It was even more a message that Kain's arrival was imminent. The trees sensed Kain's proximity, and were greeting him as a forest mage.

"Be still, my comrades," Vard called. "This is nothing to fear. Take a breath. and be at peace!"

His words fell on deaf ears, but he couldn't explain what was occurring in just a few words. "Take control of your mounts and calm yourselves! That's an order!"

At last, his command penetrated the panic, but it stirred again as a vast shadow swung overhead. Vard could just make out the underbelly and wings of a black dragon. Men and elves drew bow and arrow as it hovered.

"The first to loose an arrow is a dead man," Vard bellowed, relieved to see bows lowered. "Stand down! At ease!"

Vard feared for those above. One stray arrow could mean disaster. Ropes were cast down, and two figures descended. One was Kain Arenil, and the other was a woman. He spared a glance at those near him. Though calm, extreme wariness poured off them in waves.

"They are friends!" Vard snapped again. "My orders stand!"

The two dragon riders completed their climb several strides away, and stood, obscured by trees.

"Is it safe to approach?" It was Kain Arenil's voice.

"Your Highness, please join me," Vard said.

Kain wended his way through the trees, and Vard saw Katrine Aranati with him. She went up in his estimation if she could ride a dragon and descend a rope like that.

They stopped before him. He bowed at Kain and nodded at Katrine.

"Your Highness, My Lady, this is Tholdrek Opalgrip, leader of my scouts, and elder of the dwarven people." Opalgrip cast Vard a side glance, but bowed to Kain. He also nodded at Katrine.

"Your Highness, glad I am to meet ye, and you, My Lady. Brave ye must be to ride that beast."

Kain grinned. "It takes a little more concentration than riding a horse, and the fall is a trifle further. Luckily, Nugoriem makes it as safe as possible. How come you to be in the kingdom? My sister mentioned nothing of the dwarves' involvement."

"Ah, your sister, Gwaethe Arenil? We have had small chance to enjoy her company since we arrived in Amitania. We probably slipped her mind."

Kain nodded and turned to Vard.

"Well met, Lord Anton. We came as soon as we could to assist your search and rescue. Lady Katrine insisted on being involved, partly to aid in communication back to Brightcastle. I'm very sorry we meet again in these circumstances. I assure you, the queen is bearing up admirably."

Vard nodded. "Thank you, Your Highness. I'd be there to support her, but this is where I need to be. I hope we can locate my father. You think the *Sis Lenweri* may have taken Iona?"

Kain inclined his head. "Or someone working with them. There are other theories, of course, and the queen is following those through. We can't afford to narrow our focus at this time."

"It must be killing Alecia." Vard muttered.

Kain led him aside and motioned Katrine to join them.

"What information have you to share, Vard?" Kain asked.

Vard pulled his thoughts back from Alecia and Iona to the situation at hand. "We found evidence that Lyam traveled north from the battlefield and through the Usetar Mountains. He must have been with the *Sis Lenweri* who returned to their home after the battle. Why they took him, I don't know. Anyhow, Sam and I tracked them, and then asked for help from Amitania. There's no way we could find and attack the *Sis Lenweri* stronghold unaided."

"Gwaethe thought I could help," Kain said, "and Nugoriem can aid us in locating the elven strongholds. There may be opposition from the other dragons—the green, red, and gold. The black will take our side against them. He previously led the dragons, being the oldest among them. However, the green has challenged Nugoriem for the position."

"There's no love lost then," Vard said. "Why do you believe Iona's disappearance is linked to Lyam's?"

Kain shrugged his shoulders. "Something niggles at me. Your daughter disappeared under strange circumstances. There were deep gouge marks on her windowsill. It reminded me of Gorin's rescue." Kain spoke of the *Sis Lenweri* prisoner Prince Gorin, son of High Prince Faenwelar who had started the war between humans and the *Sis Lenweri*. It was eventually learned that a dragon rescued him from his tower prison.

Vard nodded. "It could be. Iona was well guarded, but with the excitement of the coronation ball, it would be easier to steal her away under the cover of darkness and the noise of festivities. What of the sock?"

"It was definitely Iona's," Katrine said, "and was found near the home of the noblewoman Melanis Stenmore. She can't be located. We think she may have been involved."

"What does James think?" Vard asked.

Katrine raised her chin. "At first he was skeptical. He thinks he knows her well. However, as a member of the spy service, she would be privy to much information, including the details of Iona's care. The fact remains, she is missing, and no one, including her servants, appears to know where she is."

"Are you sure you aren't suspecting her because… she was once engaged to James?" Vard watched as Katrine stiffened. Of course, her suspicions must be partly because of that rivalry.

"That has nothing to do with my assessment of her. No matter how I dislike the thought of the two of them together, at that time he was free to carry on with her as he pleased."

Vard stared at the noblewoman sorceress. "And your *friends*? Where are they?"

Katrine quirked an eyebrow. "I suppose you need to know as the leader of this mission. They follow a day behind. It is hard to keep up with a dragon, but they can travel day and night."

"They must indeed be special to perform that feat of endurance." Kain fell silent, staring at Katrine. "Wait," his voice lowered to a whisper. "Do we speak of the night hounds? *They* are your friends?"

Katrine's head snapped up, her eyes glowing in the shadows. "How the hell did you work that out?" She motioned at Vard. "Did *he* tell you?"

"I'm not stupid, My Lady. I can draw conclusions. Can we trust them?"

"The last time I asked her that," Vard said, "the reply was, 'they fight for us for now'."

"That hasn't changed," Katrine muttered. "The hounds are loyal to me, and I support the kingdom."

"What if something were to happen to you, My Lady?" Kain asked.

Katrine drew a long breath. "I can't be sure. If I died, I believe they would flee. They may disappear as they did in the past. I've been unable to find much about them in the archives, but it seems they usually had a master or mistress. That too is debatable, as those who have held that position in the past likely kept it a closely guarded secret." She fixed her swirling blue gaze on first Kain, and then Vard. "I expect both of you to keep my secret, or I cannot aid you."

Vard was quick to agree. "You have my word, Lady."

Kain held up a hand to forestall more agreement. "Wait a moment, Vard. Secrecy may be a promise neither of us can keep."

Katrine took a step forward, hands clenched. The silver sparkles in her irises rioted.

"Prince Arenil," she said through gritted teeth. "My hounds aided the kingdom in the last battle, and I almost paid for their aid with my life. Magic remains outlawed in Thorius. Putting myself forward to help in this mission is a risk. Can you guarantee that neither I nor my hounds will be exposed?"

Kain was silent for several beats as he stared at the sorceress. Vard tried to relax. They would do what they must—with or without Katrine and her beasts.

Finally, he nodded. "I'll do my absolute best to protect you, My Lady, to keep your secrets. I also vow to watch over you and reduce the personal risk you face."

The sorceress stared, and Vard wondered what thoughts occupied her. Kain's promises should be enough to reassure even the most demanding ally, he thought.

"Very well." Katrine turned and strode into the forest.

Kain let out a long breath. "I hope we can trust her."

Vard grasped his shoulder. "She's a prickly character, but has only ever been a friend to Thorius. Her hounds will be a boon for us when we find the *Sis Lenweri*. And both she and them will need your protection. If the hounds are harmed, Katrine will feel their pain as if it were her own. James told me what happened in the last battle. Shock almost took her, and James had to kill the suffering beast to save her."

Kain's gaze snapped to his. "Brave man!"

Vard nodded. "Indeed, but he loves his lady more than his own life." He surveyed the skies. "Where is the black dragon?"

Kain smiled. "Nugoriem advised he was headed for the nearest peak he could land on. Said he was 'peckish'."

Vard grinned. "You think we can trust him? Seems we have many allies newly come to us, and it has been decades since elves or man interacted with them."

"Nugoriem has proven himself. I'm content he can be trusted. Shall we make camp?"

Rejoining Opalgrip and Sam, they found a forest stream to camp beside. Vard ordered a watch set while the camp was being set up and a meal cooked. Then he walked into the forest, determined to complete a flyover of their position.

CHAPTER THIRTEEN

ALECIA stood in the royal seamstress's workroom, outwardly calm, but struggling for composure. No recent news had arrived of the expedition to the northern mountains, and nobody had discovered anything new in Brightcastle. Iona had disappeared with no trace besides her sock and the scrapes on her windowsill.

Alecia swallowed down panic and tried to listen to the dressmaker, Isadore Bellemont. The petite dark beauty was discussing the dress she was adjusting for Alecia's wedding. Alecia wasn't sure about the color of the gown, but, with the turmoil present in her life, she couldn't bring herself to care.

Isadore had suggested a burned orange and cream creation with a modest neckline in keeping with her new station. It was really two dresses—a cream underdress with a spectacular overdress complete with pearls and gold thread. The sleeves were simply divine—floaty cream creations which left her hands free. There was a headpiece which matched the overdress, and to which her cream veil could be attached. The veil was of the same material as the sleeves. The dress maker assured her she would be breathtaking.

Alecia knew the burned orange would look well on her, but she preferred lilac and had thought she would be married in it. If not for the catastrophe of Iona's abduction, she might have fought for her preference.

Isadore stood back to admire her work.

"Oh, Your Majesty, you are breathtaking in that color. The gold embroidery makes a statement, that's for sure. And the sleeves! You'll look like you are floating down the aisle." Isadore folded her fists beneath her chin, and her eyes sparkled. "I think this might be my best gown ever!"

Inside, Alecia quailed at her enthusiasm, concerned that the wedding might yet have to be postponed. Clearly it couldn't go ahead without Vard. Worry for Iona dragged at her, robbing her of the joy she should feel at her impending marriage. But all might yet be well, and she must try to be enthusiastic even if only for Isadore.

She drew in a deep breath and put a smile on her lips. "It is truly beautiful, Isadore. Thank you for your efforts." Even to her ears, her words sounded forced.

Tears appeared in the seamstress's eyes. "Oh, Your Majesty, I know it must be hard to think about your wedding when your darling Iona is missing. That's why I'm here—to take the pressure off you. I've worked hard to create a simply stunning dress, and you must trust and depend on me. As you must lean on your ladies."

Isadore spoke of her ladies-in-waiting and her advisors, all of whom had tried their best. But no matter how much they tried to support and distract her, the fact remained that her daughter was gone. There was no guarantee she would ever see Iona again. Alecia lay awake at night imagining how scared Iona must be without her—if she was even alive. Then she would tell herself that her child was indeed in the land of the living. There was a purpose to stealing Iona, and it would do the perpetrator no good to kill her.

But what if that was exactly what had happened? What if... Alecia cut her thoughts off there, short of imagining her daughter dead. Her vibrant, cheeky, rambunctious child had a full life ahead of her.

Alecia nodded and smiled again. "I'm trying to do as you say, Isadore." She swallowed convulsively at the well of grief that rose to swamp her. "How are the attendant's gowns coming along?" *There!* That was better. At least she had asked a question that didn't involve Iona's disappearance, or the quest to retrieve Lyam. Much better to focus on Linnet, Meriel, Katrine and Alique who had agreed to stand up for her.

Isadore beamed. "You won't believe how gorgeous your ladies will be. I dressed them in the burnished orange, but have slightly differing shades for each of them." She pulled out some fabric swatches and fanned them out so Alecia could see the colors. "I have reserved the paler shades for Linnet and Meriel as they have the striking red hair, and stronger orange for Lady Alique with her gorgeous blonde tresses. Lady Katrine's gown is a medium shade. Their gowns are based on your underdress, with a wide V-neck, and full fitted sleeves that end in points. I think they will love them. I'm yet to decide on the embellishments."

Alecia had a flash of inspiration. "Perhaps a jeweled waist band and matching headdress?" She suggested. "Merielle especially adores sparkles on her clothes." Alecia made a mental note to check that the four ladies were happy with their gowns.

Isadore nodded. "She is a stunning woman, and I agree with your suggestion. I'll certainly consult with them on this."

Alecia hid a smile as the dressmaker packed away her pins. Isadore was a force to be reckoned with when it came to gown design. Usually, she got her way, especially if the subject she dressed was easy going— which was why Alecia would advocate on their behalf if needed. For herself, she was pleased to agree to Isadore's suggestions on the topic of her wedding gown. The woman had good taste, and Alecia was glad to wear something different on her special day.

The fitting over, Alecia wished Isadore a good day and left the chambers, joining her female guards for the journey back to her office, which was on the ground floor. Even though her life had stopped, Thorius had not, and there was a myriad of decisions and paperwork to attend to. When she arrived, Linnet was there, poring over what looked like an inventory.

"Good morning, Lin," Alecia said, leaving her guards outside. "It's good to see you."

Lin dropped a moderate curtsey, impressing Alecia with her elegance. Anyone would believe Lin had been born into the nobility, instead of being handed her title recently by Alecia.

"Good day, Your Majesty. You're late."

Alecia smiled. "Always the one to keep me on my toes."

"Someone has to." Lin's gray eyes turned serious. "How are you? Any news?"

"You know full well that you'd be among the first to hear if news of Iona reached us. And I'm as well as can be expected. I've been having a wedding gown fitting."

Lin grimaced. "How did *that* go?"

Alecia sighed. "Better than you might think. Isadore has done a magnificent job, despite choosing a color I've never worn."

One eyebrow rose. "The burned orange *is* unusual—I'll give you that. At first, I hated it, but the woman altered the shade to one that suits me, and I adore the design."

As Alecia sat behind her desk and lifted the first paper from the pile, Lin handed her the document she had been reading.

"I fear we will bankrupt the kingdom with this wedding. Are you sure all these people need to attend?" Lin asked.

"I'm the first Queen of Thorius in hundreds of years. Of course, many people must attend my wedding. I've invited the heads of all the neighboring kingdoms and their entourages. I just have to trust that Iona is found, and Vard returns in time." She slumped in her chair, head in her hands. If Iona wasn't found, the wedding didn't matter one little bit.

Lin sat across the desk from her and reached out to place a hand on her forearm. "We'll find Iona. Please believe that."

Alecia raised her face to her advisor and plastered on a smile. "I'm trying."

Lin nodded, a frown on her forehead. "I'm hearing mutterings about Vard's suitability as your husband."

"Of course you are. He's not of royal blood, and no matter how much faith Uncle Beniel had in him, few will see him as suitable. I've never cared what people think of my choice of husband."

There was a loud tap at the door. Admiral Nikolas Cosara strode into the room. He swept a bow, then advanced to stand before her.

"I'm sorry for the interruption, Your Majesty, but we have news of Melanis Stenmore." He looked at Lin. "Pardon, My Lady, but I need a private discussion with the queen."

Lin looked at Alecia, who nodded her permission to depart. By the time Lin left the room, Alecia's insides were ready to explode.

"What is it, Lord Cosara?" she asked.

"Melanis Stenmore has been found, battered and unclothed on the steps of her townhouse. I have her outside."

"Bring her in!" Alecia said, rising and rounding the desk. She waited, checking the knives hidden about her person as the admiral left the room.

In moments, he returned, accompanied by two soldiers and a figure covered in a cloak with a sack over their head. The men dragged the prisoner to the middle of the room, and pulled off the sack. A bedraggled Lady Stenmore sagged between the two men, her eyes closed. All she wore under the cloak was a tattered white shift.

Alecia stepped forward, but Nikolas placed his body between her and the woman. "Care, Your Majesty. Remember what crimes she is accused of."

"I hardly think she is in any condition to attack me." She watched with relief the steady rise and fall of the woman's chest. They needed her alive to extract whatever information they could. "How come she to be in this condition?"

Nikolas's aqua eyes hardened. "This was how we found her. I assure you I'm not in the habit of beating women."

Alecia raised her chin. "I never suggested you were, but somehow she was injured, and is close to death, if I am any judge." Despite the caution of her advisor, Alecia stepped closer until she could lift Lady

Stenmore's eyelid. She was pale and freezing. "Lay her down before the fire," Alecia hissed. She looked up at Nikolas. "Fetch Lady Benae. Tell her it's urgent! Send my guards to me."

For once, Nikolas didn't argue and strode from the room. Once her guards entered, she sent them to bring blankets and stoke the fire as well as fetch warm broth. By the time Benae arrived, Melanis was resting on a thick bear skin by the fire, wrapped in blankets.

Benae gasped and fell to her knees, her hands gently probing her patient. She pulled the blankets aside so she could examine her, then looked at Alecia. "Please ask your guards to step outside, My Queen."

Knowing Benae would want privacy for her ministrations, Alecia did as requested. When she turned back to Benae, the healer had laid hands on her patient. She closed her eyes for long moments, after which a little color returned to Lady Stenmore's face. Then Benae pulled ingredients from her basket.

"How is she?" Alecia asked, as Benae mixed dried berries and powder into a goblet of boiled water.

"Gravely injured. She has so many broken bones, I stopped counting. Many of her ribs are broken or cracked. She has a broken shoulder and pelvis, and I believe there is bleeding in her skull. How she isn't already dead, I don't know. Add to that shock and exposure, and... it's a miracle."

Or perhaps not, Alecia thought. Perhaps there was a reason Melanis hadn't succumbed to her injuries. "Can you save her?"

Benae's worried eyes lifted to Alecia's. "Perhaps. I will do all I can. I realize you need to question her."

Alecia smiled. "You always do your best, no matter the situation. If anyone can help her, it's you. Perhaps Alique can assist? I'll send for her." Without worrying that she was stepping on Benae's pride, Alecia rose and spoke to her guards outside.

When she returned to the injured woman, Melanis groaned and rolled her head to the side. Alecia's heart leaped. She kneeled and touched the pale face of the woman. Her eyes snapped open and burning golden orbs speared her. It was such a shock that Alecia almost fell backwards. Golden eyes, much like Vard's. This woman's eyes were normally blue if her memory served her. Was she a Defender?

"Where am I?" Lady Stenmore's voice was weak but alert.

"You're in the keep, in my office, Lady Stenmore," Alecia said, unable to keep the chill from her voice. "You've been missing for days, and now you appear outside your mansion like this." Her hand swept the length of the woman's resting place. "Care to tell us where you've been? What has happened to you?"

Alecia drew a deep breath. She couldn't lose her temper, or say the wrong thing for fear this interview would fail.

The golden orbs of the other woman had subsided. Alecia could now see pale blue through the gold. If she was a Defender and had been injured while in animal form, that could explain how she survived injuries that should kill a human. Nikolas Cosara entered the office and joined her, looking down on the woman.

"It's time to explain your absence, My Lady," Nikolas said, "if you are able. Tell me where you've been the past several days."

Melanis kept her eyes straight ahead, flinching as Benae applied a paste to her abrasions. "Can't you see I'm in agony?"

Nikolas crouched beside her. "Regardless, you will answer the question, and any others we ask."

Melanis clenched her jaw and, rather than being tempted to slap her, Alecia stood and moved away. Let Nikolas see if he could extract his information.

"Answer me!" Nikolas snapped.

Lady Stenmore's eyes met his. He gasped. "Your eyes!"

His gaze flew to Alecia's, and she nodded. Vard had informed her that Nikolas had seen him during or soon after the change from hawk into man. He would know what a shapeshifter's eyes looked like after the change. Nikolas's antipathy for Vard bordered on hate, and this was the reason. Vard's essence threatened Nikolas in the extreme.

She returned to his side and placed a hand on his shoulder. "Perhaps we should question the patient when she is feeling more herself?"

He shook his head. "Now is the time to get answers, My Queen. If it doesn't threaten her life." He looked at Benae, who performed another check.

"She is stable, Admiral. You may question her. I'll stop the process if I'm concerned." Benae rose and took her box of tinctures to the table, where she went about mixing another potion. "I'm preparing a pain medication. You may question her until I complete it, and then she must rest."

"Princess Iona is missing, Lady Stenmore," Nikolas said. "Do you know where she is?"

Lady Stenmore's jaw clenched. "How could I know that? This is the first I've heard of her disappearance."

"Ah, yes." Nikolas squatted before the woman. "You've been at your country estate. How convenient."

"We looked for you at your country home," Alecia said. "Your servants had not seen you and had no knowledge of your whereabouts."

Nikolas scowled at her, and Alecia returned it. How could she stay quiet when her child was missing? But she must try. The admiral was more experienced in these matters.

He turned back to their prisoner. "Where have you been for the past week?"

Silence greeted the question, but Nikolas waited, motioning to Alecia with a hand that requested her silence too. She clamped her teeth together and breathed deep to control her temper. He certainly was a man used to getting his way.

Finally, Lady Stenmore spoke. "I was indeed at my country estate. I told the servants I didn't wish to be disturbed. Roth, my butler, is very good at protecting my privacy."

"We searched your country house, along with your city mansion."

Her eyes snapped to his. "You had no right!"

"We had every right, My Lady. We had reason to suspect the princess had been near your mansion. Now why did the men tasked with searching your country estate not find you there?"

She drew in a slow breath. "I visited a sick relative when I was away. It must have been that day your men visited."

"I don't believe you, My Lady," Nikolas snapped. "I believe you kidnapped the princess from her cot, and that you took her somewhere after that. Where is she?"

Now fully in control of her emotions, Melanis turned cold blue eyes on him. "You would be better served looking at her family rather than focusing on me. I have nothing to do with Princess Iona's disappearance."

Nikolas stood abruptly and turned in time to block Alecia from approaching Melanis.

"Can I speak with you outside, Your Majesty? Lady Benae, I am finished questioning Lady Stenmore for now. I'll arrange to have her transferred to the prison." He escorted Alecia from her office, and closed the door behind them. She sent three guards in to watch the prisoner then turned to Nikolas.

"She's lying!"

He closed his eyes as he took a deep breath. "I agree with you. However, we learned something about the lady we didn't know before today. I'll not speak of it, but you know what I mean."

Alecia nodded. "And you think that means she's guilty? She may have had nothing to do with the crime, or she may be fully responsible, or know who is."

"Oh, she's responsible for it."

Alecia drew herself up and faced him square on. "We can't afford to narrow our focus. If she's not the perpetrator, the real criminal may get away. Iona doesn't have unlimited time!"

He sighed again, his jaw tense. "You're correct, of course, but what would you have us do?"

Alecia's shoulders slumped. "I don't know." She lowered her voice. "If we could discover what shapes she can change into that might help."

Benae stepped from the room at that point. "Your Majesty, you cannot house that woman in the prison. As her healer, I forbid it." The petite brunette's green eyes blazed.

This was one of Benae's attributes that Alecia truly admired. The healer was a staunch advocate for the sick. "I'm sorry, Benae, but she is dangerous, and could be responsible for Iona's kidnapping. Lady Stenmore must go to the prison under full guard." Alecia suppressed a shudder at the thought of Melanis morphing into a raging beast and tearing those close to shreds. They couldn't risk that. Nor could they risk her escape.

Benae stepped closer, and Alecia held up a hand. "You're excused, Lady Zorba. I'll let you know when the prisoner is moved. Please use extreme caution around her." She left Benae in the hall, staring at her, storm clouds in her eyes.

As Alecia returned to the office with the admiral, she had an idea. Leaving Nikolas to oversee the transfer, she went in search of Hetty.

CHAPTER FOURTEEN

ALECIA found Hetty in the kitchen, mixing a foul-smelling concoction over the fire. She chased the kitchen staff from the room, and stood beside her friend and advisor.

"What has possessed you?" Alecia asked. "You'll have all the staff gossiping about your witchcraft."

Hetty dropped a deep curtsey. "Your Majesty. You're in a mood this morning. I'm helping Benae with a tincture."

Her words stunned Alecia. "You're helping Benae? She hates you."

Hetty quirked an eyebrow. "I was bored. All those servants I now have in my new home leave me with nothing to do."

"You're my advisor! That should be enough." Then she reflected on how close Hetty was to Iona. "I'm sorry, Hetty. You must be just as scared for Iona as I am."

Hetty huffed. "I'm not scared. The child will be found safe and well."

Alecia gulped as a wave of fear and sadness rose. And she had thought she was doing well at keeping her terror under control.

"Yes, we must believe that." She pushed her fear away and took the spoon from Hetty. "I have another task for you. Send one of the kitchen staff in to finish this chore, and come with me."

Alecia explained her plans to Hetty as they waited for Ramón to arrive. He and Benae lived close to the keep in a modest manor house that had once belonged to a disgraced noble. Things were tense between Alecia and Ramón, but he must attend the queen since he was one of her advisors. Vard would be angry when he found out about Ramón's position. However, Alecia always thought of the saying "keep your friends close, and your enemies closer".

Besides, Ramón was perfect for this chore. He knew Lady Henrietta was also a witch, and had dealt with her before. Alecia could use him as security for this trip to the jail. Ramón was a brilliant swordsman, almost as good as Vard. He would be adequate protection for the two ladies.

Hetty paced across the room, eyes narrowed, finger tapping her pursed lips. She hadn't spoken since Alecia explained her task.

"Well," Alecia said, "do you think you can discern whether Lady Stenmore is a shifter? And perhaps which animals she can assume?"

"Something always itched about that woman," Hetty said. "I dealt with her when I raised support for you. She brushed me off, didn't want to be in the same room as me, it appeared. I thought she was looking down her nose at me."

"Ha!" Alecia said. "She's frightened of you, of what you might expose."

"Perhaps." Hetty kept pacing, talking as she walked. "I might be able to confirm her as a shifter, merely by looking into her eyes. But knowing which animals? We'll need samples for that."

"What samples?"

Hetty paused before Alecia. "Hair for one. That shouldn't be difficult." Her eyes further narrowed. "Skin, saliva, blood, and urine to be safe."

Alecia's stomach turned. "How much?"

Hetty scoffed. "Not much, girl—I mean, *Your Majesty*—a few scrapings or drops of each, and several strands of her hair."

Contemplating the gathering of the samples, Alecia wrinkled her nose. She looked around the room and spied an exquisite vase on a plinth near the window. As Ramón entered, she was hefting the vase to look inside. She grabbed the cloth that had lain under the vase and used it to wipe the inside of dust.

"Good morning, Ramón," Alecia said, as he bowed low to her and then Hetty. "Remind me to get the cleaning staff to give this room an extra dusting."

Ramón frowned. "That's hardly my job, Your Majesty. Don't you have a chief housekeeper to order those tasks?"

She shook her head. "Never mind. I need you to accompany us to see Lady Stenmore. We have samples to gather."

"I heard she had been found. Did you discover anything useful?"

Alecia could hardly come out and accuse the noblewoman of being a shape shifter, not to Ramón.

"She hasn't admitted to anything, but wasn't cooperative. That's why we need the samples. To… to discover her true essence. Currently, all we have is our gut feelings that she's guilty."

"You think Lady Stenmore had something to do with Iona's disappearance?" Ramón looked decidedly uncomfortable. "Wait a minute. You're going to make an enchantment? A truth spell?"

Alecia nodded, not quite able to meet his gaze. She couldn't tell him the truth, not if it turned out Melanis was a shifter. "Something like that. Can you accompany us to the jail?"

Ramón sighed. "I suppose I can do that. What's the vase for?"

"For the collecting of samples," Alecia said. "Lady Henrietta, are you ready?"

Alecia strode from her office, with Hetty and Ramón following. Her guards trailed her from the keep, but Alecia made them hang back a respectable distance.

Ramón kept glancing at her, but she wouldn't explain more than she must. This was her business, and he was merely the muscle this time.

The guard in charge of the prison bowed when he saw her approach.

"I wish to see the prisoner, Lady Stenmore," she said.

The man frowned. "Yes, Your Majesty, I understand, but the admiral said no visitors under any circumstances."

Alecia fixed him with a cold eye. "And you think that applies to me? The ruler of this kingdom, and your ultimate superior, not to mention the admiral's?"

"Um, well, no, Your Majesty. I suppose it don't apply to you." He looked at Ramón and Hetty. "It could apply to them, though."

Alecia inwardly rolled her eyes. It was a fine time for this man to develop a brain.

"Guardsman," she said. "I guarantee no harm will come to you if you allow myself, Lord Zorba, and Lady Henrietta to visit the prisoner. Will that suffice?"

"Begging your pardon, ma'am, but how can you guarantee that? What if some harm befalls you because I let you down there?"

Alecia gritted her teeth to prevent a swearword escaping. "Lord Zorba will guarantee my safety, my good man. Now, let us pass."

She stood, arms folded and foot tapping. The others followed her lead. Finally, the guard moved to unlock the gate that led down to the cells.

"Thank you," Alecia said as she descended the steps. "I'll reward you for your common sense today." She could almost hear Ramón's teeth grinding. Hetty was, thankfully, silent. It wouldn't take much to set Ramón off.

The stairwell was lit by torches every few paces, and the corridor they descended to was also well lit. In no time, they found Melanis Stenmore. The guard unlocked the barred gate into the cell and entered.

"Visitors for you, My Lady. See that you behave. The lord here has a sword and knows how to use it."

"That will be all, guardsman," Alecia said.

As the man exited, Melanis pushed herself up from the pallet on the floor. "What do you want?"

Ramón stepped forward. "I suggest you mind your manners, My Lady. Can you stand?"

"No, I can't stand. I'm lucky to be alive."

Alecia joined Ramón. "And how did you come to be in this condition, Lady Stenmore? Broken bones, clothes missing, blood and dirt all over you? You were missing for days."

The woman remained seated, but glared up at Alecia, lips compressed.

"Never mind. You don't need to speak to us. We'll let your samples do the talking for now. Ramón, please hold her shoulders."

Ramón did as she asked, and Alecia plucked a few long blonde strands from Melanis's head, transferring them to the vase. The woman flinched, but remained silent.

"It will be interesting to see how you tolerate the rest of our sampling," Alecia said, pulling a knife and a small vial from her sleeve. The woman's eyes grew wide, but Alecia struck so swiftly Melanis had no time even to call out before the knife flashed across her grubby palm. Alecia squeezed several drops of blood into the vial.

"Ramón, lay her down on the pallet and hold her." Alecia forced her finger inside the woman's cheek and scraped out a smear of saliva which joined the blood. Then she took the knife and shaved several layers of skin from the woman's cheek and added them to the vase.

"Now for the final sample," Alecia said, striding across the cell and grasping the slop pot. It was empty, thankfully, but none too clean. She lifted it and strode back to Melanis.

"You will use this pot. I want a sample of your urine."

Melanis glared at Alecia as though she'd like to strike her dead. "You must help me rise."

Alecia took a step back and motioned to Ramón, who appeared none too keen to be involved.

"Your Majesty, surely you have enough samples?" he asked.

"No, she must urinate in the pot. Now!"

Ramón sighed and helped the lady rise, then maneuvered her over the pot, so she was squatting, the white shift bunched around her thighs. When she was finished, Ramón helped her back onto her pallet. He was quite solicitous of the woman, Alecia thought, but then Ramón had always been respectful of females.

"Now, are you satisfied with your 'samples'?" Ramón snapped.

Alecia raised her brow at him. "Perfectly, thank you." She looked at Melanis. "I appreciate your cooperation, Lady Stenmore."

"As if I had a choice!" Melanis spat, then turned her head to the side, away from her visitors. They filed out of the cell and closed the door, the guard coming to lock it.

Alecia's insides squirmed with anticipation of the results of Hetty's testing. Finally, they might learn how Iona was taken, or at least who Melanis Stenmore really was—friend or foe?

Alecia rejoined her guard outside the jail, and Ramón mounted, ready to escort her back to the keep.

"We have a change of plan, Ramón. I will no longer be returning to the keep, but will escort Lady Henrietta into the city where we will process these samples." She mounted her horse and reached for the vase holding the samples that Cretia carried.

Ramón scooted his horse close to hers. "You're not entering the city with a guard of only three women, *Your Majesty*." The honorific was ground out as if said reluctantly, but Alecia thought it was more irritation with her that made him torture the words.

She gazed back at him impassively. "That choice is not yours to make, Lord Zorba. However, you may accompany me if you're concerned."

His baby blue eyes flared with anger. He was a ball of frustration these days. Oh well, he would overcome his moods in time, when he finally accepted his new status. Perhaps.

"Very well," he snapped. "Move out."

"Just like a man to take control of my guards when Arelle is completely capable," Alecia muttered. She shrugged at Arelle, who shook her head, her normally placid nature not on display.

It was an uneventful ride to Firedrake Alley, the location of Hetty's old cottage. She had kept the premises after joining the queen's advisory body, and Alecia had it patrolled regularly. She didn't want anyone moving in and taking over the dwelling. It soothed Hetty to know she had a "bolt hole", as she called it, to return to if needed. This was one of those days.

The guards and ladies stayed outside while Ramón entered the two-story dwelling to ensure all was safe for Alecia and Hetty to enter. Nothing was out of order, but a thick layer of dust covered the furniture and shelves.

Hetty entered the kitchen, and began laying out ingredients while Ramón started the fire and brought in more wood.

"You really are most useful, Ramón," Alecia said, smiling.

"Someone has to do the chores, and it can't be you," he said, then sneezed. "If that's all for now, I'll wait outside."

Alecia nodded and went to help Hetty while Ramón exited the kitchen.

"That boy is as grouchy as a bear after winter," Hetty muttered, as she laid out all the samples.

Alecia wrinkled her nose. "With Iona missing and so much else on my mind, I can't spare the emotion to care. Besides, he deserves a little grief for his past actions."

Hetty stopped and speared her with an intense black gaze. "I swore I heard the boy found Vard when he was more wolf than man. Didn't he risk life and limb to bring your child's daddy back from the forest so that you could see him one last time? And didn't that result in Vard saving Iona's life, and yours?"

Alecia refused to be cowed or feel guilty. "Enough, Hetty. You do your job, and I'll take care of mine. I've forgiven *you*, haven't I? Perhaps with time, I'll be able to do the same for Ramón, and even Benae. I'm not unreasonable."

Hetty narrowed her eyes at Alecia, then bent her head to her work.

As Alecia watched, Hetty made two concoctions of the blood, saliva, urine, hair, and skin.

"Why the two pots, Hetty?" she asked.

"Well, I have two spells in mind with slightly different ingredients. I thought I would try both in case one is wrong."

"What are you using?"

She indicated one of the pots. "This one, apart from Lady Stenmore's samples, has ground skull bone, sparrow's entrails, snake's eyeballs, and campfire ash." As she mixed the ingredients, Hetty chanted words over the pot, then moved onto the second sample pot. "This one has ground skull bone, dandelion root, blackthorn, poison mushrooms, and moss." She mixed that one, saying slightly different words over the pot.

"Here, take this pot and place it in the large cauldron over the fire."

Alecia did so. Hetty placed the other pot beside it and extended her hands toward the cauldron, muttering harsh-sounding words.

Betherane, mundine, catersaw, belil.

Undrane, forthri, nufor, bewah.

Alecia shivered. She had heard spells before, back when Hetty was trying to help Vard control his bear form, but these were different. They felt wicked, even though she knew Hetty was not.

Hetty's dark eyes reflected the dancing flames of the fire as she repeated the words with more emphasis and volume.

Betherane, mundine, catersaw, belil.

Undrane, forthri, nufor, bewah.

A red mist seeped from the pot Alecia had placed in the cauldron. From the other pot, a slimy green ooze rose, creeping over the sides of the cauldron, and pouring into the hearth.

Hetty stepped back and motioned her to do the same. "Don't let it touch you."

As Alecia watched, the red mist began forming shapes, swirling and sweeping in the air over the cauldron. Alecia stepped further back as the mist grew too large for the fireplace to contain. She and Hetty retreated to the doorway as the room filled with red mist and green ooze. The smell was hideous, like all the odors of decay and foulness combined.

"Nothing like this has ever happened with these spells!" Hetty's voice contained a good measure of fear. She grabbed for a bucket of water sitting by the doorway and went to hurl it onto the green slime.

"Wait!" Alecia grabbed her arm. "The mist is forming a picture."

The red mist had wings! It was all Alecia could think of to describe the shape. And along with the wings came a sharp beak and talons. The mist was a hawk! Its head turned to focus on them. There came a "jump" in the mist, and the form doubled in size until flapping red wings of vapor filled the room.

"Out! Get out!" Hetty shouted, clawing at Alecia to follow her. They both turned and charged from the cottage, bursting into the street, sucking in great breaths of fresh air.

"Get away!" Alecia screamed to her guards and Ramón. She turned to check on Hetty and saw her old friend had stopped to close the door. "Get the horses out of here."

The beasts leaped and swung on their reins as a rumbling began in the house. Alecia grabbed her mare, and hauled her up the street into an alley. The others followed, Ramón leading his and Hetty's horses.

"I don't like this," Hetty muttered. She walked backwards as if she couldn't take her eyes from the cottage. The rumbling escalated, and people poured into the streets from taverns and shops to see what the noise was. Spurts of crimson mist oozed from the window, and from under the eaves. Green slime seeped under the front door and into the alleyway.

A roar punched the air, and, with a rumble and snap of breaking timber, parts of the roof blew into the sky, followed by a thick ball of red mist. The vapor coalesced into the shape of a gigantic dragon. It gave one ear-splitting roar, and shot away over the roofs to the west.

Silence fell on the street as townsfolk stood, mouths gaping and eyes wide. Alecia knew how they felt. She glanced around the alley and streets flanking Hetty's roofless house. Shards of timber littered the cobblestones, and one unfortunate fellow clutched a huge splinter that protruded from his arm.

Her guards seemed to have escaped injury, as had the horses. Hetty was quiet, which was always a concern. A deep gash dripped blood at Ramón's left temple. She joined them.

"Ramón, you need to get Benae to check that," Alecia said. "And take that injured fellow with you."

Ramón's shocked eyes met hers. "What did you do? Bizarre things occur around you, Alecia, but I think this wins the prize."

"It doesn't matter. No one died, and the house can be rebuilt. I'll get the ladies to set a guard on the place."

Ramón goggled at her. "You will return to the keep, Your Majesty, before someone attacks you for what just happened." He stepped closer to her and lowered his voice. "It was clearly witchcraft that caused this… this… explosion. Leave the area before someone spots you, and blames you for it. Ladies, take the queen and Lady Henrietta back to the keep now!"

There he went again, ordering her guards. But he was right, unfortunately. This was a dangerous situation. "What are you going to do, Lord Zorba?"

"I'll see you safely away, then secure this area, and deal with any injuries. Now go!"

Alecia mounted Silver as Ramón helped Hetty aboard her horse. Then the lady guards closed in around Alecia, and they left via the alley they had sheltered in. The man was infuriating, especially when he was right.

"Are you well, Hetty?" Her friend hadn't said a word since the explosion.

"I'm well enough, girl. Now keep quiet until we are back in the keep."

Alecia paced back and forth in her sitting room, too agitated to sit and sip her tea as Hetty was doing. She was concerned for her friend, but she also needed answers.

"Speak to me, Hetty," she said, voice hushed so the guards outside wouldn't hear. "What happened?"

"You saw what happened," Hetty snapped. "What I don't understand is why. I must be out of practice. It's all this royal advising I'm doing. It's not natural, and my spells are suffering."

"We can deal with that later," Alecia said. "I need to understand what the results meant. Is Lady Stenmore a shape shifter?"

"I could tell that from her eyes," Hetty snapped. "Close to the transformation, a shifter has that golden halo to their irises, and they smell different."

Alecia frowned. "You never told me about the smell."

"It wasn't important before. This time, with the Stenmore woman, I wanted more proof. Now the mist, before I lost control of it, shaped itself into a hawk."

"I saw that, it was definitely a hawk."

"That's one of her forms."

Alecia gasped. "I remember Vard telling me he was looking for a hawk shifter back before the king died. He never did find the culprit. It could be her."

"You're missing the point, girl."

Alecia scowled. She would have to stop Hetty calling her "girl". It wasn't appropriate. She reflected on what the point might be. There was the hawk, and then it transformed into…

"The dragon! Melanis Stenmore is a dragon?"

Hetty nodded. "It seems to me she can take both those forms. And if she can transform into a dragon, she could have taken Iona from her room."

"The scratches on the windowsill?"

Hetty nodded again. "She may be solely responsible for the abduction, and she could have transported Iona anywhere in the time she was away."

Alecia sat in the nearest chair—or slumped would be a better description. "She *could* be anywhere. How can I know if Melanis in dragon form could've cared for my daughter during the flight? She might have dropped her!" She closed her eyes, reaching inside for the strength to overcome this shock. Unwittingly, a vision of Iona's battered little body slipped into her mind. *No!* She would *not* think like that.

"How do we explain to Ramón what happened?" Alecia asked.

In that moment, the door to the chamber crashed open, and Ramón entered, slamming the door behind him.

Alecia surged to her feet. "I beg your pardon, Lord Zorba! Explain yourself!"

"*You* explain to me what just happened. You could've been killed." His cut had re-opened in his agitation, and blood trickled down the side of his face.

"I told you to get that tended to."

"Benae is busy with several other injured. She'll see me in due course." He pulled out a handkerchief and mopped at the blood. Heaving a deep breath, he met her gaze. "What *was* that?"

"The spell appears to have backfired. We don't quite understand what occurred." Alecia didn't wish to explain any more than she must.

"Tell me again what the spell was. I fail to see how that debacle had anything to do with discovering the truth."

She joined him in the middle of the room, and they stood toe to toe, both breathing heavily.

"I'll let you know once Hetty and I assess what happened," she snapped.

"That won't do! Questions will be asked, especially by eyewitnesses and the injured." He drew breath and went on more quietly. "Dozens of people saw that mist dragon. Already I have fielded questions about its origin. The community is fearful it will return and damage their homes, or kill them."

"Ramón," Alecia said, battling her own anger, "I can't answer those questions right now. The mist creature won't return to do any more damage."

His eyes narrowed. "Can you be absolutely sure of that?"

Alecia glanced at Hetty, who failed to meet her eyes. Apparently, they couldn't be sure of no further consequences. She sighed and turned back to Ramón.

"It's too early to say. The mist creature and the slime resulted from a spell using various ingredients and incantations. It included the samples we obtained from Melanis Stenmore."

"We can't tell the people that!" Ramón said.

"No, we can't. You see my dilemma."

"*Our* dilemma," Ramón said.

"Did anyone see me, do you think?" Alecia asked.

Hetty spoke from her chair. "Someone is bound to have seen you. If so, it will have to be put around that the queen was on a mercy mission to a sick resident and happened upon the disaster. That it was simply bad timing your being there. When the explosion occurred, you were hustled away for your own safety, leaving Lord Zorba to attend to the populace, especially the injured."

Alecia nodded. "Yes, that could work. As long as people don't associate Hetty, the owner of the cottage, with Lady Henrietta, my advisor."

"I wasn't taking much notice," Hetty said, "but, since I went there in disguise as Lady Henrietta, it will be safe, providing no one saw either of us enter or leave the house."

"I was watching closely," Ramón said. "I don't think that's likely, but we certainly can't be sure you weren't seen."

Alecia huffed. "I can't concern myself with that, with mights and maybes. We have the first new lead since we found Iona's sock. We must speak with Melanis Stenmore."

Ramón faced her, hands on hips. "How does the explosion and the mist dragon implicate Melanis?"

Alecia stubbornly refused to answer.

Hetty sighed then stood and joined them. "Boy, use your brain. We used samples from Lady Stenmore in the spell. The queen and I were virtually certain she was a shapeshifter, but we needed to know what forms she could take."

Alecia gasped and pulled her advisor to the side. "Hetty, what are you doing?"

Hetty's dark gaze bored into her, turning her cold. "I'm sick of the secrets," she whispered. "He needs to know."

"Easy for you to say," Alecia said. "This secret doesn't affect you as it does… others."

They both turned to Ramón, whose usually tanned complexion had turned gray. "Lady Stenmore is a shapeshifter?" He considered, and his face became even more pale. "A dragon shifter?"

Alecia gave up her protest. "Yes, and also a hawk, if Hetty's spell was true."

"We think she stole Iona from her room as the dragon, causing the deep gouges on the windowsill. Then she flew away, possibly landing on her mansion, dropping the sock on her way, and ending up at a place unknown."

Ramón turned and began pacing across the room as the ladies watched. He was taking this much better than Alecia had expected. Then he stopped and faced her.

"We need to have another look in that mansion, and at her country estate. Iona may be hidden in either place. This time, we'll look specifically for secret passages."

Ramón and Estevot traveled to the Stenmore country estate while Alecia and Nikolas Cosara searched the townhouse. Merielle came along to help. Nikolas hadn't approved of Alecia's involvement, but this time she refused be denied, as she was heartily sick of inaction.

As they turned over the lower floor of the mansion, pulling up carpets and knocking on walls, the admiral's face was stormy. His conduct was little short of disrespectful, and Alecia's temper simmered.

Merielle approached. "You must forgive my husband, Alecia. He is too used to getting his way in all things. He should understand you need to be involved."

Clearly, she wasn't quiet enough.

"I understand the queen needs to be involved, beloved," Nikolas said. "I'm concerned for her safety. Tell me again why we suspect Iona could still be in one of the Stenmore properties? You have evidence of how Lady Stenmore may have removed the princess from her nursery?"

Alecia frowned. "You'll think me insane."

His brows drew together. "How so?"

Nikolas had seen Vard transform from hawk back to man, so he knew shifters existed. What was the harm in telling him the truth?

She met his stern gaze. "I'm almost positive that Melanis Stenmore is a dragon shapeshifter."

Nikolas's mouth dropped open, and his gaze narrowed.

"I said you'd think I was insane."

If Nikolas's face was stormy before Alecia's declaration, then it was now a life-threatening blizzard. Suddenly all the fight went out of Alecia. Nothing they did seemed to get them any closer to finding Iona. She walked over to an overstuffed chair and sat down, inviting Nikolas and Merielle to do the same.

"I prefer to stand," Nikolas said, his voice cold.

Merielle took his hand, led him to a love seat, and pulled him down beside her. They whispered together for a few seconds, during which Alecia closed her eyes and tried to pull her ragged emotions under control. All she could think about was their utter failure. Despite their efforts, Iona was missing without a trace. She must face the genuine possibility that she would never see her daughter again.

Nikolas cleared his throat. "I saw her eyes the day we found her. I can believe she's not what she seems—but a dragon shifter?"

Alecia forced herself to meet the admiral's eyes. "I believe a dragon was used to take Iona. Now Stenmore has been revealed—I can't say how—we can't discount her involvement."

"Then why isn't Iona anywhere on the Stenmore estates? Why would she be involved in such a scheme?"

"James Tomel uncovered rumors that her estates are impoverished. She has been selling valuable artifacts to keep up the pretense of wealth."

Nikolas frowned. "I hadn't heard those rumors. But this could be a wild goose chase. I struggle to believe your theory unless you can provide me with the evidence that damns Lady Stenmore. At least reveal how you came to confirm her shifter essence."

Alecia stood, scowling at the admiral. "I can't do that. Magic was involved, and I know how you feel about that. I won't reveal the source of the information, but I was an eyewitness. If the word of your queen is not enough to convince you, then perhaps I have the wrong man leading my naval fleet."

Nikolas huffed, appearing completely flummoxed. Finally, he met her gaze. "Right then. Say Melanis *is* a shifter. What do we know that links her to Iona?"

"That's just it!" Alecia said. "There's no good reason that Melanis would take Iona unless there was money in it for her. And that means there must be someone else involved."

Merielle moved to the edge of her seat. "But who?"

Alecia met her worried gaze. "I think Kain is right. The *Sis Lenweri* were involved in both Lyam's kidnapping and Iona's."

"If that's the case, should Kain and Vard's mission be successful, we shall also retrieve your daughter."

Alecia nodded. "And yet we have heard nothing new, since those vague reports of Nugoriem's disappearance." She stood. "We should return to the castle in case word arrives."

CHAPTER FIFTEEN

AFTER three days of trekking the deep forest trails, Vard was beginning to doubt they would ever locate the *Sis Lenweri*. The quest to find the rebel elves and his father had become a trial to get through each day. Mornings dawned bright and cool, and the night guards reported nothing besides the creatures of the forest, and the wind through the leaves.

The scouts found only evidence of the animals which inhabited the region. There was nothing to indicate a population of *Sis Lenweri* lived anywhere in the area. The lack of success weighed heavily on them all. But most ominous was the absence of Nugoriem. He had flown off on day one to hunt, and they hadn't seen him since. Kain wore a perpetual frown, as if the dragon's disappearance was his personal fault. Vard feared they would never recover Lyam. As for Iona, if they couldn't find the *Sis Lenweri*, they would never know if her disappearance was linked to Lyam's.

After spending hours each day in either the hawk form or the wolf, Vard was nearing exhaustion. His search for evidence of the presence of *Sis Lenweri* had drawn a blank. Either his senses had let him down, or there were no *Sis Lenweri* in these forests.

And, as if matters weren't bad enough, Katrine had revealed yesterday that she couldn't locate her hounds. They should have been with her by now, and no matter what she did to sense them, nothing worked. At least she had spoken twice with Hetty, and let Alecia know their location and progress—or lack of it. Vard had seen Alecia in the fire, beyond Hetty, her glorious lilac eyes full of fear. She and her advisors had made no breakthrough in Brightcastle—no Melanis Stenmore, no ransom note. Nothing.

Sam dropped back beside him. "You need to get more rest, Vard. You're almost asleep in the saddle."

Vard drew in a deep breath. "I can't sleep. Whenever I close my eyes, I see Iona as I last saw her, playing with Alecia. I can't stand this lack of progress. Where are the enemy? And where is that blasted dragon?" He lowered his voice. "Not to mention the hounds."

"We'll find them. We have good people here. The dragon probably lost track of time."

Vard grunted. "Maybe. I can imagine such an ancient creature having his own schedule. Still, surely he knows how critical he is to the mission."

"Of course he does!" Kain joined them. Dark circles lay under his eyes, and his skin had taken on a gray hue.

"Then, where is he?" Vard asked, his tone not what he had hoped for. Bickering would gain them nothing. "Sorry, I meant no disrespect."

Kain shrugged. "None taken. This lack of progress is eating at all of us." His eyes suddenly stared fixedly, and he appeared to be looking inwards. His throat bobbed, and he swayed in his saddle.

Sam clapped a hand on Kain to steady him, his puzzled gaze finding Vard's.

"Kain! What's the matter?" Vard turned his horse to study the *Lenweri* leader, and saw the moment when he again became aware of his surroundings.

"Nugoriem is wounded! He needs my help." With those words, Kain spurred his horse between Sam and Vard, and galloped up the track.

"Damn the man!" Vard said. "He could be running into an ambush. Sam, take twenty men, and catch him up. Tell the others what is happening. I give you command until I return." With that, Vard dismounted and handed Sam the reins. "Look after Trax for me." He bolted into the trees to the right, finding a dense patch of undergrowth. Quickly forming the hawk in his mind, within minutes Vard was winging away to the north in pursuit of Kain.

* * *

Sam tried to keep his mind clear as he led his party of twenty north. Kain's path was easy to follow, even when it veered to the right onto an overgrown deer trail. The Lenweri leader was going to break his mount's leg, or his own neck! Obviously, he shared a telepathic connection with the dragon, unless he had lost his mind. No. Kain Arenil was not the type of man who succumbed to insanity, although he had been through much change in the last year or so. Much as Sam had.

Sam shook the thoughts from his head, and concentrated on negotiating the thick bush. There was no way they could be stealthy, charging through the forest like this, but they must stay with Kain. He just hoped there were no *Sis Lenweri* close, right at that moment.

After a half hour of madness, Sam slowed his mount. If there was a *Sis Lenweri* encampment ahead, he didn't wish to charge straight into it. The forest had opened a little, and he heard a waterfall. Cool air caressed his sweat dampened brow and he wished he had the time to appreciate it.

A few more moments passed, and Sam spotted a clearing through the trees. Weak sun streamed down upon the body of a huge black beast. Nugoriem. He urged his companions to stop, and chose three to accompany him. He tied his horse and Trax to a boundary tree beside Kain's mount, and stepped into the clearing.

Adjusting his weapons as he approached, Sam kept a wary eye on the beast, even though it appeared to be dead. He was yet to spot Kain.

"Don't come any closer." Kain's voice came from behind the dragon.

Sam froze, his eyes sweeping over the beast. Deep gouges marred the iridescent sheen of the black scales on his visible legs, and all along his body. His tail ended in a bloody stump, and his closest wing lay on the grass, twisted at an unnatural angle. Nugoriem's eye was closed, and his body unmoving.

"Is it dead?" Sam asked, sword in his hand, just in case.

Kain appeared at the beast's head, his hand placed gently on the snout.

"I strongly advise you not to call him 'it'. He detests that." Kain closed his eyes, as if concentrating. After several moments, he looked at Sam. "He's alive, but barely. The other dragons attacked Nugoriem, and he has lain here at death's door for almost three days. When he awoke, he called to me."

"Can you help him?" Sam asked.

"My presence seems to lend him healing, yes. I don't understand how. It happened before when I shot him down and inadvertently saved his life."

"That wing looks painful."

"My next task is to straighten it. Then he should be able to heal it. Give me a hand, please."

Kain approached the bent wing, and, with Sam's help, placed it in a more natural position. His companion grimaced as they worked, as if he felt the pain of the wing.

"Are *you* well?" Sam asked.

Kain sucked in a breath, and rolled his shoulders. "I have a dragon in my head, screaming in agony. Let's get this over so he can heal. The other wing's almost as bad."

They walked around the dragon's mashed tail to the other wing. This side was extensively burned, including the wing which was ripped in several places.

Sam sucked in a breath. "Surely he can't heal those tears?"

Kain shrugged. "We may have to sew those." He placed his hand on the crusty burns above the wing, and closed his eyes. Sam watched, amazed, as some of the superficial crusts dropped to the ground, leaving soft gray scales beneath.

Kain slumped on the grass, panting. "Get a needle and the cow gut twine from my horse, please."

Sam summoned his men to watch Kain while he went to get the supplies. He also fetched a water bag and dried meat. When he returned to the elven prince's side, he found the three soldiers gaping at being so close to the fearsome beast.

"Take position around the dragon, eyes facing out," Sam snapped.

The men jumped to do his bidding, and Sam kneeled beside Kain, handing him the food and water. He then threaded the large needle, and prepared to sew the rents in the wing.

A hand halted him, and he turned to Kain.

"It must be me," Kain rasped, his face ashen. "Only if I sew the holes will Nugoriem be able to heal the damage." The words seemed to take a lot out of the elven prince, or perhaps it was the thought of lending more of his failing energy to the beast.

"You're not up to this, Kain," Sam said. "What good will it do if you kill yourself healing this creature?"

Kain frowned. "I'm just tired. Move aside. I need to do what I can."

Sam finished threading the needle, and handed it to Kain, then turned to wash down the largest tear. When he finished, Kain sewed the edges of the cut together, muttering under his breath.

"What are you saying?" Sam asked.

"Nugoriem has taught me some incantations. They help with the healing, though most of the process comes from our bond, which is stronger than when we first encountered each other. Now let me work."

Kain went back to his task, the muttering resuming. Sam watched, ready to pick the prince up if he collapsed. When one rent was repaired, Kain straightened, swaying on his feet, and moved to the next one.

Sam grabbed his arm to steady and restrain him. "Kain, you must rest. Is Nugoriem out of danger?"

The *Lenweri* leader's eyes closed as he conversed with the dragon. When he opened his eyes, he nodded. "He'll live." He let out a heavy sigh. "Perhaps I should do as you say."

Kain handed Sam the needle and sat down, took a drink from the water bag, then rolled himself inside his cloak, and closed his eyes.

"Well, that was easier than I thought," Sam muttered to himself. He gathered wood for a fire and fetched food from the saddlebags. One man had a pot, plates, and utensils with him, and fixed a meal of dried meat and vegetables while Sam cleaned the other tears in Nugoriem's wing.

By the time they had eaten, Vard walked into the clearing. He had the golden eyes of recent transformation and avoided the men, who had returned to sentry duty.

Vard glanced at Kain, then ran his gaze over Nugoriem. "Well met, Sam." He helped Sam to his feet. "Is the beast alive?"

Sam nodded. "You wouldn't know it, but yes." He motioned Vard away from Kain. "I don't know how it can be alive, but saving it has exhausted Kain." He paused, clenching his jaw. "How can the dragon help us now? It will be weeks before it can fly, if ever again."

Vard's eyes returned to Nugoriem. "What does Kain say?"

Sam shrugged. "He's been preoccupied with healing since I arrived. I didn't wish to distract him." He observed Kain sleeping. "But the healing is taking its toll. He can't sacrifice himself this way."

"Surely he knows his limits?"

"Sounds like this is only the second time he has healed Nugoriem, and the first time he was unaware he was even doing it. I don't think he knows how far he can push himself."

"We have to trust all will be well," Vard said. "We need both of them."

They let Kain sleep, hoping that would refresh the elven leader enough to finish his healing.

* * *

Vard had found at least one *Sis Lenweri* camp whilst scouting in hawk form. He also narrowly missed being shot down by an arrow. The bird's residual terror fluttered inside him. How many more close shaves could he risk before his luck ran out? He shut the fear away, and turned his attention to Nugoriem.

The magnificent beast certainly appeared dead. And as Sam had already said, how could he help them in this state? Time was ticking, and they must rescue his father and, likely, Iona, before they were traumatized permanently—if they were still alive.

He summoned Sam from his sentry post.

"I found a nest of *Sis Lenweri* to the northeast," Vard said. "I didn't get too close, but it appears a permanent camp. They have built huts, as well as the usual tree houses. It's a hive of activity. I intend to wait until night, then get a closer look."

Sam clapped him on the back. "Let's hope our hostages are in there."

Vard's mood dropped. "No guarantee of that, but judging by the path the retreating *Sis Lenweri* took, it could be the right place."

Sam growled. "It better be. We all need some good news, and a few heads to bash. Any sign of the night hounds?"

"Not a scent. Lady Star will be going out of her mind unless she's been able to re-establish a link with them."

"Let's hope she has."

Kain groaned and rolled over, rubbing his face. He pushed himself to his feet and laid a hand on Nugoriem's chest. After several moments, he nodded and exhaled. "He's improved." Kain walked all around the dragon, often laying hands on it.

Once finished, he approached Sam and Vard. "Thank you for tending Nugoriem while I rested, Sam. And Vard, any news?"

"I've found our first encampment of *Sis Lenweri*."

Kain smiled, but his eyes were cold. "That's welcome news. I'm in a good mood to teach the *Sis Lenweri* a lesson. Though why I should need to, so soon after their defeat at Brightcastle, I don't know."

"How are you feeling?" Sam asked.

"The rest did me a world of good. If there's food left, I'll have a meal, then sew that wound, and finish healing Nugoriem."

Sam pushed a plate of food at Kain, and they fell silent as the elven prince filled his stomach. He gulped down water from his bag, and turned back to the dragon.

"I wish there was something more I could do to help," Sam said. "Kain, are you sure I can't do anything? Fix a poultice, or a potion?"

"I'm no healer, Sam," Kain said. "If Alique were here, she might suggest something. All I can use is my bond with Nugoriem, and whatever magic I hold."

Vard felt the hairs stand on his neck as a deep voice rumbled in his mind.

You are powerful, shifter. Your magic could augment my elven friend's. The strength of the bear is well known to you.

I'm happy to help, Nugoriem, but how?

Aiding me will risk exposing your secret. You must partially morph into the bear and lay your hands on all injured parts. Are you able to do this?

Vard wanted to help. They needed Nugoriem in their quest, and if he could contribute to the healing… but could he? And what if he exposed his shifter abilities to Kain? This was asking a lot.

Well, shifter? I would be in your debt.

The dragon didn't sound humble. But to have a magical beast owe him a favor? It might be worth the risk. Certainly, saving this beast could only be a boon.

He reached inside himself for the bear, the way he must if he wanted to control the extent of the transformation, and stopped on the verge, half bear, and half human. Power surging through his limbs, Vard approached Nugoriem. He started at the muzzle, working his way down the far side of the body, laying hands on the dragon and feeling the beast draw upon his power. He avoided the side where Kain was stitching the wing.

It took all his concentration to stay in that plane, bear in mind and spirit, but still human in form. He made it to the tip of the dragon's bloodied tail stump, spending some time on the macerated tissue. When he had finished, though still shortened, the tail was healed. Vard started up the other side, trying to look like he was examining the creature. From the corner of his eye, he observed Kain look up at him and frown.

"What are you doing?" Kain asked.

Through the fog of concentration and balanced on the precipice of the shift, Vard registered the question as he would a buzzing mosquito. Until Kain blocked his path.

"I asked what you were doing."

Vard cursed under his breath, clenching his jaw before he responded. "I'm checking the beast." His voice came out half a growl, difficult to understand, even to his ears.

Sam joined him on his other side, and Vard risked a glance into his friend's eyes. He saw the moment Sam registered what was going on by the widening of his eyes. Sam took a ragged breath, and slipped around Vard to Kain.

"How about we move to the head of this glorious beast, Your Highness," Sam said, placing his arm on the man's shoulder, and guiding him away from Vard.

Clearly, Kain was reluctant to move because Sam repeated the suggestion. Eventually, Kain moved away, and Vard focused on the rest of the wounds, including the wing Kain had sewn.

The rumble of the dragon sounded in his head.

Thank you, shifter. Your magic has helped heal my hurts. I am sorry for any trouble this causes.

Vard swept his hand down the beast's muzzle, on the side where the socket was eyeless and scarred.

It was my honor, Nugoriem. Don't forget you owe me!

The rumbling laughter in his head was mocking, not reassuring of future benefits at all. Vard took a deep breath and stepped away, while

Kain took his place, laying his hands on the dragon. Vard focused inwards again, and put the bear to rest, releasing the power back to dormancy.

Sam called to him. "Are you well, Vard?"

Hoping he was whole again, Vard joined Sam while Kain examined the dragon.

"Thank you, my friend," Vard said. "We will talk later."

"We'll talk about this now, Anton," Kain snapped. "What were you doing? You were not yourself."

How could he know? He had never looked the man in the eye, only Sam.

"Your Highness," Sam said, "Vard would never hurt Nugoriem."

"Enough, Delacost," Kain said, chopping his hand at Sam. "I will hear from Anton, and he will look me in the eye and tell me what I just witnessed."

When Vard remained silent, Kain spoke. "I'll start if you like. I felt something when you touched the dragon. It was like a… swirling vibration. Nugoriem began humming, and at first I thought that was what caused it. But it came from *you*. I *know* it did."

Vard closed his eyes, trying to sweep the vestiges of his partial transformation from his gaze. He did *not* need to reveal himself to another person.

"Anton!"

He opened his eyes, staring at the ground before raising his gaze to Kain. The man stiffened, eyes widening slightly. "What *are* you?"

Sam stepped between them. "Look, we don't need to get into this now. Has he harmed the dragon in any way?"

Kain's gaze became unfocused as he communicated with the beast. Then he was back.

"Nugoriem is well. He says he'll be able to fly inside the next hour. Though his shorter tail may affect steering."

"There!" Sam said. "The dragon is well, and ready to fly. We must prepare to infiltrate this camp Vard found."

Kain's hard eyes bored into Vard's. "Delacost is right. There will be time later for talk. I like to understand the men I fight with, but you may keep your secrets. For now." He stalked away, and Vard felt relief that his essence remained hidden.

"With luck, he'll never know," Sam said under his breath. "Though I think you could trust him."

"The fewer who know the better," Vard ground out. "Already too many know, or suspect what I am. That doesn't include you, my friend. It's a relief you're aware."

Sam clapped him on the back. "Let's get packed and return to the others."

Nugoriem was indeed fit to fly within the hour after Vard loaned his magic to the beast. Loaned! As if he would ever get that energy back. And it had taken its toll. Either that, or the fear of being revealed had sapped his strength.

At least he had no trouble keeping his distance from Kain. The elven prince flew Nugoriem, keeping a watch on their progress from the skies. It was growing late, and they hoped to make their assault on the *Sis Lenweri* stronghold after dark. There was just time to grab a meal, and lay out a plan. He tried to concentrate on that rather than on the distasteful scene with Kain.

Vard's party rejoined the others, and continued their march along a trail that led northeast. As soon as they found a suitably large clearing, they tended the horses and made camp. For once, Vard left Trax's care to another, and pulled food from his saddlebags. There would be no fires this close to the *Sis Lenweri*.

Opalgrip stomped up to him. "'Tis glad I am to see you returned, Lord Anton. Lady Star has been like a cat on hot stones since you left. Keeps wanting to take off into the forest. You should speak with her."

Vard frowned at the dwarf. "Thanks for dealing with that, Opalgrip. I'll see what I can do."

Before Vard had washed down the last of his dried beef and cheese, Katrine appeared before him.

"Lady Star," Vard said, giving a small bow. "How are you?" He studied the swirling silver specs in her dramatic blue irises. Many avoided the sorceress when she was agitated.

Katrine took a deep breath, and visibly struggled to compose herself.

"I have found the hounds, Lord Anton. They are well. They *say* they went for a night hunt and became lost."

"You don't believe them?"

"They may believe they merely got lost, but *I* think something has interfered with them." She lowered her voice further. "You know the hounds choose who to be loyal to?" Vard nodded, a chill chasing down his spine.

"Well," Katrine said, "I think someone, likely the *Sis Lenweri*, has tried to steal them from my protection."

"And you base this theory on?" Vard asked.

She narrowed her eyes and the silver specks flared. Lady Star had never liked being questioned. "I've had strange dreams since they vanished. Normally the hounds pop in and out of my dreams…" She paused, frowning. "Anyway, what is normal doesn't matter. Lately I've had nightmares of the beasts being tortured. I'm very connected to them. It doesn't seem to be a physical torture, more a mental compulsion they are struggling with."

"And they are back now?"

She nodded. "I sent my mind out into the forest today, and I found them. They're close, and they're well. But I need to touch them to be sure." She turned and glared at Opalgrip. "That dwarf hasn't allowed me out of his sight, but I want to see my friends. Alone."

Vard considered the request. She should be safe in the company of the beasts, if whatever had tried to coerce them had given up for now. "You're free to meet up with them, but don't be long. I want you back here before we're ready to leave. Before dark."

They made plans for the covert invasion of the elven camp. Vard sent Opalgrip, Frostforge, Tanulia, and Ara to scout. Their primary aim was to get an idea if any prisoners were being held, and of their location. That should be something they could do from the fringes of the camp. Once they returned, Vard could make more solid plans for a rescue.

"It must be a secret operation, if possible," he said. "We're too small a force to fight a battle. We get in, get the prisoner, and get out. Perhaps the dragon and the hounds can provide a distraction if needed."

"What if Lyam is there and injured?" Sam asked. "How will we transport him?"

"Nugoriem has a harness," Vard said. "We could fly him out."

"How do we summon the dragon?" a soldier asked.

Vard contemplated that. Any sound, such as a horn, would draw attention to their location. Lady Star could shoot a fireball, but that would also draw attention. If Iona was in the camp, they must control her rescue with the utmost care.

Kain walked in, taking them all by surprise. As he approached, Vard steeled himself for more questions about his identity. He'd tell Kain if there was no other way.

The elven prince's dark eyes were intense as he stopped before Vard.

"Nugoriem says he can speak into your mind as he does with me," Kain said, quietly. "If you need him, you need only think of him, and he will consider your request."

Vard laughed. "I'd rather not rely on being able to do that. And even if I can speak to Nugoriem that way, how can I trust him to help?"

Kain gritted his teeth. "It may be all we have, Anton. And as to trust? He has risked his life for us. He has confirmed my guess that you leant him energy to heal. Do you not think your help has gained you a boon?"

Vard shrugged. "Perhaps, perhaps not. The dragons are a law unto themselves. They serve no one, certainly not you or I."

"His help is all we have. Now what would you have him do? I'll help where I can."

Sighing, Vard laid out the plan.

Kain remained quiet for some time. "I can't believe they are causing trouble this soon. It seems even the loss of their two most senior leaders hasn't dented their mischief making."

"It would seem so," Vard said. "Let's get any hostages out, and you can arrange a parley, if possible."

Kain walked a few steps away, and then back. "I'm tired of their scheming."

"Look, Kain," Vard said. "I'm sure Alecia will help you put your troublesome cousins in their place. And your sister, too. She'll be equally upset about their behavior. All will be well."

Kain nodded, though his jaw remained tight. "I must get back to Nugoriem. Good luck."

As Vard watched the elven leader disappear into the trees, he sent up a prayer to the Goddess that they would succeed this night.

CHAPTER SIXTEEN

THEY moved like ghosts through the forest, swinging around and approaching from the east. Hopefully, this would be an unexpected direction of attack. Even though Vard knew his people were positioned on either side of him, he struggled to see or hear anything of them. *Good.* Their scouts had found a likely shanty amid the elven encampment which could contain his father and daughter. Of course, it was far from the edge of the camp. Vard had known it would be. Opalgrip and the others had seen *Sis Lenweri* coming and going with medicines and bandages, along with water and food.

He pushed the thoughts of his kin from his mind and concentrated on the mission. Get them out, and then see to their injuries. Fear would *not* distract him.

Finally, Vard reached the first line of tents. Male and female elves moved between the tents, though few. It had taken them an hour to travel through the forest, and only a fraction of the population appeared to be awake. They needed to delay until only the sentries were up.

Vard signaled those on either side of him to settle down and wait. The message was passed on to the others.

The scent of dog floated to him. Katrine's night hounds surrounded the camp a little further into the forest. He hoped they wouldn't need them. Vard morphed partially into the wolf, so he could fully use the heightened senses. Yes—night hounds, the vague scent of the dragon as it flew high overhead, overwhelming smokey fires, the remnants of baked bread and nuts, and, far off in the forest, horses. A pity the elven ponies weren't picketed close to the prisoners. They could have been loosed and let run through the camp, creating a convenient distraction.

The activity in the camp wound down as more elves retired to their beds, and sentries dispersed to their posts. Vard had tasked Opalgrip and his crew with incapacitating the *Sis Lenweri* sentries. He heard a faint grunt far off. Opalgrip had been as good as his word.

Another half hour, and the camp was quiet enough to move in. Vard signaled to those on either side of him and crept forward. He used his wolf sight and senses to scan the area he moved into. He would be the first to go into the hut.

He spied a sentry directly ahead, and sent Sam to dispatch him. His friend moved on silent feet, clubbing the sentry over the head to fall at his feet. They moved on and took another two elven guards out of action.

Vard stood before the hut, teeth clenched. They must be inside. They must be!

He ghosted to the door and tested it. It was tied shut on the outside, which suggested the prisoners were inside with no guard. At least it might mean that. Vard's guts roiled, and his heart thumped hard. He untied the rope that held the door and pushed inside, shutting it behind him.

It was even darker in the hut, but slowly Vard made out the shapes of a pallet with a man-sized lump covered by a cloak. Very faint snores came from there. *Lyam!* He cast about the rest of the small structure, noting two buckets, a low table, and a pair of boots.

Vard slipped across the room and kneeled beside the sleeping form, reaching his hand to what he thought was a shoulder. He squeezed, and the form rolled away from him, a face revealed in the movement. Barely revealed! It was a mess of bruises and scrapes, so grossly swollen he wasn't sure if it *was* Lyam.

"Vard?" The sobbed word was music to Vard's ears.

"Father, what have they done to you?"

Lyam wept, and Vard grasped his father's shoulder then rubbed his back, giving what comfort he could.

"Father," he said, horrified at the state Lyam was in, "I'm getting you out of here, but I need your help."

He made Lyam focus on his face, and held his gaze for a long moment. Finally, Lyam gave a shuddering breath, then another, and nodded.

"Where is Iona?"

The man's eyes flared wide. "Iona? What do you mean?"

Vard's heart lurched, and he thought it would stop altogether. Iona wasn't here? He took a hold of himself. "She went missing four weeks after you did. We thought she might be here, that the two incidents were related."

"No! I haven't seen her." Lyam's face crumpled. "That poor little child." His face snapped up. "Alecia! How is she?"

"She is well. Listen to me. Can you stand?"

Vard gave Lyam space, and the man pushed himself to his hands and knees. He was horribly feeble. The scent of fresh blood and putrefying tissues assailed Vard. His father had been exposed to horrific torture.

He helped Lyam to his feet, but supported him. Together, they shuffled to the door. It flew open as Vard reached for it. Instead of a *Sis Lenweri* soldier or one of their rescue team, an elven woman stood there. He had met her before. In Amitania.

"You!" she hissed, launching herself at Vard like an alley cat.

Nails raking his face, Vard let go of Lyam to defend himself. He must ensure the woman didn't raise the alarm. He partially shifted into the bear and forced the woman down to the ground, eyes blazing and hand over her mouth. She stiffened under him, eyes going wide. From the corner of his eye, Vard noticed Sam in the doorway.

"Get something to use as a gag," he snapped.

Sam pulled something from his pocket and thrust it at Vard. It turned out to be a woolen sock and Vard forced it into his prisoner's mouth, securing it with a dirty scarf Lyam tossed him. He experienced a brief flare of gratitude that his father was well enough to contribute even this small thing.

Keeping his bear shift, Vard glared down at Failora. She trembled, but her dark gaze was defiant.

"This is how it is going to play out, Failora," Vard said. "I'll leave you here trussed like a chicken. If you raise the alarm inside an hour, I'll track you down wherever you are, and make you wish you had died this day."

Her eyes widened, and she shook her head from side to side. Vard moved to the corner of the room and cut lengths of rope from two lines tied to spikes in the ground. Lyam's shackles. He must have grown too weak for them to be necessary of late.

As he tied her hands behind her back, Failora let out a panicked squeak. Vard secured the knot and moved to her feet. They were suddenly flailing so he couldn't grab hold of them.

"Sam!" he whispered.

Sam joined him, and together they tied Failora's ankles, though her struggles kept up.

"We can't count on her to stay quiet for an hour," Sam said. "Slit her throat, or she must come with us."

Vard jerked at the suggestion, and Failora started another round of whimpering. She sounded like she was trying to say something.

He rolled her onto her back. "If I loosen this gag, will you promise not to sound the alarm?"

She nodded instantly.

"Vard!" Sam hissed.

Lyam moaned quietly.

Vard held up his hand against the protests. He pulled the gag out. "Speak."

"Take me with you." Failora sounded desperate, and her eyes held terror.

Something was off with her. "Why do you want to come with us?"

She frowned and hesitated.

"This is a bad idea," Sam growled.

"No!" Failora's quiet protest sounded genuine. "I want to leave this camp. My family has disowned me because I am *Sis Lenweri*. And because I was Faenwelar's mistress, and the wizard's before that, I have been treated as a slave here." She spoke of the sorcerer Leck, whom Vard eventually killed.

"Why did you attack when you saw me?" Vard asked.

"That was instinct," she said on a sob. "It has been my task to care for this man, who I eventually learned is your father. I was told I would be held responsible if he escaped. When I saw you here, all I thought of was foiling this escape and getting revenge for the wizard's death."

"Then why did you not cry out immediately and raise the alarm?" Sam asked.

She glared at him. "There is no time for this. Decide."

Vard immediately turned to Lyam. "Is what she says true?"

Lyam nodded. "As far as I know. They have been harsh with her."

"You go with us as a prisoner," Vard snapped. He replaced the gag, pulled her to her feet and thrust her at Sam, who was muttering under his breath. "Shut it, Sam! Move her out."

As Sam thrust the woman before him, Vard helped Lyam out of the hut and pulled him between two tents as a patrol jogged by. He knew it was a terrible idea to bring Failora with them, but at least that way he could control her. She wouldn't raise the alarm. He pushed his doubts of Failora's trustworthiness to the side, and surveyed the camp. Apart from the usual sounds of camp life after dark, there was only the muted call of sentries, and the thump of their booted feet. And the crashing of Vard's heart. He drew his sword.

When Vard thought all was quiet, he motioned Sam to cross open space between the tents, heading south. As they reached the shadows of a large tent, a high-pitched whistle sounded to his left, and a half dozen *Sis Lenweri* materialized out of the darkness.

Nugoriem, we are discovered!

Vard sent the urgent thought to the dragon as he hustled his father further behind him, and launched an attack at the nearest enemy. Sam was engaged in a sword fight with two elves, having pushed Failora behind him. Vard scored a cut to the ribs and, in a lull in his fight, saw that Sam had a clear passage through the tents.

"Go!" Vard cried, shoving Lyam at Sam.

Sam didn't hesitate and pulled his two charges after him, Failora helping Lyam. Vard watched Sam hand the elven woman a knife before they passed from view.

He did well enough in the fight until more enemy joined the fray. With numerous shallow cuts and facing at least five *Sis Lenweri*, Vard prepared to morph into the bear. A menacing growl sounded from behind the elves and a handful of night hounds landed on the backs of the enemy. They bore the *Sis Lenweri* to the ground, clamping their jaws around necks or whatever they could reach. The sound of the cut and thrust of swords was replaced by screams and the gurgling of blood through ruined throats.

Vard spun and took off in the direction Sam had disappeared, catching up to the other three on the edge of the encampment. They melted into the forest as the camp came alive with screams and whistles.

"They'll be on us in minutes," Sam rasped. "Keep moving!"

"Father isn't capable of running," Vard said. "It's a miracle he's made it this far."

Vard let the bear go, and a wave of weariness overcame him. He went down, smashing his ribs on a rock. Even Sam heard the crack of breaking bone.

"Perfect!" Sam said. "Now we must carry *you*."

Vard wheezed as his breath caught with the pain, and he tasted blood. He knew the signs of a serious chest injury all too well. Perhaps if he shifted into the bear, he would survive.

"I need to shift, Sam. Take Lyam and Failora, and leave me here."

"Don't be insane. I'm not leaving you."

"I'll be fine," Vard said. "I'll take refuge somewhere and heal, then I'll find you. Get Lyam to a healer. Use the dragon." With those words, Vard began the change, and Sam's eyes widened. Without further words, his friend turned to the forest, and ushered his charges away.

* * *

The bear who was Vard shuffled into the forest to the east, seeking a small cave he remembered. There was a stream nearby. Blood dripped from a dozen cuts, but they wouldn't kill him. His chest burned, and he coughed blood.

Once he hit the stream, he drank deeply, every breath and movement spearing agony into him. He padded along the stream, hoping the hunters wouldn't track him in the water. A half league later, he clambered from the stream, made his way over a rocky outcrop, and crawled into a cave. He would go no further until he healed.

* * *

As Sam helped Lyam and Failora through the bush, a constant stream of swear words filled his consciousness. Vard was one of his few friends. If he died, Sam would never forgive himself.

Lyam went down and couldn't rise. "Leave me here and get Vard! I won't let him die!"

"I'm not leaving you," Sam snapped. "Can you rise?"

The older man shook his head. "I have nothing left. And I'm not worth saving."

"That's defeatist talk, Lyam. Vard thinks you're worth the trouble. We came all this way to rescue you."

"You came for Iona. She's not here."

Sam swore. "That's not true. Vard and I started out *for you.* Iona was safe when we left. Now get to your feet, and prove you're worth the effort."

"I wasn't lying when I said I couldn't stand."

Sam sighed. With Failora's help, he pulled Lyam to his feet and hefted the man over his shoulder. Lyam was Vard's size, but the weeks of starvation and torture had leached the weight from him.

They set off again through the forest, Sam hoping his sense of direction was true. Usually it was, but he'd been distracted at the start. He tried to see the stars through the canopy of trees, but clouds had moved in. Light rain began to fall, making the footing treacherous.

"Rest break," he said, and Failora helped him place Lyam against a tree, then sat beside him. From somewhere she pulled a pouch and ate some of its contents before offering it to Lyam. He shook his head.

It was a fine mess. Sam removed his water flask from his satchel, and took a long drink, then stood and took it to Lyam. Again, he shook his head.

"Drink, man, or I'll tip it down your throat."

"I told you I wasn't worth your effort, Samael Delacost."

"And I said you were." He stood there waiting. "What's it going to be?"

Lyam sighed and reached for the flask. Sam heard him take several long gulps before handing the water back.

"That's better. Now, if the lady has enough food, perhaps you would eat a handful."

Failora handed Lyam what appeared to be dried fruits and nuts, and Lyam growled at Sam. "You're just about as ornery as my late wife. Who put you in charge, anyway?" However, he took the food and popped it in his mouth.

"You know who did. Perhaps, after you eat and drink, you might manage to walk some. It wouldn't hurt me not to carry you all the way."

Silence followed Sam's remarks.

Then… "You shame me, boy. I won't give you excuses. I've been making your life harder when I should be helping. But I meant it when I said to leave me and fetch Vard. He's worth ten of me, and he could be dying."

Lyam wasn't giving in without a fight.

"I know Vard well. He's tough and resourceful. And he ordered me to get you out of this forest. You'll do your best to honor his wishes, and so will I." Sam extended his hand, even though he couldn't see Lyam in the dark. However, Lyam could likely see him, due to his shifter abilities.

Lyam stuck out his hand and grabbed Sam's, and he hauled the man to his feet.

"If we don't go too fast, and have rest stops, I think I can manage." Lyam's eyes began to glow in the dark, suggesting he was partially transformed into one of his animal forms. Whatever helped get them out of this Goddess forsaken wilderness worked for him.

They moved slowly, Sam often stumbling over rocks and exposed roots, while Lyam and Failora found surer footing. That led to Sam cursing his mortal weakness, and wishing for the night vision of the elves. He thought he wouldn't wish to be a Defender like Vard. That would lead to more problems than it would solve. All the secrecy surrounding his friend wore him down.

Up ahead, light suddenly blazed through the trees, and the night was filled with screams and the sound of flesh being sundered. The travelers froze, trying to understand what was happening. They crouched in the undergrowth, studying the shapes and sounds of chaos.

"To me! To me!" a kingdom voice cried.

That was enough for Sam. "Stay here, and don't move for anything. I must help where I can." He left his companions and slipped toward the fighting. As he came closer, Sam saw this was their camp. The *Sis Lenweri* had invaded it, possibly following some of their force back after Lyam's rescue. All was chaos, but he forced himself to study the battle. The kingdom soldiers and elves were holding their own, but for a knot of *Sis Lenweri* clustered around what appeared to be only three or four kingdom soldiers. Kain Arenil! If the elven leader wasn't caught in that attack, he had never been a pirate.

Leaping past the last trees and into the clearing, Sam grabbed the arm of a passing soldier and hauled him towards the melee.

"Lord Sam! You're back!"

"Never mind that! Come with me. We need to break up that knot of the enemy."

The two men charged at the cluster of *Sis Lenweri*, who did indeed surround Kain Arenil. The elven high prince looked to be holding his own. Sam sliced at the lower legs of the elven enemy before him and was rewarded with a scream as the *Sis Lenweri* fell. His companion, a man called Tagi, did likewise, opening a gap in the ring of attackers.

Sam and Tagi drew the attention of the ringed *Sis Lenweri*, and the enemy sprung at them with howls of rage. Sam dodged a sword strike which almost took his head. He must be more tired than he thought. Recovering, he spun and kicked the elf in the neck, his enemy collapsing with a crushed windpipe. And then there was no time to look out for Tagi as more *Sis Lenweri* were drawn into the battle.

Sam soon fought back-to-back with Kain Arenil, taking more nicks than he cared for. The enemy numbers slowly diminished, but so did theirs. Then a narrow line of fire sliced through the *Sis Lenweri* as they tried to retreat into the forest.

Sam looked aloft and surmised the huge dark shape must be Nugoriem. Another blast of searing flame scorched the clearing, taking more attackers with it. Sam again looked skyward. The black dragon roared defiantly and flapped out of sight.

Kain bent over, panting beside him. "I must have a word with him about using fire when I'm that close." He sounded done in.

Sam clapped him on the back, and surveyed the destruction. At least twenty charred elven corpses lay close to the trees. He found Tagi, who had fared well and suffered only a few obvious cuts.

"Collect the injured, Tagi," Sam said, "and get them attended to. Drag the dead into two piles, ours and theirs. Take an elf with you, so you don't get it wrong. Bury our dead. Prince Arenil will decide what to do with the *Sis Lenweri*."

Sam jogged into the forest and found Failora and Lyam where he had left them. He led them back to the clearing and placed Lyam with the injured. Failora, he put to helping the kingdom wounded. He shook his head as he approached Kain. Failora was a needless complication.

Kain peered at her. "I know that woman. What's *she* doing here? She's *Sis Lenweri*."

Sam sighed. "Her life hasn't been so easy since Faenwelar's death. Her people have turned on her. She begged to come with us, and Vard agreed."

Kain looked to the heavens, working his neck and shoulder muscles. "Forget her. What did you find? And where's Vard?'

"We brought Lyam out, but he hasn't seen Iona. As far as I know, she wasn't brought here. Vard was injured in the escape, and has holed up in a cave. He ordered me to get his father to safety. I'm going back to find him."

"What a damned mess!" Kain growled. He turned and walked over to Lyam, kneeling before the older man. "Do you remember me, Lyam?"

Lyam barely opened his eyes, but nodded. Kain checked him over and returned to Sam. "He's in bad shape."

Sam nodded. "That was Vard's other order. To get his father back to medical help. Lady Benae is the best, and she's at Brightcastle. Do you think the dragon will take him?"

"I'll have to go with him to make sure he doesn't fall. And that will leave Vard with no means of getting quick healing."

"It's what he wanted."

"How serious were his injuries?"

Sam met Kain's eyes. "He was coughing blood when I last saw him."

Kain walked away, casting his gaze around the clearing at the aftermath of the battle. When he returned to Sam, the elven prince fixed him with his dark gaze.

"You take some men and find Vard. I'll place a sergeant in charge here and get the company moving. Assuming Nugoriem agrees, I'll fly Lyam to Brightcastle then fly back to you when I can. You follow the rest of the company once you locate Vard. I'll find you. May your Goddess go with you."

Kain strode off, issuing orders as he walked.

Sam sought Lyam. "I'm going to find Vard," he said, squatting before Vard's father. "I'll bring him back no matter what. Kain Arenil is flying you to Brightcastle."

Lyam's gaze fired. "I won't fly to safety when Vard might be dying."

Sam clenched his jaw. "You will do exactly as I have ordered—as Vard has ordered. You won't give Kain any grief, and you will damned well get better. I don't have time to argue with you, Lyam. Give the queen my best when you see her."

Sam stood and walked away, pleased to have the last word. Kain had ordered him to take men with him, but he didn't know what state Vard would be in when he found him. Better not to expose Vard to the curious eyes of strangers if he didn't have to.

He found his and Vard's saddled horses, tied with the others amongst the trees, mounted, then entered the forest, searching for the trail they had followed into the clearing. Once he located it, he got his bearings and started along an animal trail that led northeast.

CHAPTER SEVENTEEN

VARD groaned as he rolled over. The movement caused a fit of coughing, which brought stabbing pain through the left side of his chest. When the paroxysm passed, he opened his eyes and spent long moments gazing up at the roof of a cave. As he caught his breath, he pushed his thoughts back, trying to recall what had led him here. Trying to remember where "here" even was.

The events of the past weeks were jumbled in his mind. The last thing he remembered was seeing Lyam in that hut, and… His father had been near death when they arrived at the *Sis Lenweri* camp. Where was he now? Vard closed his eyes and pushed again. He, Sam, and Lyam had left the hut, along with Failora, and been attacked as they passed through the camp.

That was how he got injured. He finally recalled sending Sam off with the others, so that Lyam could get the care that would save his life. And then the bear.

He pushed himself to a sitting position, which caused another blast of pain and a further coughing fit. The spit was slightly blood tinged. Examining himself, he noted several deep sword wounds on his arms and legs, and a fist-sized bruise on his left chest, palpable through his shirt and tunic. Vard tried to rise, but the pain in his side was too great. If he had broken ribs, he should stay still.

Trying to moisten his mouth with spit, he peered around the dark cave for his water bag. He couldn't see anything but his bloody sword. A low growl sounded from outside the cave, and he froze, reaching for the sword and pulling it into his lap. The shallow cave with its low ceiling wasn't exactly ideal for fighting with long blades, but it was all he seemed to have.

A rustling came a short distance from the cave opening, and Vard tried to make out what caused it. Then a large dog-like shape launched itself into the cave and bore him down onto his back. He got his fists up quickly enough to keep the thing from his face and neck, but already his strength faded. Saliva dripped from the beast's mouth onto his chin.

A whistle sounded and was repeated. The pressure on his chest and arms eased as the dog creature sat back on its haunches.

"Who's there?" a female voice asked. A small blue globe of light appeared near the cave ceiling. and Vard could make out Lady Star and one of the night hounds.

"Lord Anton! Are you well?"

"Since your hound jumped on my chest, and I have at least one broken rib, I would have to say 'no', Lady Star."

She pushed the hound to the side and moved closer to Vard, the silver specks in her blue eyes catching the light. They could make a man dizzy if he focused on them.

"We have been following your trail. I thought we were tracking *Sis Lenweri*. You're lucky Nightwalker didn't kill you."

"Yes, I feel so lucky," Vard said, prodding his chest gently to assess his broken ribs.

"Leave off," Katrine snapped. "You'll do yourself more damage. Let me see."

She opened his tunic and shirt, and sucked in a breath as she exposed his chest. "You certainly have multiple fractures. How are you even able to breathe?"

"With difficulty, especially after that hound's tender ministrations."

Katrine turned and sent the beast out of the cave before reaching into her pack.

"You lie down and rest while I set a fire and strap that chest. I have herbs that will help with the pain."

Vard settled back, a wave of relief washing over him that he wasn't alone. "Do you have water?"

She reached for her belt and removed a small water bag, handing it over. "Only two sips at a time."

Vard complied, watching her as she worked. In short order, Katrine had a small fire going, started magically, and a pot of water warming over it. She added herbs and powders from time to time. Finally, she added a generous dollop of honey, and gave a cupful to him.

Familiar with potions made by witches, Vard sipped cautiously. The medicine went down smoothly, much to his surprise, but then the bitter aftertaste hit.

"Fah! That's worse than anything Hetty ever gave me!"

Katrine smirked, but couldn't hide the dark shadows of concern about her eyes. "Who do you think taught me most of what I know? Hold still now."

She set aside the pots and sat cross-legged beside Vard. Pushing his shirt aside to fully bare his chest, she placed both palms over the bruise on his ribcage and closed her eyes. His chest warmed where her skin touched his, and there was a tingling sensation.

"You have three ribs, each broken in two places, so that part of your ribcage is unsupported. Surprisingly, it has already begun knitting. You're a quick healer." She fell silent for a long moment, during which the tingling and heat intensified.

She sat back. "That's all I can do. My healing skills are minimal, though perhaps one day... I've learned to delve wounds and illness, so I can tell what's wrong, but all I can do is take away a little of the pain and inflammation. I'm sorry I can't do more." She reached for her sack again and removed white rolls of narrow cloth. "I'll bind your chest so you can move more comfortably and breathe easier."

"I'm grateful," Vard said, testing his breathing and already finding it less painful. He levered himself up to allow her access for the bandaging.

"You're lucky, you know," Katrine said. "That's often a fatal wound. How did it happen?"

"I can't remember." Better to tell that small lie than have Katrine speculate on why a fall against a rock had given him such a serious wound. He didn't want to reflect on that, either.

Katrine also cleaned his various cuts, and stitched the deep ones before applying a healing balm. She frowned as she placed a hand on his forehead.

"You seem a little feverish. Make sure you drink plenty of water. Lady Benae will do much more when you return to Brightcastle. Now we must move out if we are to avoid the *Sis Lenweri*. I've seen large groups of them combing the forest."

With her help, Vard got to his feet. Shuffling like an ancient crone, he made his way from the cave and down a short incline. Katrine sent the hounds roving ahead and to the sides to take care of any small bands of *Sis Lenweri* scouring the forest. By the frequent cries of pain that floated to them on a slight breeze, there were plenty of the enemy about.

They moved as silently as they could. Vard had no breath for talk, even if that had been wise. Twice he thought he saw a huge shadow pass overhead. A dragon? Was it Nugoriem, or one of the others?

After only thirty minutes of travel, Vard needed to rest. Katrine helped him down against a fir tree, then she vanished into the woods. He closed his eyes and let his senses wander. He smelled unwashed bodies mixed with the crushed pine needles the elves used to disguise their scent. It could be *Sis Lenweri* or *Lenweri*. No human scents met his nose except for a faint rose perfume, which Lady Star preferred. And there was plenty of the rank, musky smell of the night hounds, and that of small forest creatures.

By the time Lady Star returned, Vard was rested enough to resume the trek.

"How is it out there?" he asked, grunting as she assisted him to his feet.

"We had pursuit, but the hounds have taken care of them. I detected no one close, except we should meet up with Delacost before long."

Vard swore softly. "I asked him to get my father on that dragon, not wander about in the forest."

Katrine gave him a sidelong look. "Samael is irritating, but he can be relied upon to follow orders."

"We'll see. How far away is he?"

"Another quarter hour should do it. Now hush. Conserve your breath for walking."

Vard snapped his teeth shut. She was right, damn the woman. He didn't have breath for both, and talking could get them killed, no matter how thorough the hounds were.

Soon, he couldn't have held a conversation if he wanted to. It was getting increasingly more difficult to place one foot in front of another. His chest burned like all the fires of hell. Vard worried he might still die if he didn't get proper treatment. He staggered to a halt, and Katrine turned to him, a frown on her brow.

"Are you well?"

"I can go no further. I'm as weak as a kitten and my ribs are burning. Can you work your magic again?"

She dropped her eyes and huffed out a breath. "I never seem to do any better than when I first attend an illness or injury. But I'll try."

She seated him and unbuttoned his shirt, reaching inside to find the bandages that lay over the injury. Vard looked inward, hoping… needing to feel something like healing. Beyond a very slight warming, there was nothing, and certainly no reduction in pain.

"There," Katrine said, "that's all I can do. I'll mix a cold pain tonic. Samael will be with us soon."

She smiled at him, but didn't manage to hide her fear.

CHAPTER EIGHTEEN

AFTER the fruitless search of the Stenmore mansion, Alecia, Nikolas and Merielle returned to the keep. Alecia was quiet, but her mind worked furiously. Frustratingly, there was nothing more she could do until she got word of the northern mission. If Iona was found with the *Sis Lenweri*, she could look forward to their reuniting, assuming her child was unharmed.

Sending her mare to the stables with a groom, Alecia bade goodnight to Nikolas and Merielle, and sought Hetty. After Iona's kidnapping, her advisor and friend had moved into a small chamber in the keep and Alecia found her there, pacing the room.

"Your Majesty! Thank the Goddess! I heard from Katrine a half hour ago, but her message ended abruptly."

Alecia drew in a breath to quiet the moths in her stomach before answering. "What did she say?"

"I thought she said Iona wasn't found with Lyam. However, she was so quiet, I think she was in some trouble, and then she vanished. I heard 'not with the *Sis Lenweri*', and then she kicked dirt into the fire."

Alecia's hand reached for her head, tearing the crown from her carefully coiffed hairdo. She flung the precious headpiece across the room and onto a chair. "What good is that thing if I don't have Iona? Did she have word of Vard? She could have been saying Lyam was not with the elves."

Hetty frowned. "Yes, she could. I wanted to go and fetch you, but I thought I would serve you better by staying near the fire in case Katrine should return."

Alecia huffed out a breath. "Yes, yes, you did the correct thing. I'm not angry with you. I'm scared and frustrated." She took a few deep breaths. "At least Nikolas is willing to consider Melanis might be a dragon shifter. We achieved something tonight. But Iona is not anywhere to be found on the Stenmore estates."

Hetty rang a bell, and a maid appeared. "Can we have tea brought, and a light repast?"

Alecia barely noticed as the maid bustled out. What were they to do? There was nothing *to* do, but wait for word from the north. It might be a long night.

When the tea came, they sat before the fire, Alecia staring into its depths so she wouldn't miss anything. The day had exhausted her. The next thing she knew, she was being shaken awake by Hetty. Katrine's face floated in the fire.

Alecia blinked rapidly, trying to clear the haze of sleep from her mind. Deep in the shadows behind Katrine was Vard. His face was gaunt, brow wrinkled and skin tight around his eyes. He was surely in a deal of pain.

"Vard, what's wrong?"

Her enquiry made him jump as if he hadn't been paying attention.

"I'll be right as rain with a little rest, my love." His hoarse voice told the lie. Vard was very ill, and trying to spare her.

"Don't you dare die on me, Vard Anton," she snapped.

Katrine held up a hand, frowning. "If you don't mind, Your Majesty, we must talk. We have little time."

Alecia settled back in her chair. "Go ahead."

"Lyam is injured, and on his way back to Brightcastle with Kain on Nugoriem. He will be with you in mere hours." She appeared to steel herself. "We didn't find Iona in the *Sis Lenweri* encampment, and

Lyam hadn't seen her. She may be in another camp, but we can't continue the mission. We have casualties, including Lord Anton."

Alecia swallowed hard. She wanted to force them to continue searching, but she also needed Vard. He looked like he needed her too.

"Vard, when will you be home?" she asked in a quiet voice.

He shifted, and a spasm of coughing shook him. When he recovered, he slumped, and waved for Katrine to speak.

"Lord Anton will be well, I think. He broke several ribs, and I have been unable to help much. When Nugoriem gets back after dropping off Lyam, he will fly Vard to you." She paused, her sparkling irises swirling wildly, as they did when she was agitated. "Do not delay."

"It seems the search for our daughter is in your hands, my love," Vard croaked.

"May the Goddess help you, Your Majesty," Katrine said.

The vision of Katrine and Vard in the dark forest faded until only their own cheery blaze remained.

Alecia turned to Hetty. "We must prepare. Benae will need to be ready to receive Lyam. I'll have her summoned. Then I'll meet with my advisors to determine our next steps.

Alecia gathered her advisors in the small audience hall. An early breakfast had been served, but it would be hours before Kain arrived. As she looked around the room, Alecia's insides warmed at the sincerity obvious on those faces. Not present was Hetty, who had decided to keep trying to scry Iona. Alecia felt her advisor's absence keenly.

She clapped her hands, and the room quieted.

"Thank you for attending so promptly," she said. "Lady Henrietta is following a lead, so will not join us. I've had word from the mission which has been somewhat successful. Lyam Anton was located and rescued from a *Sis Lenweri* camp deep in the northern forests. Princess Iona was not in the camp with Lyam." Her voice wobbled and she tightened her jaw then continued. "We should expect Kain Arenil's arrival on Nugoriem within hours. He will bring Lyam Anton, who is injured. However, we still do not know where my daughter is. Those deployed to the northern mountains have begun a retreat due to losses and injuries."

There was a general murmur of dismay at this news.

"What do we know about Iona's whereabouts, Your Majesty?" Lady Linnet asked.

Nikolas stood. "We know where she isn't. We have thoroughly searched the Stenmore estates, including any wall spaces, trap doors, and cellars. This keep has been similarly searched. And we now know she wasn't with Lyam in the elven camp."

"Unfortunately, that leaves many stones unturned," Ramón said. "You should know we have sent James Tomel to interview Melanis Stenmore again. They were once friends, and it is hoped she'll tell him more details of the kidnapping."

Captain Estevot huffed. "Give me ten minutes with her, and I'll have all her secrets spilling from her treasonous mouth."

Alecia felt the same. However, as queen she couldn't condone torture.

"Tempting, Captain," Alecia said, "but I prefer not to poke the dragon, so to speak."

Nikolas Cosara gave her a sharp look. "Does it not infuriate you that she has information which could lead to the princess's recovery?"

Alecia straightened. "Infuriates is too mild a word, Admiral. However, Melanis maintains she has nothing to do with Iona's abduction."

Merielle stood, fire in her eyes. "I respect your restraint, My Queen. If my child were missing, I would tear the world apart to find her. Lady Stenmore will face a terrible consequence should she be responsible." From Merielle's fierce expression, Melanis would face that consequence from the fire-haired lady herself.

Alecia took a moment to appreciate her advisors' devotion, battling emotion that would be of no use this day. "Let us hope that if Lady Stenmore is guilty, she admits her part, and leads us to my daughter."

Two hours later, the arrival of Kain, Nugoriem, and Lyam interrupted their conference. A footman announced their presence in the courtyard, and Alecia took herself in hand lest she run from the room in her eagerness. As it was, she waited for her advisors to lead the way after sending someone to fetch Benae.

As she stepped from the keep into the cool morning air, the great bulk of the black dragon dominated the space. His giant claws scraped the cobblestones while the light from torches cast a rainbow of colors from his shiny black scales. Alecia bowed her head as the dragon's eye fixed on her.

Your Majesty! It seems I have become little more than a beast of burden. His deep voice boomed in her head.

"Welcome Nugoriem, and many thanks for your help in this mission," Alecia said aloud.

The dragon inclined his head and extended a foreleg so two footmen could climb up and help Lyam dismount. Her future father-in-law was barely conscious. She hurried forward to greet him as he was lowered onto a stretcher.

"Lyam! How glad I am to see you." Alecia took his hand, horrified at how cold it was.

Lyam's head turned to her, and a ghost of a smile curved his blue lips. Then Benae hustled Lyam into the palace to the rooms reserved for his care. Alecia heaved a breath as she watched him go.

"The blessings of the Goddess be on him," a male voice murmured.

She turned to find Kain. "Indeed, Your Highness. Thank you for bringing him home. Did you see Vard before you left?"

Kain shook his head. "I'm afraid not. He was injured during the mission to release his father from the *Sis Lenweri* camp. When I departed, Delacost had already embarked on a mission to retrieve Vard."

Alecia nodded. "I have been informed of Vard's injury. When do you leave to fetch him?"

He tilted his head to the side, considering perhaps. "Nugoriem won't be fit to fly for several hours. I'll release him to hunt and rest. When he returns, we shall set off again, assuming that is deemed the best plan."

Alecia stared at him. *The best plan?* Her beloved was stranded in the forest, gravely ill with no medical care, and the only means of rescue was debating whether to fetch him?

"Inside, if you please, Your Highness. We have much to discuss." Alecia stalked to the steps, entering the keep and heading to the room they had vacated.

She wanted to appear grateful, but Kain must understand the urgency of Vard's situation.

When they were all back in the meeting room, Alecia faced Kain.

"Prince Arenil, Vard isn't in a good way. He may be more seriously injured than Lyam. I demand you fetch him back here as soon as you are able."

Kain frowned. "Care to fill me in on how you know this?"

Alecia looked around at those assembled, then stepped closer. "I can't explain that. It would betray a confidence."

Kain lowered his voice to match. "If your confidence involves Lady Katrine, then I know she has some means of communication."

Alecia heaved a sigh. "Yes, Katrine is with Vard. She has done her best to ease his pain, but he has a serious chest injury. I can't lose him, Kain."

His eyes softened. "I know that. He's tough, that one. I'm confident he can survive this." He looked at the assembled advisors. "This meeting, is it about your daughter?"

Alecia nodded. "As Iona isn't on the Stenmore estates, or with the *Sis Lenweri* you found, we must decide what to do next. Your advice would be welcome." A footman entered with a tray of food and another with two pitchers.

While Kain ate and drank, he told the assembled advisors what had occurred in the north.

Alecia's heart raced at the thought of Vard attempting a return journey on horseback.

"Your Highness," Alecia said, "you must fetch Vard. He won't make it back without Nugoriem's help."

Kain frowned. "Of course I will, if that's what you desire."

Alecia almost collapsed with relief. Ramón took her arm and led her over to a chair. "You should take more care, Your Majesty. You're wearing yourself out."

She closed her eyes until the room stopped spinning. When she opened them, she saw genuine concern in Ramón's blue gaze. "Thank you. I'm trying my best to do what is right."

Ramón nodded and stepped back. Alecia drank punch from a goblet Merielle fetched for her. The sweet liquid settled her shaking hands and drove her weariness away.

James Tomel entered the room and approached Alecia. He kneeled before her, and spoke in a quiet voice.

"Melanis broke under my questioning. She hid Iona in the forest north of Brightcastle in a small woodcutter's hut. She was taking her to the *Sis Lenweri* for gold, but didn't want to present the child until she had payment. The elves were less than pleased and beat her until she revealed the truth. She says she lied about Iona's location, but the elves have a day's head start on us in the search for her. They may already have her."

Alecia's heart cracked open. Her daughter, lost in the forest in a shack, didn't bear thinking about. "She will die of cold and hunger!"

"Melanis left her with a woodsman. Someone she used to work with. He will keep her fed and warm."

Alecia huffed. "What if he harms her?"

Ramón appeared before her. "Don't think of that. Focus on the fact that we know more now than we did a few minutes ago." He turned to James. "What did you have to do to get her to speak?"

James sighed. "Most of it was guilt. I know what buttons to push. However, I had to promise you wouldn't sentence her to death."

Alecia growled and surged to her feet. "Like hell she won't get the death penalty. Or have you forgotten we are in this predicament solely because Lady Stenmore was running short on funds?"

She stalked across the room and spun to face James. "How deeply involved is she with the *Sis Lenweri*? What *hasn't* she told you?"

Alecia boiled inside. If Melanis wasn't sentenced to death, she would find a way to escape. As a dragon shifter, there wasn't a prison that could hold her once she was well.

"I believe I have all of it. However, once we have Iona back, more may be uncovered."

Alecia nodded, trying to contain her anger at the woman who might yet have killed her daughter.

"Please eat and drink," she said. "I need to speak with Lady Henrietta." She left the audience chamber, and, once she was out of sight, ran to her advisor's suite of rooms. *Please Goddess, let Hetty discover something which can help us find her.*

She swept in without knocking to find Hetty slumped on the carpet before the fire, sobbing.

Her friend pushed herself up and faced Alecia. "I've seen Iona. It was dark and like looking through smoke, but I saw her. Alecia!" Her voice broke on a sob. "There was no sign of life, and a dark shadow loomed over her!"

Alecia choked back a cry as she landed on her hands and knees before Hetty. She pulled the old woman into a kneeling position, and cupped her face in her hands.

"Hetty, please show me. Where is she?"

"I'm spent, girl. I've nothing left in me. The connection came at the end of a long scrying. It was fleeting and dark, but it was Iona. She was wrapped in rags and lay on the hearth before a fire."

"A campfire, or in a room?"

Hetty closed her eyes, swaying. "It was definitely indoors. The wall behind her was wooden, constructed of rough planks. The fire seemed the only light in the room."

"Was it a small cabin?"

Hetty's dark eyes opened to meet hers. "It could be, yes."

"The shadow. What shape was it?"

Hetty closed her eyes again. "Human, tall, perhaps male. Whoever it was must have seen me, because they shouted. I couldn't make out the words."

Alecia gripped Hetty's shoulders. "You say there was no sign of life, but you could be mistaken. The scrying was brief. You could be wrong, Hetty. Please tell me you could be wrong!"

Hetty stared at her, misery in her gaze. "I *could* be wrong."

Alecia slumped. Her friend was only saying that to raise her spirits. *I can't lose Iona. Or Vard.*

She rang for Linnet, and strong sweet tea. Hetty needed someone with her, and Alecia must return to the audience chamber. Every minute she delayed could spell the end for Iona.

She paused outside the chamber, listening to the hum of discussion within. Taking several long breaths, she prayed for calm, or at least that she could fake it. She must not appear a distraught mother. When Alecia thought she might just be able to walk in without screaming, she bade the footman open the door.

Her eyes sought Ramón, and he walked to her. "What now?"

"Please, hear me out," she whispered. "Hetty has scried Iona in a rough wood cabin. There was someone with her, but only their shadow was visible." She would not give voice to the possibility that Iona was already dead. Ramón need not know that.

He turned pale and grabbed her hands. "That confirms what Lady Stenmore told Tomel. How do we begin a search? How do we deliver this information without revealing Hetty?"

Alecia clapped to bring the room to order. "We must start a search of the region north of Brightcastle. James has already advised you of Melanis Stenmore's testimony. What he hasn't revealed is that we have confirmation that Melanis is telling the truth about Iona's location."

James's visage revealed no surprise, for which Alecia was thankful. She hoped he could carry this off. Her words caused a stir. Everyone talked over each other.

"One at a time, please!" Alecia snapped.

Of course, Nikolas stepped forward. "Where did this recent intelligence come from?"

"I believe James is not at liberty to reveal his source. However, if James says the source is trustworthy, I believe him."

Estevot growled. "If it's trustworthy, he can reveal the source. Are we to go on a wild goose chase based on the words of two treasonous individuals?"

Several gasps echoed around the room. James Tomel had been charged with treason while head of King Beniel's spy service. Suspicion still hung over him, despite being cleared of the charges.

"Steady, Captain," Nikolas Cosara said. "A search needs to be done. If our queen is content to accept Tomel's word, then so am I."

Estevot scowled at Nikolas, but fell silent, his arms folded. He could hardly admit to not trusting his queen. Once they quieted again, Alecia began.

"I suggest we gather a force and split into small groups, spreading out for several miles. Melanis Stenmore said the location of the cabin was north of Brightcastle. We need to find and search all those cabins."

Kain stepped forward. "As I flew in, I noted several structures with signs of habitation. Nugoriem and I can sweep the area, and narrow down the likely structures."

Alecia stared at him. Could they risk using the dragon to search for Iona, knowing Vard needed him? Who needed him more? Her daughter, or the love of her life? The answer was simple. She must find her innocent child, a being who could not fend for herself. She hoped they were in time.

"Yes, Your Highness. I accept your offer. Please summon Nugoriem while we gather our search force."

CHAPTER NINETEEN

VARD rode Trax through the forest south of the last camp made by his mission, fire blazing in his chest with every small jolt. They had only been on the trail an hour, and yet it felt interminable. Honestly, he didn't think he'd survive the journey back to Brightcastle, unless Kain returned soon. A dragon flight was the only way he was getting out of this one. That and quick healing from Benae.

The thought that he might never see Alecia and Iona again sapped his strength, dragging him into the core of his pain repeatedly. He wasn't game to morph partially into the bear with people close, in case he lost himself in the beast. Likely that wouldn't happen, but once was enough. There was no point surviving if he hurt someone or never returned from the bear. And this time, only the bear could save him. It was an impossible situation.

Sam rode alongside, ready to catch him if he toppled from the saddle, which he had threatened to do several times. Katrine roamed the forest ahead with her hounds, seeking *Sis Lenweri,* and disposing of them. Every so often, he heard a scream and knew another marauder had been dispatched. She returned from time to time to check on him, even though she could do little.

As if thinking of her was a summons, Katrine appeared on foot on the trail in front of Trax. The horse snorted and stopped, jolting Vard's ribs unbearably.

Katrine did her best to examine Vard by getting Sam to dismount and boost her to his level. Her eyes tightened, and the silver sparkles in them gave away her agitation.

"Where is that damn dragon?" she asked. "Surely, he has had time to drop Lyam off and return. He is supposed to be magical!"

Vard grunted. "Nugoriem may be magical, but after his recent brush with death, I'm sure Kain won't wish to push him past his limits."

Katrine clucked, sounding like an annoyed hen. "How can you be so understanding when you…"

"Might be dying?" Vard supplied.

Katrine stiffened, but straightened her shoulders and met his eye. "You have already almost died once. If we can't get help, there's a high chance…" She shook her head. "There isn't much more I can do."

Vard slowly brought his hand up and clutched her shoulder. The movement sent a bolt of pain stabbing through his unstable chest wall. "You've done your absolute best, and I'm grateful. Perhaps a pain tonic would help?"

A voice came from below. "Would you mind finishing what you're doing, Lady Star?" Sam said. "You're not as light as you think."

Vard smirked, but refrained from laughing.

Although Katrine frowned, her eyes softened and the wild swirling in her irises settled. "I can do that." She squeezed his hand. "You may let me down, Sam."

"Thank the Goddess," Sam grumbled.

Katrine quirked an eyebrow at him, and left to brew her medicine.

"I hope she makes it good and strong," Sam muttered. "We can't afford to have these breaks every hour. We'll never reach Brightcastle. Can I help you down?"

Vard shook his head. "I can't get down. It may kill me. And if I survive that, I likely won't be able to remount."

Sam grimaced. "As bad as that?"

Vard tossed his head. "I've been close to death before and I know how it feels." He gripped Sam's shoulder. "If I don't make it, promise you'll tell Alecia and Iona I died thinking of them."

Sam covered Vard's hand with his own. "Let's hope it doesn't come to that."

"But if it does—"

Sam held his hand up. "If it does, Alecia and Iona won't be under any illusions about your love for them. And should Iona still be missing, I'll move mountains to find her. Alecia will also have my support whenever she needs it." Sam's green eyes blazed at him, serious when he usually had a lighthearted quip in even the most difficult circumstances.

Vard nodded. "Thank you."

"But it won't be needed. Now here's your potion. Drink it so we can be on our way."

* * *

Alecia sat on her horse while Estevot sorted the assembled riders into search groups. It wasn't only soldiers involved, but nobles, and the townsfolk. Despite her urgency to depart, Alecia kicked her mare forward to inspect those present. She spoke to many, thanking them for attending, for caring. Her words brought smiles to grim faces, and promises to find her daughter whatever it took.

Pulling Silver around at the end of the line, Alecia spied two familiar and unwelcome faces joining the search parties. She spurred her mare forward to intercept them.

"What are you doing here?" she asked.

"Why," Adriana said, "we are here to help. And our servants and retainers will complete our group."

Piotr smiled at her from the back of his bay gelding, a spirited animal that danced and snorted in the cool morning air. "I thought you could do with all hands on deck, so to speak."

Alecia fixed him with a hard look. "So, this was your idea?"

The dowager queen narrowed her eyes. "It was a joint initiative, Alecia. I would have thought you'd be glad we are supporting you in your moment of need."

Alecia huffed out the breath she had been holding. She couldn't afford to reject anyone who wanted to help—but these two? What was their motivation?

"I would be glad of your help, Aunt, but I must object to Piotr." If she could separate them, at least they couldn't scheme against her.

"Cousin," Piotr said, heeling his bay closer. It nipped at Silver, who squealed. "I assure you I have no motive but a desire to aid the search. Let us put aside our enmity, and find your daughter if we can."

Alecia patted her mare's neck until she settled. "You maintain you know nothing of Iona's disappearance?"

Piotr frowned. He appeared hurt that she could think such a thing, but Alecia didn't trust him one bit. The thought of these two searching for her child made her shiver. Perhaps she could have Estevot or Nikolas watch them? No, not Nikolas. As Adriana's cousin, he'd be unlikely to suspect her of doing potential harm. Estevot then.

"Cross my heart, Cousin. I was not involved in the poor mite's disappearance. I believe Melanis Stenmore is solely responsible for that. Is she not?"

Nikolas rode up, looking every bit the kingdom admiral. "Adriana; Your Highness." He bowed from his saddle, but Alecia noted his jaw tightened when he greeted Piotr. "I wasn't expecting you to attend. Or is there another concern that brings you here? If so, it must wait."

Adriana tossed her head. "We are here to help in the search, Niko. Alecia has already given us the third degree over this. I don't expect a grilling from you as well."

Nikolas held up his hands as if in surrender. "I gratefully accept your help."

"We don't need to be placed in groups. We have our own," Adriana said, her green eyes flashing.

Again, Nikolas held up a hand. "As you wish."

Alecia ground her teeth. "Thank you for your help." She rode away in search of Estevot, scowling at Nikolas as she went. As you wish indeed! He wouldn't understand what was upsetting her, but that was his problem.

She quickly found Estevot, and reined in beside him. "My aunt and Piotr Zialni have brought their own search team. Make sure you ride near them." He nodded distractedly, and she rode away before anyone could mark her brief discussion with him. Then she second guessed what she had told Estevot. Did he understand they couldn't be trusted? Would he be watching them closely enough? Could she trust Estevot?

Alecia berated herself for dithering, and looked around for her group. She found them checking their horses and gear.

"We're ready to start," Lin said, riding up to Alecia. "What's the holdup?" Her bay mare danced with eagerness.

"I think we are almost ready. The outlying groups are leaving so they can get into position. We're in the central band, the one with the most direct route north."

"That doesn't mean it was the path Melanis took," Lin said.

"We must start somewhere," Alecia said, "and the middle is as good a place as any. Remember, we spread out, keeping ten paces between you and the next rider. My bodyguard will ride before and behind me."

"I wish you would stay in the keep, Your Majesty," Cretia said, her blue eyes serious. "It's too dangerous for you to take part."

Alecia frowned. "We've discussed this. It's just as dangerous staying home with the number of guards depleted. Besides, you, Arelle, and Kenna will watch me like hawks."

"You better believe we will." Arelle's black horse snorted as she approached. He didn't like Alecia's mare, and made it clear whenever he had the chance. "No one will come close to you."

A horn blew, and the search parties began making their way through the main gates, splitting left and right to curve around the keep walls and head north.

A triple blast on the horn was a reminder to avoid the trenches, dug for defense against the *Sis Lenweri* in the recent war.

Once past the last of the defense trenches, Alecia's group, comprising Merielle, Linnet, two soldiers, and her three lady guards, broke into a canter. There were no hunting lodges or other abodes for several leagues north, but they watched to make sure no group fell behind. Leaders like Ramón, Estevot, and the admiral had spread themselves throughout the groups to maintain order.

Though Alecia could feel Silver's desire to surge forward, she kept herself close to her guards, a sharp eye on the surrounding forest. The trees here were more sparse, with plenty of trails that wound their way through the forest. Alecia's group followed the ancient road to Amitania until they reached the archery field.

From here, there were huts and lodges dotted through the forest, some owned by the nobility—Jacques Vorasava's family owned one such—and others crude shacks used by woodcutters, fur traders, and travelers. Most had been standing for centuries—added onto, or repaired as needed. Iona could be in any of them, or none. She sighed. No point in allowing melancholy to seep in yet again. She was doing something to find her child, something physical, and she *would* make a difference.

The huge black dragon swept low overhead from time to time, Kain Arenil on his back. Kain would wave a white flag and blow his horn once if he found a cabin that needed searching. She had heard the horn twice—once off to the east, and most recently to the west. If Iona was found, the dragon would fly over the entire field of the search, Kain waving a gold flag, and there would be triple blasts of his horn. To inform Kain once Iona was found, each group leader carried a gold flag and a horn they would blow three times. Linnet was their group leader, as much as it grated on the soldiers with them.

Merielle shouted from where she rode. "I see something ahead, Your Majesty. I will go forward and inspect."

"Be careful!" Alecia caught the eye of one soldier and sent them with the crimson-haired lady, though she could certainly look after herself. In the recent battle against the *Sis Lenweri*, Merielle was ferocious. It sounded to Alecia that her friend was a berserker. For a wonder, her over-protective husband, Nikolas Cosara, said nothing when she insisted on being in Alecia's search group.

The gloom swallowed Merielle and the two soldiers. Alecia and the others picked up the pace in case the three needed backup. By the time they arrived at the small woodcutters' hut, Merielle emerged with one soldier while the other completed a search of the outer building and adjacent forest. Merielle led her horse over to Alecia and Linnet.

"Nothing inside, but the fire was laid, and there is food on the shelves. Would this be normal for a shack in the middle of the forest?"

Linnet answered. "Yes, My Lady. It's expected that those who use these huts leave them ready for the next occupant if they can."

Merielle frowned. "Oh, I hoped it meant someone was coming home, and we could question them."

"I'm afraid not," Alecia said, studying the woman. Merielle's knowledge of Thorius was often limited. She hailed from a far-off kingdom, according to rumor, so perhaps things were different there. Her friend was full of mystery. "Are we done here?"

The second soldier waved, and mounted his horse. They headed north once again. Kain swept overhead, followed by another blast on his horn seconds later. Another hut had been found.

And so, they moved north, searching the crude residences they came across, listening eagerly for the triple horn blasts that would announce success. The only horns heard all day were the single blasts notifying searchers of another outpost discovered. Those blasts came less frequently as the day wore on.

As dusk settled in, Alecia scanned the woods to left and right, noting the scattered riders in both directions. Some were quite a distance ahead, while others had fallen behind. Regardless, their method should be effective. If Iona was out here.

Alecia's mood dipped as the day wore on. Perhaps it was largely weariness, but there was a good dollop of despair as well.

Before starting the search, they had decided that, at nightfall, all search parties would stop for a meal. Linnet called a halt, and they dismounted. Alecia groaned as her foot hit the ground, and she heard several others do the same.

"I haven't ridden that long since the battle," Merielle said, knuckling her lower back. She led her mount over to a tree, and tied him up, before removing his saddle and giving him a rubdown. Then she placed a nosebag of oats for him to nibble. Arelle and one of the soldiers started a fire, and boiled water for tea while the others tended to their horses.

Through the trees, Alecia saw other groups doing the same. She gave thanks to the Goddess for the dedication of these, her people. They had ridden all day, many of them much older than she, all looking for her daughter. Once finished with Silver, she sought the fire. It was chilly now she had stopped riding. She wouldn't be surprised if it snowed soon.

Ramón rode up. He dismounted and bowed to her. "I just spoke with Kain Arenil. There's a large hunting lodge up ahead about an hour. Might be the Vorasava lodge, I think. I'm going to take my group to search it. We'll eat in the saddle." He bowed again, mounted, and rode off.

It was a measure of her despondency that Alecia waved him off with no word of disapproval for him not following the plan. At that moment, all she wanted was to hold Iona in her arms. Perhaps she would be in that lodge, and Ramón would bring her home. It would be fitting, as he had helped to save Iona when she was born. She looked up and noticed the others frowning at her.

"What?"

Linnet smiled. "Nothing. We expected you to object to Lord Zorba's plan."

Alecia shrugged. "Perhaps I'm learning to pick my battles."

Merielle, Linnet, and the lady guards all laughed at that, to the great surprise of the two soldiers. Alecia joined in, and then the men. It had been too long since she laughed.

Having eaten cold trail rations, but feeling a little renewed, Alecia's group remounted and continued their trek north, checking two crude huts along the way. They were completing the second search when a soldier from Ramón's group cantered up.

"Your Majesty!" he said, bowing from his saddle. "The large hunting lodge showed signs of a break in and recent habitation. Lord Zorba asks that you attend the scene." With these words, the man reined his gelding around and trotted off.

Alecia spurred Silver after him, her guard clustered around her. Merielle and the soldiers pushed ahead. Alecia's heart pounded fit to burst. Signs of habitation? What had Ramón found?

When they pulled up at the lodge, Alecia flung herself out of the saddle and rushed through the entry to find Ramón standing in the center of a living area, brow furrowed. He joined her.

"Your Majesty, the door was forced, and there is bedding disturbed, including a small cot over in the corner."

He held aloft a burning brand. Alecia looked where he pointed, then crossed to examine the tiny bed. Heart in her mouth, she searched through the blankets. A few dark hairs lay on the small pillow, and there was a faint smear of blood on the cream sheet. She ran her finger over the stain as if she might discern if it was her daughter's.

Tears leaked down her cheeks. "Iona must have been here." The words were barely audible, but Merielle kneeled beside her, hand on Alecia's shoulder.

"How long ago do you think they left?" Alecia asked, pulling back the blankets and peering under the cot.

Ramón sighed. "I'd say less than twelve hours. A tracker has confirmed that." He crossed to Alecia and drew her to her feet. "We're close to finding her, Alecia," he murmured.

"Why the blood, Ramón? Why is she not here? Are there signs of violence?"

"Nothing, Your Majesty," one of the soldiers said. "A horse was stabled in the back though. Fresh dung."

Alecia looked around at her people. "What chance the *Sis Lenweri* discovered this place, and my daughter is now on the way back to their stronghold?"

Ramón's frown deepened, and his jaw tightened so much that Alecia was surprised she didn't hear it creak. "It's possible, but remember—there's no sign of bloodshed."

She pointed to the door. "That damage could have been done by elves breaking in."

"Or it could have been whoever was minding Iona," Linnet said. "Lord Zorba is right, we're getting closer."

Alecia couldn't help seeing her daughter in the clutches of the *Sis Lenweri*, riding on the back of a dragon to who knew where. Frightened, alone. They would use her however they liked. She possessed magic the elves could exploit… eventually.

Then she pulled herself together. "Kain Arenil and Nugoriem must be advised. Summon them. The rest of us will continue north." She would find her daughter, and somehow, she must hold on to the strength she would need to accomplish that.

Alecia approached a large clearing a little to the north of the hunting lodge. Kain awaited her, while Nugoriem circled the forest above, eerily silent except for the sound of his wings beating the air. She dismounted, handing Silver's reins to one of her ladies.

Kain strode the few steps to meet her. "What do we know?"

"The Vorasava lodge is a possible holding site for Iona," she said, fists clenched behind her. "It was recently occupied, and someone made up a small cot, as for a child."

"You think it was for Iona?"

Alecia allowed his words to hang in the clearing's quiet. "It's difficult to say. The hairs on the pillow are the right shade." She paused again. "There was a streak of blood on the sheet."

Kain rubbed his jaw. "Any signs of violence?"

She shook her head. "The front door was forced. There was a horse stabled there recently. Nothing else."

Kain walked away from her, gazing up into the night sky as if looking for something. He returned to her. "At dusk, I saw a dragon in the distance to the north. In the last half hour, I'm sure I've seen furtive movements on the ground, but each time I do a flyover there's nothing."

Ramón spoke. "Surely, if the enemy was out there, they would've fired upon you."

"Perhaps, unless they wish to crawl closer before announcing themselves. It's a dicey situation if there is a large party of *Sis Lenweri* out here. We didn't come prepared for a battle."

Alecia's heart sank. Just when they were nearing answers regarding Iona, Kain's commitment appeared to be evaporating. "Does this mean you will withdraw your help, Your Highness?" She swallowed hard at the words, struggling to keep her voice even.

His gaze snapped to hers. "Nugoriem is keen to seek his revenge for the recent attack on him. I couldn't pull him out of this if I tried."

"Seems a little foolhardy to me," Ramón said, frowning.

Kain shrugged. "And will *you* tell Nugoriem that?" He raked a hand through his hair. "Still, I'd rather not attract undue attention. My plan would be to find the princess, and get out of here, sending in scouts to assess the level of incursion after we have withdrawn."

"Agreed," Alecia said. "We're in a vulnerable position as it stands, and we have no idea how the elves are situated. Let's resume the search. Kain, keep your eye out for the enemy."

Alecia remounted and resumed her place in the line, riding north through open forest. Her group entered another shack, but found nothing. More horns came from the west, a sign that Kain had seen structures needing searching. However, those hunting to the east appeared to be in a region with few habitations. She was about to signal a rest break, which would be sent along the lines to the other parties, when a great screech echoed through the forest.

"Dismount! Seek shelter!" Alecia cried, throwing herself off Silver and leading her to the nearest thicket. She cringed at the thought of the trees on fire. Though it was cold, dragon fire was powerful. "Hoods up. Grab whatever protection you can find." It would be precious little.

Silence lay over the forest. Even the sounds of crickets quieted in the wake of that angry call. Was it Nugoriem, or one of the other firedrakes who trumpeted? A sweep of giant wings came from behind, and Alecia looked up. There was enough moonlight to see Nugoriem barreling across the sky, heading north. Kain clung to his back, his horse bow drawn. Nothing more was needed to announce the enemy. But was there another dragon, or maybe even two? Kain had seen at least one.

"We must know what is going on!" Alecia threw off her cloak, and made her way to a mountain ash that stretched its branches through the canopy.

Arelle appeared beside her. "With respect, My Queen, I can't allow you to climb that tree! Permit me."

She tossed her cloak aside and removed her steel gauntlets, then placed herself between Alecia and the ash.

Alecia stood with hands on hips. Yes, it *was* dangerous, but she was an excellent climber, having prowled the rooftops when her father was alive and wreaking his carnage. And she had climbed many a tree before Vard mastered his bear. High up a tree was sometimes the only place of safety.

"I can do this, Arelle. Why would I allow you to risk your life?"

"Ah, because you're now queen, and you will *not* risk yourself!"

Alecia opened her mouth to object, then closed it again. Just when she thought she had mastered this new position of hers, she slipped back into the old ways.

She stepped back and stuck out her hand. "By all means, ascend the tree, and tell me what's happening out there."

Alecia shaded her eyes as sticks and leaves rained down from Arelle's ascent. The girl could climb, she gave her that. Almost as well as Alecia. It was quiet for a time, and she feared the tree wasn't tall enough. It was difficult to judge in the dark.

"What do you see?" Her other guards and Linnet joined her, all gazing up. "Arelle?"

Another screech came from the north.

"Red dragon!" Arelle cried down to them. "I saw its color when it breathed fire. Prince Arenil has engaged the beast. It's smaller than Nugoriem, but angry."

* * *

Teeth gritted, Kain clung to Nugoriem, buffeted by the wind of the dragon's furious flight. Only years of army discipline kept him from panic as he contemplated fighting the red dragon and its riders—in the dark!

I hope you can look after yourself, Kain Arenil, came Nugoriem's thought, as he closed on the red beast. It was smaller, but fierce, if his memory served him right.

"I hope I can too," Kain muttered, too distracted to speak to the dragon at that point. It was taking all his concentration to stay mounted and watch for arrows from the *Sis Lenweri* dragon riders.

In seconds, Nugoriem had met the red dragon and rolled to the right, allowing the opposing beast to slide under his left wing. Kain took a shot with his horse bow at the lead rider and winged him. A return arrow narrowly missed, Kain feeling the draft of its passing by his ear.

In a flapping of enormous wings, Nugoriem banked, swinging back to come at the red dragon from behind, but the smaller beast was nimbler. As Nugoriem and Kain emerged from their turn, the red had spun and was flying straight for them.

Kain hung on for his life as their adversary twisted, its talons raking along Nugoriem's side, just behind his seat position. He twisted and fired off an arrow which hit the rear enemy rider in the back. The elf slumped in his straps, but the winged forerider raised his good arm as if to signal—just what, Kain wasn't sure. To the dragon? To troops on the ground?

That was close! he thought to Nugoriem. *You nearly lost me. Are you well?*

Hold on, elven lord! Nugoriem screamed, and banked to the right, maneuvering to attack his enemy at right angles.

Again, Kain gritted his teeth and held fast to a nearby protuberance on the dragon's back, frantically searching the skies for the red. There it was, climbing higher and higher above them until Kain could barely see it. He glanced around while he had time, assessing the skies for the other dragons. He damned well hoped there was only the one!

And then, without warning, Nugoriem lifted his nose and climbed toward the foe, his powerful wings gaining altitude with each stroke. The force flung Kain backward, leaving him holding on with only one hand. He let the horse bow slide down to his shoulder, and, after three tries, grabbed another protuberance, but his legs still flapped in the breeze of Nugoriem's flight.

Level out, or you've lost me! he mind-shouted to Nugoriem. The beast laughed in his head, but his flight did level out enough for Kain to regain his seat. He gripped the dragon tightly with his thighs and kept both hands on the boney knobs. He wouldn't be shooting his bow at this pace. Just staying on was taking all his concentration.

He had barely time to catch his breath and steady his thundering heart before Nugoriem shrieked and renewed his upward climb. He barreled toward the red dragon, which careened down from its superior elevation right at them. If one of them didn't turn aside, they would collide.

Nugoriem! Kain sent the distress call seconds before the red opened her maw and spewed out fire. Kain redoubled his grip just as his mount came to an abrupt stop, wings beating to keep himself at a stable altitude. Nugoriem spewed a gout of his own fire at his enemy, and the two flaming trails met midair in a blazing explosion of heat and light.

Lend me your power, Kain Arenil! Kain didn't wonder how he could do this, but joined his will to the dragon's instinctively. He watched with amazement as Nugoriem's fire power increased, seeming to push back against the red, taking the intersection of their fire trails closer to their enemy.

Within seconds, the blazing node of flame had almost reached the red dragon. Kain was wondering how much longer he could keep up his augmentation of Nugoriem's strength when the red pushed back, her fire power suddenly doubling. Narrowing his gaze, Kain saw the outline of the red's leading rider. He wondered if the sudden increase in power was also because of rider augmentation.

Sending a prayer to the Goddess for safety and accuracy, Kain retrieved his bow from his shoulder and fitted an arrow, a move that required both hands. He nocked the arrow and sighted, letting the dart fly.

Even as a powerful gust buffeted him, he reached for another arrow and sent it toward the rider, then grabbed for a handhold, trying to judge if he had been successful.

At that moment, the red dragon's stream of fire faltered, and Nugoriem pushed his blast through to hit the red beast in her head and chest. If the rider hadn't been dead before, he would be now. His body toppled off and dropped out of sight. The red dragon screamed and fled, her agonized call sending a chill through Kain.

Nugoriem laughed in his head. *I wasn't named 'eternal fire' for naught. Are you still there, Kain Arenil?*

I'm here. Kain heaved a deep breath. *We should ensure those on the ground are safe.*

Hold on! Nugoriem allowed Kain a few seconds to brace himself, then launched into a mad dive toward the ground.

* * *

Alecia's stomach landed in her throat. The red dragon was the one she had fought in the battle. It had promised the next time they met she would not be so lucky to escape.

"The prince and Nugoriem have won!" Arelle cried. "The red dragon has fled. You should have seen it."

Alecia was about to give a sarcastic reply, about being forced to stay on the ground, when cries sounded up and down the line. An arrow streaked through the air close to Alecia's head.

"To horse!" Alecia called. "Arelle, we need you!"

Alecia bolted to Silver, leaving her cloak where she had tossed it. She mounted and called her group to her. They formed up in two lines, Alecia behind with her guards and Linnet, and Merielle and the two soldiers in front.

"Keep your eyes open," Alecia muttered.

The soldiers wore light armor, and Merielle never rode without her shield. But Alecia worried for her friend. If only they were a larger group. They needed to combine with those to each side if they were to survive. That was assuming the woods weren't swarming with *Sis Lenweri*.

A group of two dozen *Sis Lenweri* appeared from the north, running at them on foot and shrieking fit to freeze the blood. Merielle yelled "charge" and led their small group at the enemy, riding straight into their midst, laying about her with her sword and using her shield to club others out of her way. The soldiers fought to either side of the crimson-haired berserker.

Alecia had little time to appreciate Merielle's violence before the enemy penetrated to the second line. She used her sword to club an elf on the skull, while Silver struck another with her foreleg. Both went under the trampling hooves of her mount. Her lady guards and Linnet were similarly occupied with combatants of their own. But they were losing ground, and growing more desperate as the elves surrounded them. Soon they were fighting with their horses in a circle, rumps in the center. It was difficult to avoid each other in the frantic battle to kill and maim.

Something struck Alecia on the head and pain blasted through her skull. A tall elf with a maniacal grin pulled her from her horse. He raised his sword for a killing blow which she desperately tried to block.

A sword tip appeared through the elf's chest, and surprise swept his features. Ramón hauled her to her feet as the enemy collapsed to the ground. And then it was over. Ramón's and the admiral's groups had come to the rescue. The enemy ambushers lay dead or mortally wounded.

She looked around at her people. All had sustained cuts and bruises, and she asked one of Ramón's lesser wounded soldiers to tend to the injured. It appeared most could ride back to the keep. Suddenly, she didn't feel well. She walked over to a moss-covered log and sat down. Her head hurt, and when she touched the sore spot, her fingers came away bloody.

Someone offered her a waterskin, and when she looked up to see who, two Ramóns scowled down at her.

"How come there are two of you?" She blinked to try and clear the illusion. It didn't help.

The Ramóns squatted before her. "You've sustained a head injury, Alecia. There is only one of me."

"Thank goodness! I don't think I could cope with two!" She chuckled at her joke. Unfortunately, her laughter soon turned to tears. If anyone had doubted before that she was in her right mind, they would certainly have no doubts now. "What are we to do, Ramón? I can't lose my daughter. And now the enemy almost certainly has her."

Ramón grabbed her hands and leaned closer. "They are falling back to the north, Alecia," he whispered. "We can continue the search for Iona. But *you* will return to the keep for healing."

She pulled her hands from his grasp, and bunched them into fists. "I can't return to the keep. I must be here. Where is Kain? Arelle saw him conquer the red dragon."

Ramón's frustrated sigh answered her. "I don't know how Prince Arenil has fared, but if he still lives, we should know soon. For now, let's assess the damage and plan our next move."

The skies had gone quiet—no more firedrake shrieks, wing flaps, or fire blasts were heard.

"We must resume our search," Alecia said, pushing herself to her feet. She wavered, the forest whirling madly around her. A firm hand gripped her arm. She held onto it for dear life until the spinning stopped.

When she opened her eyes, only one of Ramón stared down at her. "I don't recommend you do that, Alecia," he murmured.

At least he kept his voice low, so that those close to them couldn't hear. Perhaps he was learning diplomacy, or maybe just learning how to stay on her good side.

"That's not your decision, Lord Zorba," she said, "though I thank you for your guidance." She fixed him with a firm look. "Mount up!"

Her voice rang through the clearing, and though she was the recipient of several wary glances, all did as she commanded.

Ramón stalked away, a muttered "stubborn…" floating back to her. She ignored him. He would be just as determined were it Solomon out there instead of Iona.

As she wobbled to her mare, her ladies followed, Linnet hurrying to hold Silver's bridle. It was merely a show to enable her to be close if Alecia fell. At least she understood the need for decorum. Her three guards clustered at her back as if she would fall on her face at any time.

She rounded on them, and dizziness struck her anew. "Cretia, you may assist me to mount. You others get on your horses." She must have looked a sight, but her words had an instant impact. Arelle and Kenna spun and headed to their mounts while Cretia lingered near Alecia's stirrup. Surprisingly, the guard held her tongue as Alecia struggled into the saddle. Perhaps this really was a terrible idea?

Head pounding, Alecia and her group rode north, wary eyes on the forest, expecting a clutch of *Sis Lenweri* to spring at them at any moment. It only made her head ache harder, all the watching and waiting. *Should* they turn back?

They kept going, the forest slowly lightening as the new day dawned. Unfortunately, Alecia's head pounded harder as the first early rays of the sun hit her. She was contemplating ordering a halt to discuss a return to the keep when Nugoriem appeared, heralded by a whoosh of his giant wings. He flew low, and Alecia was happy to see Kain on his back. The high prince blew three sharp notes on his horn and pointed to the east. Then he blew the notes again as he flew west. There was no sign of a golden flag to indicate Iona had been found. Alecia looked around at her people.

"Do you think he means someone has found Iona?" she asked. "Or is it something to do with the *Sis Lenweri*? Perhaps another mob of them to the east?"

Linnet's face was sober. "I think we had better turn to the east and investigate. Be ready to fight, people." She reined her bay mare to the right, and trotted away through the trees. Alecia caught the eye of the soldiers and Merielle, and sent them after her.

"I don't think I can take another fight just yet," Kenna mumbled, rubbing her right shoulder.

"Me either," Cretia said. "Let's hope it's Iona they've found. That's why we are here, after all."

Alecia was too tired and sore to answer them, though she should have tried to lift their spirits. Instead, she bent her will upon seeing Iona, and on staying in the saddle. With every one of Silver's steps, she expected to topple off. The clop of Silver's feet seemed to mock her, and she heard Ramón's words in the beat—*back to the keep, back to the keep, back to the keep.* Certainly, she must have injured her head!

An angry female voice sounded from close by. "Get your hands off me!"

That voice startled Alecia out of her stupor. Was that her aunt? Had she found another clutch of the *Sis Lenweri*? The riders ahead of her pushed forward, but Alecia's guards held her reins and crowded around her.

"Let me go. I must see what the fuss is about."

"If we let you go, you'll fall on your head, Your Majesty. Trust us in this. You're barely able to sit straight." It was Kenna's voice, but sounded as if it was coming from a long way away.

They moved forward so slowly it felt they were pushing their way through sand. But finally, they came upon the source of the commotion.

Adriana Zialni stood by her horse, being restrained by two burly soldiers, while Piotr Zialni sat his horse with a handful of archers surrounding him, their arrows nocked and drawn.

"Of all the—" Alecia said, then she spotted Ramón.

"Iona!"

Ramón held Iona! She kicked Silver forward, then threw herself from the saddle and launched at Ramón. He caught her with one arm while cradling her daughter in the other.

"My baby!" Alecia reached for her daughter, tears pouring down her face, and began patting her all over. Iona was dirty and scared, but seemed otherwise healthy.

Alecia looked up into Ramón's eyes. "Is she well?"

He smirked. "I've not had much time to assess her, but I believe she is hale. Which is more than I can say for her mother."

Alecia's head chose that moment to make her dizzy again, and Ramón tightened his hold on her. He guided them over to a fallen tree and made Alecia sit, then placed Iona in her arms. Someone handed her a cup of milk, and Alecia offered it to the little girl. She slurped thirstily. The poor child. They would never know what she had been through.

Ramón strode away, having placed Kenna and Cretia in charge of Alecia, who had eyes only for the daughter she had believed she would never see again.

After a moment, Ramón's stern voice floated to Alecia. "What were you doing with the child?" then "Heading east…" and "How long?"

Looking up, Alecia saw her ladies appeared shocked at something, but none spoke. "What's going on? Linnet?" she called.

Her advisor made her way between Kenna and Cretia. "Yes, My Queen?"

"Do you know where Iona was found?"

Lin scowled. "It appears she has been in the company of her great aunt and Prince Zialni for several hours, Your Majesty."

Her words made little sense. *Several hours?* What else had she heard? *Heading east?*

"They were taking Iona *away* from Brightcastle?"

"It appears so, Your Majesty," Lin said. "I'm sure we will learn more in due course. For now, I think we should get you and Iona back to the keep."

"Not before I see my aunt! Help me up, please."

Lin took Iona and handed her to Kenna, which resulted in a burst of tears from the child. She helped Alecia to her feet, and guided her toward Adriana Zialni.

Adriana appeared as fresh as if she had stepped from her saddle after a peaceful morning ride. She spotted Alecia and bowed low. When she rose, she started talking.

"I found my great niece, and was bringing her to you when this pack of louts intercepted us. I thought they were bandits, and we tried to elude them. How was I to know they were your soldiers?"

"By their uniforms," Alecia snarled. "They may be a little grubby, but that's because they've been fighting the enemy. You, on the other hand, look clean. Why did you have my daughter?"

Adriana drew herself up. "I saved your daughter, and this is how I am repaid? With suspicion and disdain?"

Adriana recoiled as Alecia raised her hand. Oh, how she longed to slap the dowager queen. Her fingers itched to exact retribution on her aunt but... she didn't know the full story. Adriana could yet be innocent.

"Take them both back to the keep," Alecia ordered her soldiers. "Lock them in Adriana's chamber until they can be properly questioned. And Aunt, be thankful you are not on your way to the dungeon."

She spun and almost fell over. The last face she saw was Iona's before the dark took her.

CHAPTER TWENTY

A FIERCE throbbing woke Alecia. She scrunched her closed eyes, and the stabbing increased. Gritting her teeth, she opened her eyes, fighting back a wave of nausea. Wherever she was, it was dark, with just a candle burning in a far corner of the room. From what she could see, she was in the bedroom of a country manor house.

A door opened, and Benae entered. "I thought I heard a groan," she said, bustling over to the bed. "How are you feeling?"

"Like a woodpecker is hammering at my brain." Alecia struggled to sit up. It was no good. She was too weak. "Where is Iona?"

"So, you remember? I thought you might struggle to recall the most recent events, so severe was your injury."

Alecia hissed. "Iona?"

Benae smiled, her eyes tight with weariness. "She is back in Brightcastle, none the worse for her recent adventures. I'm hopeful she'll even be too young to have nightmares."

"Adventures! That's a fine thing to call kidnapping."

Benae sighed. "I'm sorry. Ramón returned with your daughter while I traveled here to tend to you. I was already on my way north, and Kain guided me to the Zorba hunting lodge to heal you. It is as well Ramón sought the nearest safe house rather than try to get you back to the keep. You would not have survived that journey."

Alecia frowned. "It seems I owe yet another debt to your husband."

"When will you understand that he only has your best interests at heart?"

"Perhaps in time we'll mend the trouble between us." She studied Benae. Had she been too harsh on the woman? "My thanks for healing me. I fully appreciate how much care you dedicate to others."

"Then we may be friends in the future as well," Benae said, a smile curving her lips. "Lady Alique was to see to Iona's needs. She will give your daughter a full examination, though, from my brief look at her, she will be well. Children are resilient."

Alecia nodded. "How long have I been here?"

"More than a full day. It is now mid-morning."

"When can I leave? I need to see Iona."

"You will be fit to ride tomorrow morning, though another day's rest would be better. That was a very nasty knock you took."

"I'll leave as soon as I can. How are the injured? I assume some remain here?"

Benae smiled. "All are recovering well. We have a dozen recuperating who will all be safe to move tomorrow." Benae helped Alecia to sit up and adjusted her pillows.

Alecia had only one more concern. "Where is Vard? Have you heard from him?"

At her question, Benae sobered. "Kain has flown north on Nugoriem to meet those who infiltrated the northern forests. He will bring Lord Anton here."

Alecia's heart thumped hard. "You think he will be too late?"

"I didn't say that. I have no way of knowing. Lyam described Lord Anton's condition to me, and it was very serious. However, he is as tough a man as I have ever met. I think he will come back to you in time for your vows."

Alecia huffed. "The wedding is the least of my concerns. All I need is Iona and Vard. The three of us back together as a family is more than I thought possible only yesterday."

"Oh yes, but you are queen now. A queen can hardly live in sin with the man of her dreams. Bad enough you already have a child with him."

Alecia gasped. "Your bedside manner leaves much to be desired!"

Benae smiled, and patted her shoulder. "I'm half joking, Alecia. But you get my point. You wanted this after all. The position, the power, and the responsibility."

Alecia scowled, but try as she might, she couldn't fault Benae's logic. "Yes, I did."

"Now, I'll fetch your lunch, and hopefully that soothes your temper." With those words, Benae swept from the room, calm and composed as she always seemed to be.

Alecia took a deep breath and relaxed on the pillows. Benae seemed different today—more prepared to stand her ground against Alecia. In the past, she had often let Ramón fight her battles. Alecia decided she liked this version of Benae much better. Perhaps they *might* be friends one day.

There was a knock at the door, and a maid bustled in with a tray. "Good afternoon, Your Majesty. I have luncheon for you. And Lady Benae says you must try everything on this tray."

Or perhaps she and Benae wouldn't be friends after all!

Alecia had almost cleared her tray, including the foul potion for her headache, when there was a commotion outside. She was getting out of bed when her door burst open, and Sam appeared with Vard. He looked dreadful!

Alecia was beside him in a heartbeat. "Vard," she said, taking his free arm and trying to support him. He hissed in a sharp breath.

"That's his injured side, Your Majesty," Sam said.

"Oh! I'm sorry! Where's Benae? Has she seen to you? You can have my bed. I don't need it. I'm fit as a fiddle."

Vard didn't seem to hear her, and she peered around him at Sam. "Is he…" She couldn't bring herself to ask any of the questions about his condition.

Sam kept guiding Vard to the bed, and lowered him onto it, careful to spare his injured ribs.

"He's tough, Your Majesty, but it's been an arduous journey. First on horseback—"

"Damn near killed me," Vard croaked.

Alecia climbed onto the bed, and took his hand. "I can't believe I have you back. And we have Iona safe and sound!"

Vard smiled, but the pain in his eyes scared her. She had never seen him like this, though she imagined he had experienced similar before.

"Kain told me, but it's good to hear it from your lips, my love," Vard said, groaning as he tried to get comfortable.

Alecia couldn't believe the changes in Vard since she waved him off only a few weeks ago. He was terribly thin, but more than that, his pale face was pinched, and gray streaks marred the black of his hair. He appeared to have aged at least ten years.

Sam continued. "I flew with him on the dragon's back, and that was no picnic." Sam's green eyes were full of concern, no matter how he tried to reassure her. "But now we're here, all will be well."

Alecia wished she could believe that in her heart, but Vard had barely looked her in the eye since he arrived. Was it because he knew he was dying? Or was he in too much pain to do anything more than struggle with each breath?

She pushed herself up and off the bed, then hurried out of the room. Benae met her in the dining room. She gripped her fists in her nightgown, using the contact to ground her.

"He's dying!" she said. "I've never seen him like this. Do something!"

Benae smiled, even though Alecia realized she probably wanted to slap her. "I assessed Lord Anton as soon as he arrived," she said, patiently. "I believe I can save him. But he will need you to be strong."

Alecia sucked in a breath. "I can be strong, if you get in there and do your job!"

Benae nodded and carried her bowls and a bag past Alecia, a maid following with a kettle. Once in the room, Benae prepared a tea for Vard, and took it to him.

"Drink this, Lord Anton. It will relieve your pain and help you sleep. When you wake, you'll feel more yourself."

Vard grunted, but took as much of the mixture as he could. "I've not eaten much over the last few days. Pain was too much to stomach anything." He lay back on the pillows and closed his eyes as Alecia watched on. Where was her fit and healthy lover? Terror curled around her heart, and she didn't have the strength to fight it, no matter what she told Benae.

She left the room, unable to witness Vard's struggle any longer. Seeking a moment to gather herself, she looked into the flames of the dining room fireplace, wondering if she was too weak to go back in there.

A face formed in the flames, and suddenly Hetty was glaring at her.

"What are you up to, girl? You look like you've seen a ghost."

Alecia swallowed and tried to draw her shoulders back. "It's Vard. He's here and… Hetty, he's so ill! I've never seen him like this."

"Is the healer with him?"

Alecia nodded. "Yes, but… I fear she's too late."

"I've seen that man of yours at death's door. He can fight this, whatever it is."

"He has a chest injury, but I think it's more than that. For Vard to be so far down…"

"His strongest form is the bear," Hetty said, her voice a harsh whisper, as if Alecia's words had finally struck fear into her heart. "Remember that."

"Alecia?" Benae appeared at the door to the sickroom.

Hetty's face faded from the fire.

Alecia felt her loss keenly. If only Hetty was here to lend her a shoulder, even one to cry on... she might even help Vard.

"Alecia, he's asking for you."

She spun around. The look on Benae's face sent a chill through her. She started past Benae, but the woman grabbed her arm. "I'm sorry. There is little I can do but make him comfortable. I was wrong in my assessment." Benae appeared crushed at her failure, but Alecia had no words for her. She pulled her arm free and entered the bedroom.

Vard's eyes were open, but he appeared much worse than when she had left only minutes ago.

"You came," he croaked.

"Of course I came," she said, trying and failing to keep her voice even. "What do you need?"

"Alecia, I'm dying. I wanted to tell you what you will need to hear over the coming years."

She shook her head. "You're not dying. I won't allow it. And I won't hear those words now. You'll tell me in the years to come." She took his hand and kissed it. It was cold and clammy like an old man's. She didn't understand. His injuries were severe, but this was a wasting illness. Like something was eating away from the inside out. Could it be poison?

She turned to Sam. "Get Benae back."

He shook his head. "She's already done all she can. I was here and watched."

"Get her!"

He gave her a look full of pity, but left her alone with Vard.

"Listen to me, my darling," she said, her lips close to his ear. "We are going to give this one last try. But you must be brave and reach deep inside for the last of your strength."

"No strength left," he whispered.

Alecia gritted her teeth. "You won't leave us like this. Iona needs you. *I* need you. You will *not* give up. Did you give up when Iona was born? No! You returned from the wolf to save us both. You must do it again."

Clarity returned to his gaze. "What do you mean?"

"Two things. I think you have poison in you. Otherwise, this makes no sense. And the second… You need to become the bear to beat this. It's your strongest form."

His throat moved convulsively… from fear? Or hope?

"I don't know that I can control the bear in this weakened state," he said.

"The bear will also be weak. Perhaps we can manage him."

"That's a big unknown. I'd be risking all of you."

"I'm willing to take that risk," Alecia said. "I think the others will be too."

"I'd be exposed, vulnerable. If it goes wrong, you'd have to kill me. I don't want that burden for you."

"But if it should work, then you and I and Iona get a second chance. Think of that."

Vard fell quiet as Benae returned with Sam. Alecia explained her theory about the poison.

Her eyes widened. "You could be right. I thought of it and discarded it as a possibility. It would have to be a very slow working toxin." She crossed to Vard and laid her hands on his chest, then on his head, and, finally, on his abdomen.

Benae took in a deep breath, then nodded as if reaching a decision. "I need you to understand my healing and promise me something."

They all agreed quickly.

"Speak, Benae," Alecia said.

Benae stared at her as if weighing up her decision. They were, after all, enemies of a sort.

"My healing is not merely of herbs and other medicines. I use a direct magical delving to diagnose, and often to treat. This is not something I want known outside this room. Only Ramón is aware. My life is in danger if others find out. You must promise to keep my secret, even from those closest to you."

Vard nodded instantly, with Sam also readily agreeing. Alecia thought about Hetty, and not being able to tell her the essence of

Benae's healing. Knowing the old woman, she probably already knew that Benae possessed healing magic.

"Your secret is safe with us," she said.

Benae released a long breath. "I can detect something miniscule throughout Vard's body, now that I have looked for it. All his organs have slowed, including his blood flow. This is leading to his organs beginning to fail." She turned to Vard. "And that is why you are dying, not your chest. There must have been something on the blades that cut you."

Vard's eyes narrowed. "It's possible. Can you do anything?" He had his own secrets to protect, and Alecia was about to expose them all.

"I'm not sure," Benae said, her voice lacking its usual authoritative quality. "I'm sorry, Vard, but, even knowing this, I think you're too weak for more healing. What I do is hard on the body. Again, I'm sorry."

"What if he was stronger?" Alecia asked.

"But he's weaker than a kitten," Sam snapped. It appeared Vard's friend had finally lost his calm acceptance of the world.

Alecia looked at Vard, knowing the question was in her gaze. She raised her brows, giving him the power to reveal or conceal the truth of his essence.

There was another convulsive move of the throat, then he gave the slightest nod. Even giving his permission, this was a struggle for her love.

Alecia drew a deep breath and began. "What I'm about to reveal cannot leave this room." She looked at Benae. "Your own secret is safe with me and Vard, as he has an even greater secret." She included Sam in her look. "Do you agree to hold this in your heart, and not to expose this to a single soul?"

Benae frowned, but slowly nodded. Sam also agreed, though he was racking up topics he wouldn't be able to discuss with his beloved Esta.

"Then I will begin. Vard is a shifter. His strongest form is the bear. He has two others of which you don't need to know. As the bear, I believe he can beat this illness." She turned to Benae. "Especially if you again attempt your healing."

Benae's eyes were wide. "You want me to heal a… bear?"

Alecia nodded. "We do. We hope that Vard's control over the bear will make this safe, but, in his weakened state, this might not be true. He will likely have enough strength in his bear form to…" She was going to say "to knock you across the room", but thought better of the graphic words. "To harm you. But Sam and I will be here to keep you safe." She didn't add that they would kill Vard if needed. She couldn't put that part of the plan into words.

Sam's eyes were also wide, but he didn't seem very surprised. *He already knew about Vard.* But knowing and seeing were two very different things. Vard was private about his form changes, rarely even allowing the love of his life to witness his transformations. She doubted if Sam had ever seen Vard shift.

Sam cleared his throat, and reached to squeeze Vard's shoulder. "I'll do everything I can to bring you all safe through this. Even if I must lose my life."

"No!" Alecia cried, confronting him. "That's not the point of this. You will not lose your life to save Vard. And neither will Benae, nor I. I know you're an honorable man, Samael Delacost, but you won't sacrifice your life for Vard's. That's too much to ask. You have a wife and son."

"And you and Vard have a daughter. Vard and I have an understanding. It goes both ways. Our families will always be protected."

Benae held up a hand. "That's enough talking. I agree to help Vard in his bear form. We can only hope he is weak enough not to threaten us, but strong enough for this to work."

Sam nodded. "One minute while I fetch my weapons."

His words brought home the somber reality of what they were about to do. Eyes wide, Benae prepared her potions.

"You won't be able to give him anything to make him sleepy, Benae," Alecia said. "Vard must be fully awake to control the bear."

She nodded, but her shoulders stiffened. "I understand."

Alecia faced Vard as Sam returned. "I trust you, my beloved. You can do this. Keep a tight hold on the bear, and he will bring you through this. I love you more than I can ever say."

A tear glistened in Vard's eye. "No sad words, my love. I'll do this with your help, and that of our friends."

Alecia smiled, somehow staying dry-eyed, even though her composure teetered on the edge of a precipice. "We will succeed, and I'll bring you back to Iona and Lyam." Perhaps it was her head injury that enabled her to ignore the gaping chasm that opened beneath her—the real possibility that she might lose the love of her life.

With a smile and a nod, Alecia turned to Benae. "We are ready."

Benae approached the bed with a goblet and helped Vard drink. "This should open the small blood vessels and expose the toxin," she said. "You will feel weak after you drink it. Tell me when the weakness stabilizes, and then you may become the bear. That is the moment I can delve you."

Vard stiffened at her words, and Alecia gasped. "He can't afford to be weaker!"

Benae continued to help Vard drink the mixture. "This is the best way to rid him of the poison, Alecia. Let me do my job. I know the best way to succeed, and I'm willing to take the risk to my life."

"Let her do it, Alecia," Vard gasped.

For a terrible moment, Alecia lost all faith that he would survive. He was too weak, and this would fail. Then she heard Hetty's words in her mind. "His strongest form is the bear. Remember that."

She nodded. "Go ahead."

Vard finished the goblet of medicine and lay back on the pillows. His eyes glowed with the feral essence of the bear, and she realized he held himself on the edge of transformation. A shiver she couldn't suppress rippled through her. The bear had terrified her more than once, but Vard controlled it now.

The minutes ticked by with Alecia praying to the Goddess that Vard would be strong enough, both to survive the healing and to control his beast. Then she noticed him relax into the pillows a little further.

Benae had surely noted this, too. "Are you ready, Lord Anton?" she asked.

He gave a faint nod, his irises flaring to rival the candles, and his body swelled and contracted, the outline blurring. Alecia would have checked on Benae and Sam, but she couldn't take her eyes from the magic in front of her.

She suspected the transformation was much slower than usual. First Vard's human form swelled to twice its size with a fuzzy outline and a vague sense of the bear growing. His hands and feet swelled to dinner plate size, and his nails became deadly talons. One sweep of them could open Benae up. Alecia chanced a glance at the healer to find her eyes wide.

When she looked back at Vard, his human outline and the bear appeared to be fighting for dominance; first one, and then the other clearer, until with an audible "pop", the brown bear lay on its side on the bed.

* * *

The bear lay still, every bone and muscle aching. The ground under it was soft, softer than anything it had experienced. It was an effort to open its eyes, but necessary to discern its location. Its gaze fell on a wooden structure, and panic seized him. This was no forest. Something touched his chest, like a bird alighting there. He growled. The sound was strange, bouncing back at him from the structure around him. The bird thing vanished.

He could hardly move, his limbs sluggish and achy, and when he did move, fierce pain blazed throughout his body. And the weakness. He recalled the time the man's metal barbs injured him. That was bad, but this was worse. He must accept it, for he couldn't fight it.

The bird returned. Maybe there was more than one. If he was to die, then let the creatures of this strange forest alight on him. He would not be alone. A probing entered his chest and scorched along his soft tissues, making him take a deep breath. He groaned, but the sensation wasn't painful, just nothing he had felt before. Perhaps the birds' tiny talons pierced his flesh?

After a little while, the pain in his chest dipped, and he could take a deeper breath. He relaxed, and would have fallen asleep, except the birds moved to his belly. This was now too strange for him to ignore. Why should the forest creatures dance on his belly? Before he could move, the probing started. Parts of his belly were being squeezed. It hurt, and he roared in pain, swiping at the pesky birds with a broad paw.

He hit nothing. The sensation stopped, a great weariness settling upon him. The birds returned, but the bear was too weary to stop the probing this time. That swipe had cost him most of his remaining strength. He knew no more until pain seared his skull as though woodpeckers hammered through his eyes. He couldn't see! Were his eyes open? The birds gripped his head, pecking with their appallingly sharp beaks, and something squeezed his skull so that he felt it would explode.

This was too much. Couldn't the forest creatures wait until he was dead to eat him? With a tremendous effort, he forced his body up and spun to face the nasty forest animals.

* * *

Benae froze, hands outstretched, as the bear turned on her and roared, fit to raise the roof. Its feral gaze lay upon her as if it knew she was the creator of its pain. It crouched to spring, and there was nothing she could do to prevent it.

Alecia shouted. "Benae! Get back!"

Benae drew a deep breath and dragged one foot backward, then the other, trying not to startle the creature further. One foot then the other, her eyes fixed on the teeth that could soon rend her throat. Its foul breath turned her stomach, but she forced herself to continue her slow backward shuffle.

A body landed in front of her, and a hand forced her further away. She landed with a thud on the floor, the spell of the bear's threatening presence broken. The great beast held Sam by the throat, fangs penetrating his flesh. He had the bear by the cheeks, somehow holding it at bay.

"Vard!" Alecia screamed, and flew in from the side, whacking the monster bear with a pillow. She kept hitting the creature, crying his name at the top of her lungs until all that came out was hoarse nonsense.

The bear's eyes flickered to Alecia, and Benae gasped as the giant paw swiped the pillow to shreds. Alecia stood exposed with Sam in no position to help. Blood dripped from the fang entry points on his throat as the bear held him.

As suddenly as it began, Vard melted back into human form and crashed over onto his side, taking Sam with him, holding onto Vard's cheeks. Sam let go abruptly and clapped hands to his neck, backing off the bed, and collapsing to the stone floor. Alecia stood sobbing, hands clenched on the bottom bed rail, and breathing hard.

Benae crawled to Sam and pulled his hands away. His throat had four deep punctures and bled profusely. Benae delved him, found the bleeders one by one, and sealed them.

"You're lucky, Sam," she said. "A moment longer, and your throat would have been in tatters."

He snorted. "What do you call this?" he asked, voice hoarse. He swallowed several times and nodded. "That feels a little better." He rubbed the tender tissue where the holes had been, and his eyes widened. "Nice work, Lady Benae."

"You're not out of the woods yet. We must ensure none of the bear's foul humor remains. For that, I will fix a potion. But for now, please sit over there and take watered wine." She gestured to the wall near the door. Sam rose and tottered to his assigned place.

Benae turned to Alecia. "You're pale as a sheet, My Queen. You too should drink some wine. It has been a shock."

Alecia's gaze remained on Vard. "Check him. I need to know he's well."

Benae gave Alecia one last look, then turned to Vard. Was the bear really gone for now? It had been the most astonishing thing to see his transformation. And now here he was, a man again, and very weak.

Benae crouched over Vard, whose breath was deep and even. He appeared to be asleep. His color was a little high, as if he had a fever. She laid her palms on his chest, his abdomen, and his head as she had before. Closing her eyes, she sent spirit spiraling through his vessels, right into the most secret places of the body. There was no poison left. Perhaps he truly might recover.

Alecia joined her at the bedside, and picked up Vard's hand. "It's hot."

Benae nodded. "He has a fever which should pass in a few hours. It's a sign that his health is returning. He was deathly cold before."

Alecia swiped a tear from her cheek. "I hope you're right. I feared I would lose all of you."

"I thought I was dead when he made to leap for me." Benae turned to study Sam, who sat against the wall, head resting back, eyes closed. "If Sam hadn't intervened when he did…" She shuddered. "I'll prepare a tonic for Sam, and then we should all rest."

* * *

Vard dreamed. He was the bear and injured. Crossbow bolts in his body made moving difficult, but the body of a man lay in the forest before him. This man had shot the terrible hard bolts, but he wouldn't do so ever again. The bear was terribly weak. He knew he must act, or die.

Two great sweeps of his claws opened the dead man's rib cage, and, in one gulp, the heart was in his mouth and devoured. He drank deeply of the blood in the chest cavity, and, immediately, energy surged within. The bear finished with the liver, and knew he must rest.

For now, he was out of danger. He turned and padded away through the trees.

It was dark when Vard woke, and, for long moments, he wasn't sure where he was. There was a soft bed under him, but he instinctively knew he wasn't at home. Where was home, anyway? He had stayed nowhere long enough in the last year to call it home.

He sent his senses out, and knew Alecia was with him. Perhaps it *was* home? She slept beside him in the bed, her breathing deep and even. He relaxed. His love was well. Besides Alecia, nothing here felt familiar.

With a jolt, it came flooding back. His injuries, and the strange wasting illness he had suffered. They had found poison in him. To fight it, he had become the bear. Benae Zorba had battled with him. His bear had wanted to hurt her. Was she well? He must know.

Not wanting to wake Alecia, he pushed himself into a sitting position, and discovered he was naked. No matter. He left the bed and tottered around the room, using his night vision to search the corners for Benae. She would be nearby if she was uninjured. He couldn't think about her being dead. He couldn't.

A form appeared before him, and hands grabbed his arms. "What are you doing out of bed?" The hoarse voice was Sam's.

Relief swept through Vard. A fleeting impression struck of his teeth in Sam's throat, but it drifted away like smoke on a high wind.

"I need to know Lady Benae is well," he whispered, swaying in Sam's hands.

Sam turned him around and started pushing him back toward the bed. "She is well. I told you I'd see that nothing happened to her or Alecia, and I did." His voice sounded unnatural.

Sam put Vard back to bed and pulled up the covers like a mother with her child.

Vard clasped his shoulder. "What did I do? I hurt you. I know I did."

Sam froze, but shook his head. "It was nothing. Time enough to speak of it in the morning. Get some rest." He moved away from the bedside, and Vard watched his friend settle on a pallet on the floor by the door. Sam slept on the floor and guarded him like a damned dog. Shame roared through Vard, and he determined Sam would never again lower himself like this, especially not if he had almost lost his life to him.

Surprisingly, Vard slept well after his broken night, and woke to Alecia's body resting against him. They were alone in the room. Her violet eyes gazed up into his with more than a touch of concern.

"You're well, Vard?" she asked, a quaver in her voice.

He smiled at her and watched the worry lessen. "I'm better than I've been in some time." He reached to touch her bruised head. "How did you get this?"

She flinched. "We fought a small band of *Sis Lenweri* who ambushed us. It's nothing."

Vard scowled. "It's not nothing. That injury could've been fatal. You can't afford to take such a risk."

Her eyes flared. "And what would you have me do? Sit in the keep while others risked life and limb to find Iona? I couldn't do it, Vard. And neither could you." Her heated voice reminded him of the passion she harbored within, as if he should require any reminder.

Vard drew a deep breath and spent a little time gathering his thoughts. He didn't want to upset Alecia. It just hurt him to see her injured.

"Your courage is admirable, my love. I wouldn't expect anything else from you. When I heard Iona was missing, I knew you'd take part in the search eventually." He pushed his hand through hair that badly needed a wash. "Where *is* Iona?"

Alecia pushed herself up and leaned toward him, kissing him lingeringly on the lips. His body stirred with even that light touch.

"Our daughter is safe at home, being cared for by a bevy of servants, and by Lady Henrietta. Benae mentioned a play date with Solomon, but I fear she may have been too tired to see her friend."

Vard blew out his breath and rested back on the pillows. "Thank the Goddess for that." He closed his eyes and allowed himself to acknowledge how Iona's disappearance had scared him. "I couldn't live if you or Iona died. We've come too far, suffered too much, to lose it all now."

Alecia smoothed the frown from his forehead with gentle fingers. "All is well, Vard. Soon we'll be man and wife, and nothing will ever come between us again."

He thought of the dream and dread struck his heart. Why would that dream pop up from his subconscious? Was it merely a consequence of his troubled mind?

"What's the matter, Vard?" Alecia asked. "What has upset you?"

Should he tell her? He must, or she'd worry him senseless.

"I dreamed last night. I was the bear. You remember when the assassin attacked at your betrothal ball?"

Alecia snorted. "How could I forget? It was one of the most awful nights of my life."

Vard nodded. "Well, I was the bear, and I killed the assassin."

"What of it?"

"I don't know if I ever told you… I ate his organs and drank of his blood to save myself."

He could see the news shocked her. She was silent for several moments.

"You did what you needed to survive. Hetty told me you were very near death when you came to her for help."

"Still, as a Defender, I'm forbidden to take sustenance from a human when in animal form. There must be a good reason for that, apart from it being… distasteful. The incident had slipped my mind with everything that has happened since then. Gaining control over my bear lulled me into thinking no further issues could plague me."

"It's nothing, Vard. That was a random dream, brought on by becoming the bear so you could heal. As you said—it was a deeply sunken memory. The mind has ways of dredging those up."

"But what will come of it? There must be a reason for the rule."

"I'm sure you're not the first Defender to break it, my darling," Alecia said, patting his shoulder.

Perhaps she was right. He hoped she was, but there was no point dwelling on it now.

There was a knock on the door, and Benae entered, followed by Sam carrying a tray of food.

"Well, you both appear better for your rest," Benae said, smiling. "I'll examine you, and then you must break your fast." She continued into the room and stopped by Alecia while Sam placed the tray of food on a table by the window. His eyes sought Vard's, but what he saw must have reassured him for he grinned. Then he looked down, touched his throat, and frowned. Vard clenched his jaws, wondering if this would harm their friendship.

Benae stood by Alecia, listening to her heart, checking her eyes, and the wound on her skull. Finally, she stepped back, smiling. "I declare you fit to travel, Your Majesty."

Alecia let out a breath. "Thank you so much! I can't wait to hold Iona. Can we leave today? As soon as we have breakfast?"

Benae hustled around the bed. "Let's see if Vard is in equally good condition, shall we?"

She bade him lie down, and carefully pulled the covers away to reveal his wound. Immediately, Vard could see it was almost healed. But the wound hadn't been the real danger. Benae laid her hands on his chest, abdomen, and head, and he felt the familiar tingling of her delving. If only *he* had that gift! Far better than killing men and transforming into animals. He jerked. He hadn't had *that* thought before.

Benae's smile as she straightened was broad. "You're fully fit, Lord Anton. Oh, you may feel a little weak and hungry over the next few days, but I can safely clear you to return to normal duties."

"Yes!" Sam said, his voice hoarse. "Bring on the wedding of the century. If we hurry, we will all be in time to make the ceremony."

Alecia stiffened. "You're right! It's three days away."

She came around the bed and threw back Vard's covers, exposing him fully. He yelped and grabbed at her nightgown, placing it across his loins.

"If you don't mind," he said, addressing his comments to Benae and Sam, "please leave us to our breakfast."

Benae and Sam left, broad smiles on their faces, Benae promising to have Vard's clothes brought to him. Shaking his head, Vard dropped Alecia's nightgown, and pulled her into his arms.

"Do we have time to celebrate our reuniting, Your Majesty?" he asked.

She leaned in and kissed him long and languidly. His blood started pumping and headed south to his member. Pressing her closer, his tongue invaded her mouth and she groaned, weaving her arms around his neck. He reached for her gown and slid it up her legs. Alecia jumped back.

"No!" she said, pushing her nightgown back down to cover her thighs. "We agreed there would be no sexual relations leading up to the wedding, Vard!"

"We did?" Vard's memory of the commitment was fuzzy. "Haven't we already broken that rule just before I left to find Father?"

Alecia stood, her face turning rosy. "We did. But now we've had this time apart, I want to wait. It will make our wedding night special."

He stared at her, allowing the full force of his Defender attraction to hit her. It was playing dirty, but, damn it, he wanted her now. Alecia wavered and took a step toward him. He smiled, and she stiffened.

"What was that?" she asked, raising her pointer finger at him. "You will not use that on me. Not until our wedding night, anyway. Now have breakfast, so we can be off." She spun and headed to the breakfast table, seating herself and pouring them both tea.

Vard watched, wondering what had just happened. She shouldn't have been able to resist and only waver before rejecting him. But she was Alecia Zialni, Queen of Thorius, Defender of the Kingdom, and a force to be reckoned with.

He smiled and joined her.

CHAPTER TWENTY-ONE

A FTER a day and a half of hard riding, Alecia and Vard entered the archery meadow, the scene of their first kiss. It felt like an age ago. She had certainly grown up since that day. Vard had come into his power, too. She thought back to the previous morning when he had employed his Defender attraction on her, deliberately trying to entice her into lying with him. And she had almost succumbed. Only the desire to be on her way as quickly as possible had helped her reject his charms. Temporarily, of course. It would be worth the wait. It would. And Vard would thank her.

She snorted lightly and saw him glance at her out of the corner of her eye. "Let's go home!"

Alecia stayed with her guard during the canter home, a contrast to how she first traveled with Vard to the archery meadow. She had been headstrong and careless of her safety back then, and ridden ahead of him when he was assigned to look after her. It had been inconsiderate of her to make his task more difficult. Even though her guards and retainers still thought of her as headstrong and likely to risk herself, Alecia knew she had come a long way.

Finally, they rode into the keep's courtyard, which had been decorated with bunting in the Zialni colors. It overwhelmed Alecia to see the staff decked out in their formal uniforms and waiting to greet her.

"Don't look so surprised, Your Majesty," Vard murmured. "After all, you are their queen."

She dismounted, giving Silver a thank you pat on her neck, and went to meet Ramón, who held Iona. She felt Vard close behind her, and was glad of his support, even though he didn't touch her.

Tears filled her eyes as she took Iona from Ramón and held her child close. Then Vard gathered her and Iona in a family hug, accompanied by the cheers of all present.

The morning after her return, Alecia sat in the large audience hall. She was there for a breakfast meeting to lay to rest some of the ongoing issues that surrounded Iona's kidnapping. But, as she sipped the tea that sat on a small table beside her throne, she thought longingly of her bed.

She was tired, still recovering from her head injury, and exhausted by the emotional storm that had buffeted her over the recent weeks. Thankfully, she had spent precious hours with Vard and Iona last evening. At times, it was difficult to believe that all was now well, and she could put the gripping terror behind her.

Most of her advisors were present in the hall, and were currently enjoying sweet buns and tea. Well, *most* were enjoying themselves.

Adriana and Piotr stood at the back of the room, watched over by Alecia's lady guards and two of Vard's Rangers. The dowager queen and the prince kept glancing at her, but Alecia ignored them.

Melanis Stenmore was in prison, watched over by Vortek Cruzen. She had already tried to break out of her cell by transforming, but couldn't complete the change. However, she would soon be well enough to shift into the dragon, so they must decide her fate quickly.

Alecia raised a hand, and Linnet mounted the stairs to the dais, clapping to quiet the room. The advisors took their seats.

Linnet spoke. "Welcome to all, and thank you for attending. We are here to resolve issues arising from Princess Iona's kidnapping."

Her eyes scanned across those seated, finding Nikolas Cosara.

"Admiral Cosara, have you determined how the child was abducted, by whom, and how she came to be with dowager queen Adriana and Prince Piotr?"

Cosara stood and mounted the dais. He bowed to Alecia and the assembled guests. "My Queen, Prince Arenil, honored advisors and guests. After exhaustive interviewing of Melanis Stenmore, and reviewing all the evidence, I have concluded that..." He paused and pulled uncomfortably at his collar. "I have concluded that a dragon took Princess Iona from her nursery."

This was no surprise to those assembled. After all, dragons had again fought over the skies of Brightcastle and its surrounds.

Nikolas continued. "However, the culprit—the dragon—was not a natural creature—if you can say that dragons are natural..."

Again, the admiral faltered, then straightened his shoulders. "The dragon responsible was none other than Melanis Stenmore."

The room erupted, nervous laughter and noisy chatter filling the space.

Alecia braced herself. The existence of shifters was on the brink of exposure. She had asked Vard to stay away this morning, so he would be sheltered from this, but Sam was present, and he smiled at her.

Estevot stood, pointing at Nikolas. "Admiral, have you lost your mind?"

Nikolas scowled. "I assure you, Captain, I am as sane as you are. Melanis Stenmore is a shapeshifter. She can change her shape into that of a black dragon, but one smaller than Nugoriem."

Estevot looked at Ramón who appeared to be hoping the floor would open up and swallow him. "Lord Zorba, do you believe this, too? This mad talk of noblewomen becoming dragons?"

Ramón stood. "I... I... yes. I do. It appears we have much to learn about magical creatures." His eyes met Alecia's and he raised one brow. Had he finally realized Vard's true essence? She steeled herself to hold her love's secret close to her chest, especially from this man.

Estevot paled and slowly resumed his seat.

Nikolas cleared his throat. "Thank you, Lord Zorba. Further to this discussion, Lady Stenmore tried to break out of her cell last night by changing into the dragon. She failed as she is still too ill. Her shifter abilities are indisputable, however, and she no longer denies it."

James Tomel sat as if turned to stone. Alecia had informed him of their findings last night. Though he had questioned Melanis, she had concealed her animal transformations from him.

It must have been quite a shock to learn that his one-time fiancée had hidden such a dangerous secret. It certainly appeared to Alecia that Lady Stenmore was not a Defender, bound to protect the weak and innocent, but another type of being altogether—one who used her gift for her own ends.

Alecia stood. "My good people. What you have heard is the truth. Please take time to digest this news. Melanis stole Iona from her room, and her goal was to sell her to the *Sis Lenweri*. The elven woman, Failora, who was brought out of the enemy encampment with Lyam Anton, has confirmed this. Failora admitted to overhearing plans for the most recent invasion of the dark elves into our northern Brightcastle forests. The purpose of this mission was to collect Iona from Melanis."

She turned to Nikolas. "Admiral?"

Alecia sat, and Nikolas continued.

"We come to Iona's presence in a cabin in the forest. Lady Stenmore, in human form, left the princess with a woodsman, and went to meet the *Sis Lenweri*. When she arrived without Iona, the elves became angry, thinking she was trying to trick them, although she assured them that Iona was in a safe hiding place. The leader flew into a rage and ordered Lady Stenmore beaten, during which she transformed and escaped."

Nikolas paused. He had the room's rapt attention.

"Iona remained with the woodsman, who was instructed to relocate her if Melanis didn't come back on time."

Alecia breathed deeply, trying to keep her emotions under control. It was difficult. The thought of her little girl, scared and alone, was horrid.

A loud voice came from the back. "And where did the dowager queen and Prince Piotr come in?" It was Samael Delacost who spoke.

Nikolas motioned to Estevot. "Perhaps you can speak to this, Captain Estevot?"

Alecia nodded to Nikolas as he left the stage. He was a good man, and the possibility that his cousin, the dowager queen, had been involved in Iona's torment distressed him. Nikolas resumed his seat beside Merielle, who grabbed his hand.

Estevot bowed to Alecia and turned to face the hall. "We are yet to confirm what Adriana Zialni and Piotr Zialni were doing with the princess. They *say* they had found her and were bringing her to her mother. In fact, they swear that is what they were doing."

Alecia boiled inside. "Then why were they heading east, away from the main body of searchers, Captain?"

Estevot addressed the audience. "The dowager queen and Prince Piotr say they got turned around in the forest. It isn't familiar to either of them, Your Majesty."

The crowd muttered at this, and Alecia tried to remain calm. It would do no good for her to lose her temper. "Continue, Captain."

"The two had become separated from their group when they found the princess. No one can verify their story of getting lost, or of intending to return Princess Iona."

Alecia observed Adriana and Piotr, who had fixed their attention on Estevot.

The captain continued. "Unless we uncover more information, the crown cannot charge Adriana Zialni or Piotr Zialni with any crimes relating to the kidnapping of the princess."

Adriana and Piotr sagged against each other, and the dowager queen appeared to be crying. Alecia surged to her feet.

"Adriana Zialni and Piotr Zialni," Alecia said, her voice ringing through the room, "approach the throne." She was gratified to see the fear on their faces. When they stood at the foot of the dais, she addressed them.

"Lady Zialni, Prince Zialni," she said, her voice as cold as a blizzard. "The crown may be unable to prove any wrongdoing on your part, but we do not intend to let you carry on with your mischief." She fixed Adriana with a look calculated to chill her to the bone. "Dowager Queen, you are banished to your country estate, far to the north of Wildecoast. There you will live out your days with your staff. If you wish to leave that estate, you must apply to the crown for permission."

Adriana's eyes bulged. "Alecia, niece," she said, wringing her hands. "I did you no harm. Please don't send me away!"

"You will address me as 'Your Majesty', and you will follow my orders to the letter." Alecia turned from Adriana, unable to look at her for one more second. "Piotr Zialni, it appears you continue to be a man of mystery. I banish you from the Kingdom of Thorius, and forbid you to associate with Adriana Zialni. You have seven days to get your affairs in order and travel beyond the kingdom's boundaries."

Piotr sneered up at her, but remained silent. He bowed, backed away, and returned to the back of the room. Cretia and Kenna approached Adriana and led her away. When the guards had escorted Piotr and Adriana from the hall, Alecia sat on the throne.

Nikolas Cosara returned to the dais.

"Regarding the matter of Melanis Stenmore and her fate, unless someone here has any other suggestion, I urge the crown to sentence her to death. No other course of action can keep the populace safe from her."

Unfortunately, Alecia had to agree. She had discussed the matter with Hetty and Vard. As Melanis was an animal shifter with no moral code to follow, she was too dangerous to leave unfettered, yet they couldn't contain her in any prison. Time might bring a solution, but Melanis would surely flee. Alecia wasn't willing to allow the woman to hurt another person.

She stood again. "James?"

He rose to his feet, Katrine beside him.

"You say a dragon attacked you outside your home last year?" Alecia asked. "Could this have been Lady Stenmore in her dragon form?"

"I believe this to be the case, Your Majesty," James said. "I had just broken our engagement. Perhaps she was seeking revenge." He gazed down at Katrine, and she smiled. He looked back to Alecia. "Lady Stenmore *is* dangerous. I agree you have no choice but to sentence her to death." His voice faded away and sadness cloaked him.

Kain Arenil approached. He climbed the dais and went to Alecia's side.

"Your Majesty, I may have a solution, as I can see the fate of Lady Stenmore weighs heavily upon you." He lowered his voice. "You are aware of the bond I have with Nugoriem?" At Alecia's nod, he continued, "I have just now spoken with him, mind to mind, and *he* will take Melanis off our hands. He will ensure that she never bothers us again."

"What does Nugoriem mean by that?" Alecia asked. Despite her dislike of Melanis, what kind of queen would she be to allow the noblewoman to suffer lifelong torment?

"I'll ask him." Kain's eyes became unfocussed for several seconds, then his attention returned to her. "He says he will make her his attendant. Nugoriem believes Melanis will struggle to shift into dragon form in his presence. And if she does so, her form is that of a lesser dragon, which must bow down to him. She will endure a life of servitude to one of the greater dragons. Is this acceptable?"

"I must consider," she said. "Thank you. Please resume your seat."

Kain returned to his spot beside Alique, and Alecia turned to the guests.

"Learned advisors, I ask you, if it was guaranteed that Melanis Stenmore wouldn't escape, would you choose a life of service for her? Prince Arenil has advised me that the great dragon, Nugoriem, will take her and keep her with him. She will live out her days in service to the black dragon."

The announcement created almost as much furor as the earlier declaration that Melanis was a dragon shifter.

"How can you ensure that Lady Stenmore will remain confined?" Admiral Cosara asked.

Alecia drew a breath. "I don't suppose there are any certainties with mythical creatures and their limits, Admiral. However, I trust Nugoriem to do his best to prevent Melanis from harming us in the future." Alecia walked along the stage as she explained. "I believe sentencing her to death will alienate the nobles. This way, we can announce she is to be imprisoned, and send her away with Nugoriem. Our conscience is clear of her death. We declare she was behind the kidnapping of the princess, and that she was planning to sell Iona to the *Sis Lenweri*."

She watched those assembled digest her words. Some discussed the proposal with those around them; others appeared deep in their own thoughts. When the room slowly settled, Alecia spoke again.

"Do any have objections to Nugoriem's offer to take Melanis Stenmore into his custody?"

Ramón stood. "I agree, but only as long as the dragon doesn't torture her."

Alecia wasn't surprised that Ramón wanted to assure Lady Stenmore's proper treatment, and, indeed, she wanted that too. "Thank you, Lord Zorba. I imagine many in this room concur." She sought Kain Arenil. "Prince Arenil, please advise Nugoriem we accept his kind offer and ask that he treat the prisoner with respect."

What those words would mean to a dragon was anyone's guess, Alecia thought, but there was no point reflecting on that now. They had more joyful things to contemplate.

"Admiral, please supervise the details regarding Lady Stenmore's new arrangement, and see that she leaves Brightcastle with all haste." When Nikolas nodded, Alecia addressed the crowd. "This meeting is at an end. Thank you all for your wisdom."

Enthusiastic applause greeted her words, and her advisors filed out of the hall, leaving Alecia with Linnet and Hetty.

"My friends," she said, "let us cast aside these gloomy discussions and prepare for a celebration!" She hugged them in turn, and they left the hall together, smiles on their faces, and joy in their hearts.

THE WEDDING

A LECIA studied her reflection in the tall gilt-edged mirror. Inside she was a torrent of nerves, but outwardly she looked serenely beautiful. Isadore had been correct. The cream underdress with a spectacular burned orange overdress, complete with pearls and gold thread, was a sensation. The sleeves were simply divine—floaty cream creations which left her hands free. The headpiece matched the overdress, and had her cream veil attached. Merielle pulled the fabric of the veil out to fall around her shoulders.

"You are an inspiration," she said.

Were those tears in Merielle's eyes? In Alecia's experience, her friend rarely expressed sentimental feelings, though she was often fiercely protective.

"Thank you for always being there, my friend," Alecia said, turning to include the other ladies in her company. Linnet, Alique, and Katrine attended her besides Meri. Lady Henrietta was magnificent in a silver sheath gown. "Thank you to all of you who've seen me through dangerous times and good ones to reach this day." Grins appeared on all her ladies, even Hetty.

"Your day has finally come, Your Majesty," Hetty said. "No one deserves happiness more than you do."

"I second that." Lin smoothed her orange gown.

All Alecia's attendants wore the color, in different shades, that faded the further they were placed from the bride. Lin was the last and her dress was a pale bronzy orange that exactly matched her hair. Yes, Isadore had triumphed with these gowns.

"It's not only my day, ladies, but Vard's and Iona's. In fact, my wedding day belongs to all the kingdom."

Alique nodded. "I hear many brides have chosen this day to commit themselves to their men, just as you are marrying Vard. They come from all corners of the kingdom. I have personally heard of elven marriages being celebrated today."

Alecia's jaw dropped. "Really?" Her determination to control her emotions evaporated and tears filled her eyes. "That makes me so humbled and happy. That those women want to celebrate with me is beyond touching."

A peal of trumpets blasted through the keep. "That's Vard entering the chapel," Alecia said. "We need to go now!"

Katrine reached for her hand. "Let him wait, Your Majesty."

Alecia smiled. "I think he's waited long enough, don't you?"

In the end, it was another thirty minutes before Alecia and her attendants made their way into the chapel. They had to allow time for Hetty to be seated, and for Iona to be brought from her nursery, dressed in a frilly gown of cream lace. She tottered along in cream satin slippers, sitting down at regular intervals to pull her slippers off. Solomon joined her, looking fine in his dark gray tunic and breeches with a creamy shirt and ruffled lace collar. Benae and Ramón had charge of the children, who would bring the rings to the best man, Samael Delacost.

By the time Lyam arrived to escort Alecia to the chapel, her transformation from a calm queen to a panicky bride was complete.

"What's the matter, Daughter?" Lyam asked. "This is the happiest day of your life, and you look terrified."

Alecia took a deep breath. "I'm a little nervous, Lyam."

He squeezed her hand. "All will be well, lass. Hold tight to my arm, and I'll deliver you to your man. You'll be as right as rain."

Alecia smiled as the moths in her stomach settled a little. It really would be fine. "Thank you, Father." She had decided Lyam would be her father in every way except by birth. His recovery had been rough, and his face still bore the scars of his torture, but he had come far in the few days since his rescue. Benae had worked hard.

The bridal procession made its way from Alecia's chamber down to the chapel, Benae and Ramón ahead with the children, her attendants in the middle, and she and Lyam at the end. As they walked, Lyam spoke of his own marriage to Vard's mother, and their joy at Vard's arrival.

"I couldn't hope for a more wonderful wife for my son. He has grown into such a man as I never thought to see. And much of that has been because of you. He wanted, nay needed, to be worthy of you. And now he is."

"Oh, Lyam, Vard was always a wonderful man."

"You complete each other, much as my dear Jemma completed me."

"It means much to be accepted by you."

He smiled. "I hope you always feel that way, and the humility you show will ever be a part of your reign."

Alecia reflected on his words as she halted before the doors to the chapel, her attendants ready to enter the holy space. With another blare of trumpets, the doors swung open. Benae and Ramón ushered Iona and Solomon through, and they were announced by the master of ceremonies. Alecia smiled as she watched the couple discreetly trying to keep the young ones on track.

She couldn't see Vard yet, so concentrated on her daughter and Solomon as they entertained the crowd with their antics. Finally, they made it to the steps of the chapel, and there were tantrums as each child was persuaded to give up their ring to Sam.

Next to enter was Linnet, then Alique, Katrine, and Merielle. And once they moved off, Alecia caught her first glimpse of Vard. The breath whooshed out of her as she took him in. The golden flecks in his sea-green eyes seemed to reach out and draw her to him. She truly had eyes for no one else. Lyam squeezed her hand. It was her turn to walk down the aisle to Vard.

Her mind went wild, taking her back to moments in their past, from the very first time she gazed into those astonishing eyes of his. He had picked her up off the cobblestones, and the spark of their attraction, and later love, ignited. Heart pounding, she walked the length of the aisle, Lyam's reassuring presence at her side, flashes of their history together accompanying her...

Vard the bear staring down at her with hunger in his gaze.

Vard the wolf standing over her in their worst time.

Vard returned from the animal to rescue her daughter, and save them both.

Vard in his vulnerable moments, and in his strength, in all his love and fury, in his tenderness and concern for her.

And she recalled herself in those times, standing up to him when he didn't know himself, loving him when he couldn't love himself, and fighting for him, rejecting him, and ultimately accepting him. They had been through the gamut of emotions and experiences, arriving at this day stronger than ever.

Reaching Vard, Lyam placed her hands in his son's, and stepped amongst the men who had stood up for Vard—Sam, James, and Kain Arenil. Alecia spared a smile for the four powerful men, and then fixed her attention upon Vard.

In his gaze, she recognized her experiences, feelings, hopes, and dreams mirrored back at her. That they had weathered storm and tempest, been apart, each with their own demons to lay to rest, and their separate journeys to complete, and that they had found their way back to each other made this moment even more poignant.

The priestess stepped before them and spoke.

"Dear people, I present to you for marriage, our queen, Alecia Zialni, and her chosen partner, Lord Vard Anton. I ask you to accept them, and their dreams for a life together. I ask the Goddess to bless them with love, laughter, strength, and family.

"As they stand before me, I see the love that binds them. It is strong, and I ask the Goddess to give them the power to keep their love alive through the joys and tribulations ahead.

"Alecia Zialni, you stand here in the sheltering arms of the Goddess. Are you ready to take this man, Vard Anton, for your husband?"

Alecia gazed up at Vard, fighting tears. "I am. Vard, I love and respect you more than I can ever express. Our love has been tested, and we have triumphed, even in the lead up to this very special day. I will love you, honor you, and be your companion, all the days of my life."

The priestess nodded and looked at Vard. "Vard Anton, you stand here in the sheltering arms of the Goddess. Are you ready to take this woman, Alecia Zialni, for your wife?"

Vard smiled as he gazed down on Alecia. "I am. Alecia, you are the mother of my daughter, and the love of my life. I am ready to support you, and be your companion in good times and in troubled ones, for the rest of my days. I will always protect, love, and cherish you."

In the quiet chapel, Alecia was certain all could hear her heart beating. As Vard's words faded away, for a time, no one existed but them. Seconds seemed to stretch into minutes with Alecia content to live in this moment they had created.

"Lord Anton, do you have the rings?" the priestess asked.

Vard didn't move. Alecia squeezed his fingers and smiled. This moment had caught him as deeply as it had her. A smile curved his lips.

"Vard," she said, "the rings."

He jumped as if coming out of a trance, and turned to Sam. Some guests chuckled as their great battle leader showed a moment of weakness. Rings collected from Sam, Vard gave them to the priestess for blessing, and turned back to Alecia.

"Sorry, my love," he whispered. "I was a little lost."

"Vard Anton," the priestess said, "you may place the ring on Alecia's finger."

He did so, and Alecia experienced a wave of love and exultation as the band sealed her to Vard.

"Alecia Zialni, you may place the ring on Vard's finger," the priestess said.

Alecia took the heavier gold band, engraved with leaping wolves, and slipped it onto Vard's finger, feeling a thrill as she marked her man. When she met his gaze, the intensity of his love took her breath away.

The priestess continued. "In the pledging of their love and commitment to each other and in the exchanging of rings, Alecia Zialni and Vard Anton have shown themselves worthy to be called man and wife. I do so proclaim them! You may present yourselves!"

Alecia beamed up at her husband. Vard had never looked happier. They kissed each other on each cheek, a promise of more kisses to come when in private, then turned to the assembled guests. As they raised their joined hands, a great cheer rang out in the chapel. Joined by their attendants, the bride and groom descended the stairs and made their way down the aisle, stopping to greet friends as they went.

All Alecia wanted was to get her man alone and end all the desperate waiting and wanting, but that wasn't to be. A great wedding feast had been prepared in the grand ballroom, so they made their way to that space and stood ready to receive their guests.

Guests greeted, Alecia, Vard, and their attendants took their seats at the top table on the dais, allowing all to gaze upon their queen and her husband. It was more spotlight than Alecia wished for. She was certain Vard felt the same. Still, it gave their guests a chance to observe how happy they were. It also bore witness to the new state of the kingdom—that an ex-pirate could sit at table with a queen, that there was forgiveness for those who had sinned, and that the leader of the Lenweri blessed their union. She was excited to see what such a melting pot of supporters might bring to her reign.

Finally, when the meal was done, and the dancing was about to start, Alecia stood. The ballroom slowly quieted as she walked to the top of the stairs.

"My people, thank you for helping us celebrate our union this day. It could not have been more perfect. I would like to thank all who kept moving forward with the organization during our long search for Iona. Our daughter is recovering well, as you saw earlier, but she was too tired to stay for the party." Alecia saw many smiles at the reminder of Iona's part in the ceremony. She was beloved, truly.

"I would also like to wish a happy and long life together to all those who celebrated their love with us today. It has given me and Vard pure joy to know we are not alone. We will share anniversaries with you into the future."

Alecia turned to encompass their attendants—Lyam, Linnet, Sam, Merielle, Alique, Kain, James, and Katrine. "My friends! You come from all walks of life and backgrounds. Neither Vard nor myself have siblings, but we think of you as part of our family. We look forward to sharing many happy moments with you in the future, and hope you have enjoyed yourselves today. Thank you for supporting us during the search for Iona, and also in the recent war."

"And, finally, Vard. You have stood by me when many would have walked away. I love you more than I can ever express, and will always do so, in good times and in trouble. We are forever united, and I couldn't wish for a better partner in life and love." She crossed to the table and couldn't resist kissing Vard when he rose. But it was a sweet kiss, for this wasn't the place to display the depth of her desire for him. She turned back to the hall. "And now it is time to dance!"

Vard joined her, and, hugging her to his side, drew her down to the dance floor for their first waltz as husband and wife.

EPILOGUE

VARD entered the queen's chamber for the first time without knocking. He was her husband—her husband!—and he would never have to knock on this door again. He wanted to pinch himself when he thought about them being married. It had been a long and winding road from the first day when he found her on the cobblestones and thought her a lad.

His feet stalled. How had he ever thought her a *boy*? And now she was a queen, *and* a mother. His wife had come into the fullness of her destiny. Well, not full, but very much along the road to being a great queen and a wonderful mother… an amazing wife!

"Vard, I'm tired. Where are you?" The voice of his wife floated from the bedchamber… the queen's bedchamber, which he was now welcome to share. "How was Iona? I think she should be with us this night."

He continued into the bedroom and stopped when he saw Alecia sitting in bed, covers up to her armpits and shoulders bare. His blood moved south as his eyes explored the milky contours of his lovely Alecia. Was she naked under that quilt? Oh, Goddess, please let her be naked. She smiled, and held out her arms.

Vard went to her, sitting on the edge of the bed and pulling her against him. His hands roved down her back, discovering only skin. Naked indeed.

"You're killing me, my love," he growled. "All day I've waited to be with you like this, and to find you unclothed, ready for me…"

She pulled back and kissed him, lush lips inviting his to dance, opening for his exploration. He pushed her back against the pillows while struggling out of his tunic and shirt. Her hands fluttered over his bared shoulders, reacquainting themselves with his skin. She groaned.

"I've dreamed so long of this night," she said. "At times, I thought it would never come."

Vard nudged the covers down, exposing her breasts and belly. He sucked each of her nipples until she arched against him, panting.

"Take me now, Vard. I can't wait any longer."

"Are you wet for me, Alecia?" His fingers pushed between her legs, noting the slick flesh that strained for fulfillment. "Oh yes, you are, my love. You're so ready!"

"Lose your breeches, husband!"

Vard needed no further orders. He pushed away from her, groaning at being separated. His eager member sprang from its confinement as he pushed his breeches to the floor and slipped off his boots. When his eyes met Alecia's, he saw the lust in her violet gaze. Then he ceased to think as she pushed the quilt away and parted her knees, showing him how ready she was.

Before he knew anything more, Vard was between her legs, his cock thrust into the slick warmth of her body. He was home. She tightened around him, and they lost themselves in the glory of their union.

* * *

An hour later, Alecia lay in Vard's arms, half asleep, his chest to her back. She purred as his hand rubbed her belly back and forth. Just as she had almost given in to slumber, his hand stopped, and she jerked awake.

"What's wrong?" she asked.

There was silence from behind, and she rolled onto her back so she could see his face in the dim candlelight. "You stopped your rubbing."

He frowned. "Is there something you need to tell me, Alecia?"

Oh, no! Was their first fight as a married couple imminent? Vard looked so stern. What had she done? Or not done?

"Have I displeased you, Vard? You certainly seemed to enjoy yourself... three times!"

Amusement creased his cheeks, and he shook his head. "I mean this." He pulled the quilt from her nakedness and pointed at her belly. She gazed down at her abdomen, slightly rounded, but she had neglected her exercise in the search for Iona.

She looked back at Vard, and he raised his brows. "When were you going to tell me?"

"That I gained a little weight?" Now her temper was rising. "It's nothing more exercise won't fix."

Vard chuckled and reached to stroke her abdomen again. "I don't think exercise will fix this, my love." He reached over and kissed her belly, and suddenly it all fell into place.

Alecia pushed herself up, gasping. "I'm late! I must have lost track of time in all the worry over Iona." She met his glowing eyes. "We're going to be parents again!"

"We are indeed, My Queen. And I'll wrap you in swaddling until this little one makes his appearance."

"As long as you don't refuse me your body, Vard. I've waited long enough to enjoy you and now there is nothing standing in our way." She paused. "Is it a boy?"

He smiled and kissed her tenderly on the lips. "Too soon to say, my love. Ask me again in a few months, and I may discern the sex of our child." He frowned. "Though if he or she isn't a Defender, I may be unable to tell much."

"Oh Vard, I hope this child will be born with your special gifts, as Iona is."

"Defender or not, Alecia, I will love our child beyond measure, just as I adore you."

Alecia snuggled down with her husband. Finally, they were together, and nothing could tear them apart.

THE END

Thanks for reading *To Wed a Queen*.
I hope you enjoyed it and would truly appreciate a review on the platform of your choice.

This is the final book in the Queenmakers Saga.
To keep in touch with upcoming projects, please visit my website and sign up for my newsletter.

https://bernadetterowley.com/

You can find my books at
https://books2read.com/ap/nlkzdw/Bernadette-Rowley

GLOSSARY

Places

Kingdom of Thorius - (Thor- ee- us) the kingdom of men which encompasses the King's seat of Wildecoast and the Prince's seat of Brightcastle, along with many smaller towns

Wildecoast - (Will – dee – coast) city perched on the top of a cliff overlooking the sea on the east coast of Thorius; climate is mild but windy

Brightcastle - large inland town surrounded by forests and farms, three to four days ride west of Wildecoast

Amitania - (Am – it – ay – nia) or *Elvandang* (Elle – van – dang) in elvish- the deserted city north of the Usetar Mountain Range in northern Thorius; once a thriving city and now home to elves and humans under the leadership of Princess Gwaethe Arenil and Earl Jacques Vorasava

Usetar Range - (You – set – ar) the mountain range running across the northern parts of Thorius

Selinore - the forest home of the peaceful *Lenweri*, in the mountains north of Brightcastle

People

Lenweri - the elven people who are tall and elegant with black skin and pointed ears; live in mountainous forests north and west of Thorius, in places encroaching onto Kingdom lands; also known as dark elves; they welcome males and females in their fighting force

Sis Lenweri - the faction of dark elves that wishes to take the kingdom of Thorius back from men; only males are welcome in their fighting force

Defender - a race of shapeshifters who are created to defend those in danger; they sense those in need of their help; a Defender can shift into animal form and the ability is inherited through family lines; when they shift back into human form, they retain their clothes from before the shift; their gifts may include the ability to compel others to do their will

Guardian - a person or people appointed by the king to oversee a part of Thorius

Ranger - an elite force trained to fight and track to the highest proficiency; may include females

Characters

Queen Alecia Zialni (Ah-lee-sha Zee – al – nee) - the King's niece and daughter of Prince Jiseve Zialni who once ruled in Brightcastle and was next in line to the throne. Alecia's story began in **Princess Avenger** and continued in **Princess in Exile**; she is now Queen of Thorius.

Vard Anton - the love of Princess Alecia's life and a shapeshifting Defender; once army captain of Brightcastle in **Princess Avenger** and his story continued in **Princess in Exile**; Vard was recently the King's Blade but his new title, once he marries Queen Alecia, is yet to be decided

Iona Izebel Zialni (Eye-own-ah Is – zee – belle Zee – al – nee) - Alecia and Vard's daughter, born while Alecia was in exile; she has inherited her father's Defender gifts; she is seventeen months old when **To Wed a Queen** begins

Benae (Ben-nay) Zorba - Once Princess of Brightcastle and joint Guardian with her husband Ramón Zorba; she has now lost her title of princess and guardian since Alecia became Queen of Thorius; was once married to Prince Jiseve Zialni (now deceased) and has given birth to his child; Benae can heal with her mind and has a close relationship with her stallion, Flaire. Benae's story was told in **The Lady's Choice**

Ramón Zorba - Lord of Wildecoast and once squire to Prince Jiseve Zialni; recently joint Guardian of Brightcastle with his wife Benae; brother to Lady Alique Zorba. Ramón's story was told in **The Lady's Choice**

Solomon Daire Zorba - son of Benae Zorba and Prince Jiseve Zialni (now deceased); however, it is revealed in **Of Queens and Dragons** that Solomon is really Ramón Zorba's son; a toddler of fifteen months when **To Wed a Queen** begins

Hetty (aka Lady Henrietta Guiote) - mysterious ancient woman with magical powers; once Alecia's governess and nanny; declared a witch by Prince Jiseve and sentenced to death but rescued by Alecia; Lady Henrietta is one of Alecia's closest advisors

King Beniel Zialni (Ben – ee – elle Zee – al – nee) - once King of Thorius; older brother of Jiseve Zialni and uncle of Alecia Zialni; married to Adriana

Dowager Queen Adriana Zialni - widow of King Beniel; lives in Wildecoast; Alecia's aunt

Piotr Zialni (Peter Zialni) - son of Beniel and Jiseve Zialni's younger brother; next in line to the throne of Thorius (his father is dead) after Solomon, unless King Beniel or Alecia has a son

Izebel (Is – zee – belle) - a previous warrior Queen of Thorius from centuries ago, when females could rule; Alecia's idol; Izebel's daughter Daphini was the last queen of Thorius

Gwaethe (Gway-eth-a) *Arenil* - *Lenweri* princess, daughter of King Orionkael Arenil, who was murdered by High Prince Faenwelar of the *Sis Lenweri*. She has a golden stallion called *Rassar* (means Sunbeam) with silver mane and tail; her love story was told in **Elf Princess Warrior**

Jacques Vorasava - previous Captain in the Brightcastle army. Jacques is tall with dark hair, beard and moustache; he has an olive complexion; he is married to Gwaethe Arenil and is now an Earl, and their story was told in **Elf Princess Warrior**

Doctor Damald Monive - chief physician in Brightcastle Keep; presided over the inquiry into Alecia's father's sudden death when he was married to Benae

Millie - Alecia's maid who also helps with Iona's care

Melandrach (Mel-on-drac) Arenil - brother to King Orionkael and uncle to Gwaethe and Isiloe; a hermit who lives in isolation in the remote mountains above Selinore; he is also a Defender and becomes Vard's mentor

Lyam Anton (Lie-am) - Vard's father who has been missing for over fifteen years; he is now a Defender and can shift into wolf or bear

Katrine Aranati (Kat-reen Ar- an- arti) - sorceress and younger daughter of an impoverished farming estate south of Wildecoast; older sister is Esta Aranati; once a smuggler called Lady Star; heroine of **The Master and the Sorceress;** now mistress of the night hounds; married to James Tomel

James Tomel (James Tom-elle) - master jeweler and oldest son of a farming family; lives in Costa; hero of **The Master and the Sorceress;** once spy master for King Beniel and now head of the Queen's Intelligence Network

Esta Aranati - Katrine Aranati's older sister; she is head of the Aranati estate and was once a smuggler known as Lady Moonlight; heroine of **The Lady and the Pirate;** married to Samael Delacost

Samael Delacost - once a pirate, was captured by Nikolas Cosara, admiral of the King's Navy and is now sworn to obey the admiral or spend the rest of his life in prison; hero of **The Lady and the Pirate** and now married to Esta Aranati

Merielle Cosara - mermaid who has become human; she has vibrant red hair and is not familiar with the ways of Thorian people; heroine of **The Lord and the Mermaid;** married to Nikolas Cosara; good friend of Esta Aranati and Alecia Zialni

Lord Nikolas Cosara (Nikolas Cos-arra) – Admiral in the King's Navy; he is cousin to Dowager Queen Adriana and the hero of **The Lord and the Mermaid;** he is married to Merielle

Alique (Ah-leek) Jazara nee Zorba - beautiful blonde healer, married to Kain and brother to Ramón; cousin to General Josef Formosa. Her story was told in **The Elf King's Lady**

Kain Jazara - once general of the Thorian army, he discovered his father was Orionkael Arenil (past elven king); he has taken up leadership of the peaceful *Lenweri;* he is married to Alique Jazara and is hero of **The Elf King's Lady;** half-brother to Gwaethe Arenil; son of Orionkael Arenil, the murdered elven king; has a black horse called Snow; now lives in the elven city of Selinore with his wife Alique

Josef Formosa - promoted to general of the Wildecoast army after Kain Jazara was forced to resign; he is cousin to Ramón and Alique Zorba

Alecia Zialni's lady guards:
Lady Linnet Perfore - Alecia's second-in-command; talented scout; tall

redhead; gray eyes; now promoted to the nobility with the title of countess and is Alecia's junior advisor

Cretia - the planner of the group; blonde with baby blue eyes

Arelle - the peacekeeper; inspired by Alecia to learn weapons; black hair, blue eyes

Kenna - scout and fierce warrior; hyperactive; brown hair and eyes

Jules Estevot (Jewels Ess-tee-vow) - captain of the army in Brightcastle; has blond hair and ice-blue eyes

Reid Vetta (Reed Vet-tah) - Master goldsmith in Wildecoast and Esta's betrothed for a short time

Doctor Achan Mosard - Physician to the king in Wildecoast

Master Dunnet - Vard's man servant

Elora Arenil (Elle-Aura Arenil) - King Orionkael's widow and Gwaethe's mother

Isiloe (Iz-il-oe) - Gwaethe's cousin by Orionkael's sister; unlike most of her race, Isiloe is short with white hair and pale blue eyes. She is a captain (*Ramar*) in the elven army

Chandrelle (Shan-drel) - Isiloe's sister; tall, dark elven woman with long dark hair; warrior

Ramar Lyari Morlynn - one of the *Lenweri* leaders from Selinore

Ramar Syndra Ilirie - leader of Gwaethe's personal guard; from Amitania

Exmund Tomel - Jacques's aide and corporal in the Brightcastle army; youngest brother of James Tomel, hero of **The Master and the Sorceress**; moves to Amitania and is promoted to sergeant during fighting with the *Sis Lenweri*

Elvor Faenwelar - High Prince of the *Sis Lenweri*; enemy of Gwaethe and the humans

Niel Gorin Faenwelar- of the *Sis Lenweri*; Elvor's son

Rasalar (Raz-a-lar) - Isiloe's mother- is sister to Orionkael and Melandrach- once a soldier and still trains recruits

Master Jenkin - Brightcastle weapons master

Tyra - Benae's maid- stocky, blond; helps with healing

Julli (Ju-lee) Dovara - Alique's maid; gifted helper and healer; not a great horsewoman; gentle and caring

Ruven Magbalar - *Sis Lenweri* soldier rescued by Gwaethe and became a loyal supporter; he is now *Lenweri* elven army commander in Amitania

Théoden Leovaris - *Sis Lenweri* soldier rescued by Gwaethe and became a loyal supporter and captain of her *Lenweri* guard

Vortek Cruzen - Defender who trained with Melandrach; can morph into wolf, owl and bear; now one of Vard's elite ranger force

Tholdrek Opalgrip - Blond dwarf; leader of the dwarven mission from north of Thorius

Night hounds - beasts the size of a wolf, with short grey, black, or red hair, heavy snout, and stumpy ears; the eyes are red; there are six toes on each paw, and the back feet have retractable cat-like claws, huge and razor sharp; their current mistress is Katrine Tomel (nee Aranati)

Nugoriem - the black dragon; name means 'eternal fire'; Kain Arenil is his rider

Hirova - the golden dragon

Elven trms

Alen = lord
Gir = Sergeant
Ade = Corporal
Ramar = Captain
Saleh = attack
Elrie = half-blood

ABOUT THE AUTHOR

Bernadette Rowley is an Australian epic fantasy romance author who is also a veterinarian. After flirting with picture books, junior fiction, and space opera, Bernadette was challenged to write a romance in 2011, and she hasn't looked back.

First published by Penguin Australia and then Pan Macmillan Australia, Bernadette is now an independently published author. The Queenmakers Saga contains twelve books spanning the genres of fantasy romance and romantic fantasy.

Her favorite tropes are enemies to lovers, forced proximity, and forbidden romance. Strong themes include the horse/human bond and healing.

When not at her desk, Bernadette can be found absorbed in a good romance or romantic suspense, swimming, walking, or having coffee with friends.

CONNECT WITH ME

Subscribe to my newsletter and get a free copy of Princess Avenger:
https://bernadetterowley.com/get-princess-avenger-free/

Check out my Amazon Author Page

Join the Princess Avenger Readers Group

www.ingramcontent.com/pod-product-compliance
Lightning Source LLC
Chambersburg PA
CBHW070007120726
47909CB00003B/830